THE RED HAIRBAND

GUERNICA WORLD EDITIONS 64

THE RED HAIRBAND

Catherine Greene

GUERNICA
World
EDITIONS

TORONTO—CHICAGO—BUFFALO—LANCASTER (U.K.)
2023

Guernica Editions Founder: Antonio D'Alfonso

Michael Mirolla, general editor
Justine Hart, editor
Cover design: Allen Jomoc Jr.
Interior design: Jill Ronsley, suneditwrite.com

Guernica Editions Inc.
287 Templemead Drive, Hamilton (ON), Canada L8W 2W4
2250 Military Road, Tonawanda, N.Y. 14150-6000 U.S.A.
www.guernicaeditions.com

Distributors:
Independent Publishers Group (IPG)
600 North Pulaski Road, Chicago IL 60624
University of Toronto Press Distribution (UTP)
5201 Dufferin Street, Toronto (ON), Canada M3H 5T8

First edition.
Printed in Canada.

Legal Deposit—Third Quarter
Library of Congress Catalog Card Number: 2023934951
Library and Archives Canada Cataloguing in Publication
Title: The red hairband / Catherine Greene.
Names: Greene, Catherine (Author of The red hairband), author.
Series: Guernica world editions (Series)
Description: Series statement: Guernica world editions
Identifiers: Canadiana (print) 20230195849 | Canadiana (ebook)
20230195881 | ISBN 9781771838160 (softcover) | ISBN 9781771838177 (EPUB)
Classification: LCC PR6107.R44 R43 2023 | DDC 823/.92—dc23

Part 1: Future

Evie's Story

Chapter 1

BEHIND STACKS OF BROKEN FURNITURE, plastic containers and twisted metal, the children played their game. A boy stood on an air conditioning unit, facing away from the others, his eyes buried in his palms. The others whirled around below him, arms held out, spinning faster and faster. They muffled their giggles as their hands accidentally touched. Their woven boots dislodged plumes of dust, which caught in the stream of tepid air and disappeared into the unlit roof of the dome.

"Flood!" the boy said, turning around.

The children wobbled, shrieked and scrambled onto the piles around them. Dizziness made them clumsy and their hands grasped at the air. They slipped and slid, creating avalanches of debris.

"Quick. The flood!" they shouted to one another.

One small boy lay on the floor, unable to get up.

"I'm going to be sick," he said, rolling over and resting his forehead on the floor.

"No. The flood. You've got to escape." Evie grabbed him by the waist and hauled him onto the remains of an olden-day table.

"I'm too hot," the small boy said, spitting out dust and bile.

"It's alright, just breathe," Evie said and began tentatively stroking his back through the scratchy material of his tunic. His body tensed, until he retched again.

"That's not permitted. Put him back," the older boy said.

"He's only small."

"Evie. Put him back."

The older boy raised his arms to restore order, and the children quietened.

"The flood has come. Who's drownded, then?"

The children looked around. Two of them still had a foot on the floor.

They crept down from their piles and formed a circle around the two unlucky ones. The older boy pushed Evie's rescued friend into the middle to join them. The small boy bent double and clutched his stomach, spitting onto the floor again.

The children linked hands around them and began to circle.

"Drowned, drowned, you drowned in the flood. Drowned, drowned, you drowned in the flood," they said, so quietly that it was almost a whisper. The sound floated up, echoing around the roof, like the murmur of insects.

"What's going on here?" Their teacher appeared from behind the air conditioning unit.

The children sprang apart and formed rows, glaring at the child who should have been on watch.

"The task you were given was sorting, not playing. And you were touching." He clenched his fists inside the loose sleeves of his tunic. "Get back to your room, immediately."

They followed him through the piles of recycling, into the living-dome, passing their sleeping mats and the communal eating area, finally reaching a small pod with seats arranged in rows.

"I'm disgusted and ashamed of you all," the teacher said. "You should have the good of the community at the centre of your hearts. You'll all miss the communal meal."

The children gasped. Evie raised her hand. The sleeve of her brown tunic slipped down, exposing her pale skin.

"Evie?" the teacher said.

The children watched her. The boy she'd saved from the flood tried to reach her arm to lower it. He sprang back as the teacher turned towards him.

"We did wrong. We should have done our daily task. But do we have to miss the meal? The portions this morning were small. We—" Evie hesitated. The others drew in expectant breaths.

The teacher walked towards her. His tunic and wide trousers flapped around him as he moved.

"We go hungry today only so that there will be feasts tomorrow," he said.

Evie looked at the floor. She breathed slowly, feeling the warm air in her lungs, wishing that it might fill her stomach as well. She watched the shadows her feet made as they swung slowly back and forth.

The teacher returned to his place at the front of the class.

"It seems you still need reminding of our purpose. What must we do?"

"We must sacrifice ourselves for a better future," the class responded.

"How must we do that?"

"Free ourselves from the bonds of family, obey the Porters, and prepare ourselves for our First Task."

"And what is your task to be?"

"To survey New Britain to see if there might be other places to live, and to build links with our fellow Britainers."

"Good." The teacher sighed. "Get out your Green Tablets and tell me how you will go about your task, and what you will do."

Evie picked up her tablet and turned it on. She pulled her sleeves up over her elbows and brushed her short hair away from her face. She closed her eyes and imagined the desert stretching in every direction, imagined somewhere with food. Somewhere where being outside didn't burn. Somewhere without dust. She'd seen an olden-day picture of a giant tree once. Would she find such a tree somewhere? Or water?

She raised her hand again.

The teacher stared at her.

Evie stared back.

"Evie?"

"Has anyone found a tree before, or lots of water? Can I say I'll do that?"

The teacher's eyes softened. He gazed into the distance.

"So far, no. But all the new adults from all the domes go out to search, and one day perhaps we'll find lots of water."

"Where did you go on your First Task?" one of the others asked.

"I went to the North Country. Six of us set out, and two of us returned. Neither of us saw anything other than more desert, and more wreckage of the old world. But I made many friends in the community I lived with, and learned about their lives. And in this way, we help each other stay true to our common purpose, and learn the things that others have learned."

"But there is the sea, Teacher. Why can't we get water from the sea?" someone asked.

"There's sickness in the sea. No one can live near the sea."

"And the water is salt," Evie said.

"Yes, Evie. The water can't be drunk without much trouble so it's little use to us. We need fresh water. Now, get on with your work."

The children pressed the pictures on their tablets and watched them dissolve into words. Evie frowned, unable to find the picture for 'want.' She tried to write it with her finger instead. 'W.' She scratched a matted clump of hair and felt dust and sand falling out of it. She licked her finger and smudged the dust across her tablet. 'O.' Was it 'O' for 'wont'? She sighed. *How does anyone learn to write?* she thought, looking around the class. The oldest child used both his hands to turn pictures into words, and to make the letters work. Evie repeatedly pressed the hard screen of the tablet with her finger. It vibrated. It complained. The teacher looked up.

"Evie. What now?"

"Want. I can't find 'wont.' I want to find a tree. A huge tree that lives in water."

Later that day, hidden in the shadows at the edge of the living-dome, Evie moved closer to Annie so that their shoulders touched. The warmth from Annie's body spread into her own. Annie's breaths were shallow and quick in the heat.

"Do you think anyone knows we hide here?" Evie said.

"No. It's too hot for adults."

"But not us."

"We're tough."

Evie smiled at Annie and could just make out Annie's smile in the gloom.

"Has Teacher told you your inheritance?" Annie said.

"Yes," Evie said.

"He told me mine today. Because I'm seven now."

"Is it alright?"

"I think so. All my grandparents were good. My parents have been good. But I don't know which they are."

Evie nodded. She ran her finger through the dirt on the floor and pushed it under her fingernails.

"Will you promise not to tell?" Evie said.

"Tell what?"

"My inheritance isn't good. One of my great-grandparents was bad. Very bad. And my mother was a bit bad too."

"Very bad?" Annie's eyes widened in fear and excitement.

"I don't know."

They sat in silence for a moment. Annie gently bumped Evie's shoulder.

"I still like you, Evie," Annie said, peering into the distance.

"Will you always?" Evie grabbed her friend's shoulders and made Annie face her.

"Yes."

Evie felt Annie's sweaty fingers slipping into her own.

"This isn't allowed," Evie said.

"I don't know why not, when we get to seven."

"It just isn't," Evie said. "It's the rules. Somehow it helps to make the perfect future."

"Are you scared?"

"Of what?"

"The sending out. The First Task. Teacher's friends didn't come back."

Evie's heart beat faster. She breathed in too deeply and inhaled clumps of dust. She gripped Annie's hand more tightly as she coughed. She could hear the faint murmur of voices on the other side of the dome. If she could have stopped time, she would have done.

"I'm going to find a tree, and water. I'm going to find it."

Annie smiled. "You don't know that."

"But I am. Just think, if we had enough to eat. If we had lots of water. I'm going to do it. Then we'll all be happy, and my inheritance won't matter."

Annie rested her head on Evie's shoulder. "We just have to stay alive. Then we can be best friends always."

"Always," Evie whispered.

They hadn't heard the Under-Porter's prowling walk.

He saw something moving.

He found them, and he dragged them out.

Evie struggled against his large hands, wriggling and shrieking. His stale scent enveloped her as he clutched her around the waist and dragged the two of them to the centre of the living-dome.

Some of the adults stopped their conversations and turned to watch. The children crowded closer.

The Under-Porter dropped Evie and Annie to the floor. Evie gasped. Sharp heat spread up from her ankle. Her stomach contracted and rebelled against the dirt she breathed in. She coughed and dribbled out spit. She felt herself hauled to her feet.

The murmurs of the community rolled through her head, making it spin.

She fumbled, trying to find Annie's hand.

Annie moved away from her.

"They were hiding," the Under-Porter said. "And they were touching."

Evie heard someone speak on her behalf: *They only just turned seven.*

The voices spun a web around her, and she couldn't tell what they said. Some of the words didn't make sense.

One of the Designated Carers grabbed Evie by the shoulders and walked her towards the main entrance.

"What's happening?" Evie said.

"Outside. Ten minutes."

Evie's legs lost their strength. Her ankle crumpled. The Designated Carer hauled her up.

"Please. My ankle hurts," Evie said.

"You should know better. I'll tend to it afterwards."

"Annie?" Evie looked around, and saw her friend still standing in the dome with her head lowered.

"Annie's inheritance is different. You need a more corrective approach."

Evie shook her head. *Corrective?* She'd heard that word somewhere.

She was about to speak but they'd reached the door. It flapped back and forth as the wind pounded against it. The woman opened one of the straps. The material struggled and fought against her.

"Please. I'll be good," Evie said.

"You will be."

The Designated Carer opened the door just enough to push Evie out.

The light pierced her eyes like a knife. The heat fell upon her, knocking her to the ground. The wind threw sand against her. Evie hid her face in the crook of her arm and fumbled with the hood of her tunic. She pulled it over her head and crouched in the doorway in a small patch of shade.

The dome resisted the wind and its screeches filled her ears. The sand seemed to cut her skin, even through her tunic. Evie rolled herself up into a ball. She whimpered. The air burned as she breathed it in. She pushed her sleeve into her mouth and tried to breathe through that. Her mind lost its power to think.

She lay there for ten minutes. It felt like a day. Then the Designated Carer pulled her back inside.

She gave her a cup of water. Evie gulped it down, but it made her sick. The Carer inspected her arms and legs and wiped off the sand. Evie shivered. Her body rattled so much she wondered whether her insides were still attached. She sank down on her sleeping mat and rolled up into a ball.

The Carer stood up to leave her.

"I'll be good," Evie said, her voice losing itself in her throat. "I'll be good always."

"I'm sure you will, Evie."

Evie peered out from under her arms and searched for Annie's familiar shape.

Annie had been moved.

Evie scrunched up her hand, conjuring up the feel of Annie's small fingers. Would she ever feel them again?

* * *

A few weeks later, once the whole class was designated as seven years old, they learned another function of their tablets. They learned to report on each other. Just like the adults, after the communal meal and before going to sleep, they all reported.

"You're now trusted members of the community. And sometimes children see things that adults can't," their teacher said.

And once a week the teacher called upon a child or two for confession.

Soon enough, it was Evie's turn.

"Evie," he said, "what is it that you have to confess?"

She walked to the front of the class and stood with her hands folded in front of her. Her mind went blank. Evie couldn't think of anything she had done that week. But there must be something. He only called upon students with something to say.

"I wanted another portion yesterday. I was hungry. I was rude to the server," Evie said, her breath whistling out of her mouth with relief.

"No, Evie, that's not it."

Evie looked around at the other children. What had they said? What had she done?

"I didn't help as much as I could with the recycling," she said, watching the teacher's face for signs of approval.

"No, Evie. It's something else that I have written here." He spoke quietly, but his voice burned into her ears. Her heart pounded so loudly she was sure they could hear it.

"I ... I ... don't know. Please forgive me. I don't know," Evie said so quietly the children at the back of the pod couldn't hear her.

The teacher nodded.

"You must learn to examine your behaviour, as we all examine each other's. It is written here that you held the hand of an adult who was neither a Designated Carer nor a Medic. This is forbidden."

Evie shook her head. "I didn't. I didn't do that."

"You were seen, Evie, so it is true," the teacher said.

Evie carried on shaking her head.

"Evie. It is true."

Evie stopped shaking her head and looked at the floor. She replayed the last week. Had she? She was sure she hadn't, but if Teacher said so, she must have forgotten. He never made mistakes.

"I'm sorry," Evie said.

She imagined standing in the queue for her portion of food. It would have been easy to hold someone's hand, then. It would be easy to do it and forget. She closed her eyes and imagined. *That must have been it,* she thought. *It must have been then.*

"Why did you do it?" the teacher said.

"I don't know," Evie said, trying to imagine why she might have done it.

"You must know," the teacher said.

"I forgot I was seven now," she said. "I forgot it's not allowed."

"Alright, Evie. The community forgives you. When we acknowledge our errors, we are welcomed with love and forgiveness. But we must try harder."

Evie nodded, and scampered back to her seat. She folded her hands on her desk and watched them bouncing up and down in time with her galloping heart. Her lips quivered against each other. *I must be good. I must be good,* she thought.

The next child walked to the front.

Chapter 2

EVIE HAD LOST HER CHILDISH fear of the outside and had assumed the responsibilities that came with becoming an adult. She'd swapped the hood on her tunic for a muslin scarf that she wrapped around her head, like a grownup. It protected her as she examined the protein pods outside the dome. She caressed the yellowed buds, afraid of killing them altogether. Her fingers traced crevasses in the earth. Evie sighed, turning her eyes to the sun. She stood up, resting her hands on her knees as she did so. Teacher had chosen her, and she must do this right; she must remember everything. Wrapping her muslin more tightly around her head she walked back towards the living-dome.

The grey dome rose from the surface of the desert, a miracle, pulsing and humming with the life inside. Solar panels and rain collectors shone on its surface like daylight stars. Men crawled over them mending tears, fixing bent metal with their hands, attaching things with ropes. Bare patches showed where equipment used to hang. They said that in the old days there had been cool air all day long. Imagine.

Evie walked back to the dome, scanned her wrist at the entrance and let herself inside. None of the couple-hundred people spoke, but the room was heavy with their noises, rustling, shuffling, sighing. They turned towards her in silent anticipation. Evie breathed in the warm smell of home. Sleeping mats fanned out around the air conditioning vents, each with a small heap of personal items. Evie peered at her mat as she passed. Her second set of clothes lay untouched, with her tablet on top. She smiled; no one had yet dared search for the treasure the earth had given her yesterday—the red hairband. Good.

The crowd's black, shadowy eyes became clearer as they watched every step of her walk across the room. Others might have run, conscious of the attention, the anticipation. Evie moved slowly towards the steps and paused before climbing onto the stage made from broken olden-day furniture. Everyone watched, silently. She felt their anticipation, the excitement. The others on stage were all taller than her, bigger than her, their shadows drowning her as she took her place.

"Is everyone present now?" The warm air seemed to stifle the Porter's cold voice, thaw its edges, and people leant forward to hear.

"Yes, Porter. Except for those on emergency duties. We can finish this now." Evie wasn't sure who'd answered him.

"Evie," he loomed over her, "what did you find?"

Evie looked out from the podium, watching them all. This small community. Her family. "I don't think they'll make it."

"Why?"

An intake of breath rippled through the crowd.

"It's like the others said—they haven't been watered."

An old man crumpled at the other end of the stage. His hands clawed at his face as he rocked his head. "I did water them, I really did, you know I did! It wasn't me, I don't know what …"

"Silence." The Porter barely raised his voice, but the man fell silent. "This is really just a formality. I knew all along. As did we all. You will go for training."

The man sobbed. In the crowd, a baby cried. Evie thought she saw a woman smother the sound in her clothes.

Evie stared at the old man. Probably nearly fifty. They said that people used to live much longer. *What a waste*, she thought. *They should all move out. Think how much more space there'd be. And food.* Her arm cradled her hollow stomach. *They don't work, but still want to eat.*

The guards led the man out. No one would see him again.

The Porter turned to Evie.

"This is the first time you've been the voice of the community, Evie."

"Yes, Porter." Evie lowered her head.

"Your teacher said you were ready."

"Yes, Porter."

"Most of your classmates have already spoken."

A hundred fears filled the silence before he spoke again.

"You did well, Evie. I will tell your teacher to put it on your record."

Evie kept her eyes fixed on the ground.

"Thank you, Porter."

When she looked up, she saw her teacher smiling. She couldn't tell whether it was with happiness or relief.

The crowd dispersed, shuffling back to work. Evie prepared to return to the food processing section, but stopped suddenly near the women's area. Someone was near her mat. How dare they? Fists clenched, she moved towards them. It wasn't possible to make out who it might be, but a shadow of a person was there.

"Hey," she called out, "that's mine!"

Whoever it was turned and looked at her. Evie hesitated. She'd been expecting one of the women, but this was a man, with his muslin wrapped around his face.

"I've left something for you. A present."

She peered at him. Presents were wasteful extravagances, remnants of the bad old days. His muslin slipped, allowing her to see his eyes and nose. "Joe? Father?"

He nodded. "You did well today, but there are things you don't know. There's knowledge we must keep alive. I wish we could talk." He waved at her mat. The pattern of her possessions had changed. Evie saw a small shiny box, reflecting the dim light, almost glowing red. She moved towards it, but he held her arm. Evie flinched. The shock of it paralysed her and he pulled her towards him, trapped her with his arms around her shoulders. Evie gasped. He rested his chin on her head. Evie thought she was choking. Her throat closed up; something jumped inside her chest. Her breath came in gasps. "Don't," she said, "only Designated Carers and Medics can touch us." He let go, and Evie shrank backwards.

Joe turned away, limping towards the machine room. After a few paces, he stopped to look at her again, but Evie didn't see.

Evie grasped the box and hunched over it, hiding it in the folds of her clothes, feeling its firm, smooth, and slightly spongy texture. Plastic! Actual, real plastic. A treasure. On the front, a faded creature smiled. A creature with a semi-circular back, large legs, and cloth over its eyes. What was it? She'd seen something like it somewhere. Tortoise? It had a stick in its hand. A land animal probably. But why the stick? She hurriedly hid it under her clothes, next to the red hairband, and went back to work.

Many hours later, after the second communal meal, she crouched behind the air conditioning vent, out of sight, and examined the box. The two clips at the top still worked. It opened. Inside she found a piece of paper. No one used paper now. It crinkled as she unfolded it, running her fingers over its smooth surface. Her eyes squinted.

My dear little Joseph,

I don't know what to say. I don't know how to write this. How can I write to you about life when you can barely hold up your head yet? But I have to. I hope you are loved. I won't see your milestones or hold your hand and I have only myself to blame. I hope they don't turn you against me. I love you and I want to be your mother, but they're coming to take me away and there's hardly any time.

I voted for them with the best intentions. We wanted to save the world for our children, mend the damage. And there was so much damage. The hotter and hotter summers, water rationing all year round, and clogged and barren oceans. I measured rainfall

*in my garden; I was on the barricades around the oil companies.
I saw it. But so many people didn't care, carried on wasting and
spending and killing life.*

*But then the Great Flood. I can't imagine what they'll tell
you. I suppose all the dead will just be numbers to you, nameless,
formless numbers. Those of us who survived barely mention it. We
know what we did to survive and daren't scratch the surface of
our guilt.*

*The floods had become more frequent and washed away the
soil. This rain started on a Sunday, heavy drenching rain, and we
all ran into the streets because the ground was parched, and we
thought it would help the crops. But the rain didn't stop, it carried
on day after day for two whole months. The Thames leaked onto
the streets and the underground trains had to stop. And then the
flood came. It swept away whole blocks of houses, drowned all
our landmarks, leaving only the top of Big Ben and the dome of
St Paul's. Many people died, many more of us had to scramble up
hills and onto roofs as we watched people and animals dragged
away, screeching for our help. Helicopters hovered over crowds
of screaming people clinging to ruined buildings, deciding who
to save. Mothers held up their wriggling babies. And people elbowed them out of the way. People pushed little children into the
water to clamber into rescue boats. I watched my neighbour beat a
woman to death with a saucepan to steal a dining table she used
as a raft. There were some heroes, but not enough. We had disease
and looting, and everything that is bad about human nature. But
I survived and I wish I had died.*

*A year later the city dried out and we voted them in. We
welcomed them because they promised to save us. We'd caused the
disaster with our extravagant living and wasteful ways, our dis-
regard for the balance of nature.*

*It was only later I questioned what they told us. There were
rumours at the time, small hints on the internet that all was not
as it seemed. I ignored them, swept away in the fear. I believe now
that the Great Flood wasn't just nature's revenge. They made it*

worse; they broke the Thames Barriers. They flooded us. They killed us, and left us to kill each other, because it was the only way we'd give them such power. Once the rest of the country saw London desolate, it crumbled. I hope when you're old enough to read that sentence that the punishment for believing it isn't as harsh as it is now. They will take my life for it. And they will rip this mother from her beautiful son.

Things changed so quickly that I hardly noticed how our lives never reverted to normal. The break with the past was so complete that I forgot how things used to be. I forgot what life should be like. After the flood, we barely had rain again. We worked hard to conserve it. People learned to live with hunger. So the first measures were sensible, and we cheered them on. They banned exporting food, dug up roads and car parks and tore down empty buildings to plant vegetables and fruit, or to keep chickens and pigs. I loved the National Garden at the end of my street. We'd all hang out there after work and at the weekends to dig and gossip. I cried so much when we harvested our first crop of strawberries. We'd been living off dried emergency food for so long. It was as if we'd all come to life again. Like we'd earned our right to live. And I first kissed your father with the sweet juice of our fruit on my lips. He hardly knew me and looked so surprised, but I won him over!

I was in love, with your father and with our mission. I got people out of their houses and into the gardens. We made everyone work. Our crops grew and the country celebrated. Your father and I walked everywhere, for hours. I prided myself on my blisters and my aching legs. We turned our lights off at seven every night to save energy. We only used hot water once a week. We dug and planted and tended animals in our National Garden. We tried to live off what we grew. We stayed thin and tired. But I didn't see it. We felt righteous, holy almost. The greater the deprivation, the happier I thought I was.

So, what was it like, this life we killed? We were free. We were wasteful, arrogant, greedy—but free. We used to go abroad, to foreign countries a few times a year. I wasn't rich, but I could go, too. I went to Spain and to India, before it was mostly evacuated, and to America. Everyone had a car, many people had two and there were long queues all over the roads, as we drove so much. The government used to measure Gross Domestic Product; can you imagine? We measured how much the country produced, like that was the aim, the point of living. As I write all these things, I can only think they were wrong. I still think we were wrong, but what we built in its place has had such a terrible cost.

Families used to live in houses, one for each family. They look odd now, the few left standing in between the communal dwellings, but you should look at them if any are left and think about what it was like. After the recovery, they built communities in their place. It was more friendly that way. I moved into one with your father a couple of years after the flood. We were so excited over our two rooms. Because of his job, we got one with a good view and every morning I opened the curtains to look out on our garden. I've always liked the countryside and loved feeling like the country had invaded the city. Like nature was reclaiming the land.

We felt we were rebuilding the world. I trained as a nurse and I loved my new job. There were lots of sick children and slowly we mended them. We used to work for money, but during the recovery it changed, and we worked for impact tokens. Money isn't worth anything—you just swap it for other things. I never had enough of it. But impact tokens are simple. The less you spend, the more we heal the world. Your father and I saved most of ours; we counted them in hours of hot water, or packets of meat, and watched them pile up, salivating at the thought of the years of gluttony we were forgoing.

Then they introduced the annual Survey. Joseph, if you learn nothing else, please learn this—we did this to ourselves. They gave us the weapons, but we did it to ourselves. They never forced us, they appealed to the worst in human nature, but it was in our nature all along. It was all our fault.

All they did was put meters in each block to measure how much energy and water we used, and how much rubbish we left.

And they published the results and gave medals for the people with the lowest impact. Then those people appeared on the communication channels, were famous, looked up to, copied. That's all they did—measured us, and rewarded. And we did the rest. With a perverted fascination we deprived ourselves. Our community once lived off porridge for a week, put a stop to hot water and watched the meter, goggle-eyed with glee, unaware of our ravenous bellies as we saw it had hardly moved. But we still weren't the best. We never won any medals. This made us mean. We watched and criticised and egged each other on to ever-greater feats of deprivation. The funny thing was that although it's necessary to save the environment we never really thought about it that way. It was all about the meter, and winning.

Why am I not a monster still? I love babies, and thought until last year that I couldn't have any. Until you came along, my little miracle boy. A few years ago, the woman next to us had one, a beautiful, smiling tiny boy. She'd been Listed. She used to try to hide his cries during the night; others minded—I didn't. But over the months his cries became quieter, and yet more urgent. The little boy started to look thin and wasted. And his mother looked grey and old. I saw them every day and I knew what was wrong, and I watched it unfold. I held the little boy's hand once—small and bony like a walnut—but I didn't help. You can't help the Listed. I was scared to get too close. But I lied to myself that I was compassionate, when I was just another murderer dressed up as a friend. She felt all the eyes of the building turned on her, so she didn't use the heating, she hardly ate, and her little boy struggled to suck enough milk from her. One night I heard a little howl of anguish, a cry like no baby should make. He was dying. The next morning, I found her some food and brought it round. I did it secretly, so no one would see. I went to the National Shop and swapped impact tokens for baby milk and gave it to her. But she was too scared, and I was too late. Her little boy died a few days later and she killed herself, hanged herself. The Porter smiled when he struck two names off the list and calculated our new energy usage.

So now you know the worst of me. I hate myself, and all I can do is speak up. But no one listens. They won't remember how it used to be. And they will kill me. This is wrong, Joseph. Nothing can make this right. But I love you. I'll hide this for you. Please, never have faith in an idea, never stop using your mind, never be totally certain. And I hope that you are happy.

All my love xx

Evie's fingers rested lightly on the page. Olden-day writing was as beautiful as a full-leaved vine—but this was not allowed. She turned it over. Different handwriting, smaller, neater, the ink more transparent.

That's your great-grandmother, Evie. Joseph was my father—he passed down the letter along with his name. We aren't supposed to need families. But she was my grandmother, and I am your father. This does matter. We should look after each other. You're sixteen soon, and you'll be asked to confirm your allegiance. Of course you will, as we have no choice. But what we say and what we think can be different. I loved your mother, even after they took her away, and I will always love you, even though I hardly know you. I want an ally. They are afraid of people getting close to one another. But my only duty is to you. I'm trusting you with this; I have no idea what you'll do. But you are my daughter and it's the right thing to do. You need this knowledge. And once you have it your behaviour needn't change, but I hope I've awakened something in your mind. Things cannot go on as they are.

Evie frowned. He hadn't signed his name. No definite proof then. She folded the paper, caressing the rounded edges, and placed it gently back in the box, crawled back to her mat, and hid it again under her second set of clothes, next to the hairband. She picked up her tablet, turned it on and lay down to type. In the column 'The Errors of Others' she wrote: 'I noticed Jasmine taking scraps out of the composter. She said they were for her baby, but babies don't eat scraps. She lied.' On the next line: 'Michael wasn't paying attention when we had to write out the Community Rules. He stuck his tongue out behind Teacher's back.'

In the column 'My Errors' she wrote, without hesitation: 'I was too prideful when I spoke at the meeting. I didn't have the good of the community in the centre of my heart.' But then she hesitated. She knew she had to write something. Just enough, not too much, but enough to keep her options open. She thought of the hairband and wrote: 'I was given something. I didn't ask for it, but I liked the present. I want to keep it just for me.' She pressed 'send' and lay on her mattress, pretending to sleep.

Evie struggled with strands of thought winding and twisting through her brain, uncontrolled and unmanageable; probing, twisting, snaking through her memories.

Silly to care about a baby so much; they weren't useful for years, except for picking protein pods. A feeling of nausea filled her belly. *What if the crop really does fail?* she thought. *Surely now they've found the negligent one, it won't. It couldn't fail, it just needed water. Just a bit more water, surely?*

What will we do if we have no harvest?

What's an internet?

What was my mother like? she wondered. Not that it mattered. No one saw their mother much. Evie closed her eyes. There had been so many mothers, crouched over squealing infants, their faces hollowing out. Not helping with the daily tasks.

Was it a memory she had of her mother holding her, or a dream, or a warning? Of the woman's heartbeat close to her ear, soothing her to sleep.

She clenched and unclenched her sweaty hands, rubbed them against the scratchy cover.

We must keep to the rules, to get a harvest, to make the food, to keep the dome intact, to survive the storms. We must sacrifice ourselves to build the future.

What do strawberries taste like?
What does that mean, to use my mind?
She pulled the short hairs at her temple, pulled them until they hurt. Her heels drummed silently on the floor.
What does it mean? If we don't stick together, we die.
What do I say?
This is so, so dangerous.

Evie stumbled into the education room, her head heavy on her neck, eyes burning. Her hand shook as she placed her tablet on her desk. Her legs bent too easily, collapsing her into her chair. The others chattered as always. She turned away from them.

"Evie, where did you get it?"

She pretended not to hear.

"I saw it. It's from the olden days. Elastic."

"I heard she dug it up."

"There's cloth on it, too."

"But it should have been Zoe's."

Evie turned around, focusing her eyes on the girl. "No, it's mine. It was given to me." Which was true, in a way. While digging yesterday, Zoe's spade had hit a rock. Evie had lifted the rock, and there it had been. The red hairband. Even when dirty it had stood out from the ground like a small pool of blood. "It's mine, and if anyone talks about it I'll tell Teacher everything I know about all of you."

Her fierceness made them hesitate.

"Did the earth give us anything else yesterday?" The boys jumped and hopped around the room, shouting to each other.

"Not really, just some bones for making fertiliser."

"Is that what we're doing today again? I'm sick of digging."

"You will do whatever the community needs you to do." At the sound of *that* voice, the class scrambled into their seats and composed their faces into those of eager, willing students. The teacher

turned on the communication screen, temporarily blinding everyone with its light. His eyes blinked in his pale face as he pushed
back his curly brown hair and smiled at his pupils. His fingers
twitched nervously on the remote control. He breathed in slowly.
"Today, wind turbines again. We'll do exercise two in class, and you
can do the next one on your own time. So, remind me, what are the
most common points of failure in the motor?"

During the class Evie was sure he watched her more closely
than usual. She fidgeted with her tablet, running her fingers along
its edge. The skin under her nail began to bleed and she smudged
it across the screen. She tried to clean it with spit and the edge of
her tunic.

A collective sigh of relief marked the end of the lesson.

"So, go to your duties. Evie, I need a quick word with you."

Evie stared at Teacher. He returned her gaze, his eyes calm, but
concerned. When she didn't move he sat at the desk next to her.

"So, I read your submission last night."

"Yes?"

"You're very observant, Evie. I'm always astonished at the truths
you spot in others' behaviour. And you did really well yesterday;
your confirmation is just a formality now. People know they can
rely on you."

"Thank you." She lowered her head. He picked a small lump of
mud from his sleeve and dropped it onto the floor.

"So, what were you given?" he said. Evie stared at the floor, following a crack from under her foot out towards the front of the
room.

"Evie?" He sighed and looked away. "Sometimes things happen
to us. They aren't things we do. And when they aren't things we do,
they aren't our fault."

"I didn't ask for it."

"I believe you. And you did the right thing telling me."

"Alright." Her eyes scanned the screen in front of them. "Are
you angry?"

His face crinkled into a smile. "Of course not. Everyone thinks these things sometimes. We'd all like to keep things, have them as our own. But we need to work hard to overcome our feelings."

"I see. I thought you'd be angry."

He placed his hand on the back of her chair. "Of course not. Why would I be angry? Will you fetch it for me now though?"

"Of course."

Evie rushed out of the room, and back into the living area. The sound of her breathing pounded inside her head. She walked towards her mattress, clutching her elbows with her hands, crushing them. She crouched down, pulling aside her mattress. The box and the hairband lay there. Both red, both beautiful, both given to her. With a sudden resolve, she scrunched up the hairband, thrust it back under her mattress, and picked up the box.

He couldn't hide his surprise as he held it gently in his hands, turning it slowly around, examining each of its sides. "This wasn't given to you by the earth, Evie?"

"No." She paused for a second and bit her lip. "It was given to me by Joe, with the limp."

"Do you know what it is?"

"It's from the olden days, isn't it? For keeping things in, I suppose." She hesitated again, looked away, shifted her weight from one foot to the other. "The clips are worn; I couldn't open it."

He placed it on his table. "Yes, I think you're right. I can see why you wanted to keep it. What a funny creature on the front though." He peered at it before smiling at her once again. "Any ideas?"

"No; it's waving a stick. It's funny."

He laughed. "Yes, it is funny. I suppose we'll never understand what went on in their minds. But we have to try. I love artefacts." He shook it; it sounded empty. "I can't wait to check this out. Fascinating."

"Yes." Evie hid her tablet in the folds of her tunic.

His body relaxed and he leant back in his seat, one hand resting on the box. "So, tell me, Evie. What is it you really want to achieve here? You're nearly old enough to decide what you want to do."

Evie smiled, but didn't look directly at him. Her eyes focused on a tuft of hair sticking up from his head. "I'd like to show my loyalty to the community."

He nodded. "And how are you going to do that?"

"I'm going to find water. Lots of water."

"Well, keep going as you are and there's no reason to think you won't. Good work, Evie, keep it up."

Chapter 3

THE CLASS LINED UP IN the centre of the communal pod. They had been washed, and their hair neatly cut. Evie wriggled inside her clothes; her body felt light and soft. She looked down the line and smiled at her classmates. They heard footsteps behind them. They froze, pulling their shoulders back and staring straight ahead. Evie clenched her fists, feeling the sweat gathering in her palms.

The rest of the community looked up at them, hopeful, and afraid.

The footsteps sounded rhythmic and solid now. Made by men who didn't wear work boots. By men never excluded from communal meals.

Everyone, even the Porter, bowed their heads as they walked into the communal pod—the Commander, flanked by his assistants. Metal patches on his uniform reflected the dim light. He shone and glowed.

The Porter bowed again and led him up to the class.

The Commander stopped, placed his legs neatly together, and addressed the community.

"You are now adults, and it is my great pleasure, as Chief Commander of London North, to announce your First Tasks to you, and your community. You are expected to serve the community in all things, and be willing to give your life to New Britain. Are you ready?"

"Yes," they all shouted.

Evie's voice leapt from her mouth. Her eyes drank him in. She watched intently, hoping that he might notice her—her in particular.

The Porter handed him a tablet, fumbling with the buttons, and pointing with shaking fingers at the list of names. He guided him to the first student.

The Commander looked the young man up and down.

"You, Robert, after due consideration of your talents and conduct have been chosen to depart to London South, and from there to make your way through the Southern outposts. You will survey the land and look for things that might sustain us. You will learn the ways of the people in those places, and record everything they tell you. Then you will return, and be of use to your community. In the name of New Britain, do you swear to give your life to your task?"

"I swear," Robert said, his head bobbing with enthusiasm. The Southern outposts, the most well-travelled part of New Britain. An easy task, a task that promised life.

The Commander nodded and moved on to the next student.

Evie clenched and unclenched her hands.

A few were sent North, others to the East. Two to devote themselves to learning new methods of desalination developed by a dome in Anglia.

As the Commander stood opposite her, Evie stared into his eyes, trying to read the news. She leant forward hopefully. She held her breath.

"You, Evie, after due consideration of your talents and conduct have been chosen to depart to Bristol, and from there make your way to our Western outpost. You will survey the land for resources, and learn what happens to the people down there. In the name of New Britain, do you swear to give your life to your task?"

Evie swallowed. Dust caught in her mouth and coated her tongue. She coughed. The West? Her legs shook inside her tunic.

Perhaps she hadn't heard him correctly. She breathed in. He smelt clean, like a newly spun blanket, or a freshly washed child.

He frowned.

Evie swallowed again. "I swear," she whispered.

He moved on without meeting her eyes. Evie no longer listened to where the others were going. She was sure the eyes of all of them were on her.

She wiped her hands on her tunic. Her cheeks stung. Tears began to blur the faces around her. She dug her nails into her leg to stop them.

After the ceremony the Commander shared their communal meal. The customary circle bowed outwards, so that he might sit at the apex.

"We thank the earth for the gifts it has given. Our gratitude is unending," they all said, and he smiled, formally. Evie watched the Porter give him a second portion of bread.

"I can't believe you're going to the out-country, Evie." Annie had crept up behind her.

"I'll do my task," Evie said.

"I'll miss you."

"Our lives haven't ever been the same, and they won't ever be," Evie said.

"What do you mean?"

"Your perfect inheritance, Annie. When we were children it didn't matter. But now I have to prove myself. And I will."

"No one thinks like that anymore, Evie. It's just a place. Maybe you really will find water there, or a tree."

"Leave me alone," Evie said.

Annie hesitated.

"Evie. It'll be alright. We'll both come back."

Evie shrugged. "Please leave me now. I need to prepare for my task."

She stood up and began to walk towards her mat to prepare her items. She hesitated, and walked through the entrance to the classroom pods instead. She placed her hands on the shiny material of the doorway. Evie ran her hand down it, to where she used to hold it when she was small. She closed her eyes and tried to conjure up the feeling of being small, and the dream of finding a tree. Tears gathered in her eyes. Evie swallowed, trying to gain control of her body. She breathed in the smell of the pod, imprinting it in her lungs.

"Evie?"

She looked up and blinked.

"Teacher. I didn't think you'd be in here."

"I'm finishing my reports for the class."

"Oh."

Evie asked her body to turn around, but it wouldn't. Her eyes rested on her desk. She followed the lines of it, the odd way that one of the legs bent. It used to rub against her shin. She longed to feel it.

"Are you ready for your task?"

"I've sworn to give my life to New Britain." The words hung on her tongue.

"I heard you. Are you disappointed with your task?"

Evie looked at her teacher. She weighed her options. She balanced the need for comfort against the risk of error.

"I will do what my community demands," she said.

"Sometimes it is hard, though. But the hardest tasks are those that show us at our best."

Evie nodded.

"Return to us, successful, and you'll be lauded for the rest of your life," he said.

"Will it …" Evie clenched and unclenched her hands. "Can it erase my inheritance?"

Her teacher frowned.

"None of us can escape our heritage. But we can prove ourselves to be different."

Evie nodded. Her teacher began to rearrange the desks, destroying the pattern that defined the room. She turned away and walked back to her sleeping mat. She put her tablet and spare set of clothes into a cloth bag and prepared to go to sleep. All the students would leave, together, first thing in the morning.

Chapter 4

A S SHE SAT IN THE transportation vehicle, Evie rolled the teacher's phrase over. *The hardest tasks are those that show us at our best.* But did they know how great this distance felt? Would they have sent her if they did? The vehicle clanked and jolted along. Then it screeched. Evie instinctively gripped its walls, curving her fingers around its metal rivets. She felt the young woman next to her wince. The young man opposite wriggled in his seat before wiping his face in his sleeve. They shuffled, breathing in the warm air. Evie squirmed in the puddle of sweat on her seat. She rubbed at the red hairband, which she'd wrapped around her arm under her tunic. Still unwashed, it itched and scratched. She hadn't dared take it off since the Designated Carers had looked, but failed, to find it. The transport moved smoothly again, and they relaxed against the walls, raising their faces to the ventilation hatches. Dust streaked down from them in neat lines, making tunnels of light. The air tasted of hot metal and grease. Evie breathed it in, felt it swallowing her, and closed her eyes.

"We should have more water." Evie opened her eyes, wondering whether it was the vehicle or her head that was spinning. The young man held out a wooden cup, with a film glimmering on the surface of the liquid.

The woman next to Evie took it and smelt it. "You're sure it's fresh?"

"It's from the tank," he said, shrugging.

"It looks funny." The woman sniffed it again. She dangled her fingers over the edge of the cup.

"Don't touch it as well!" Evie slapped her hand out of the way.

"Hey!"

"Well, you shouldn't touch it." Evie scowled.

"She's right," the man said, "but we're thirsty. My head hurts. We should drink."

"You think?" The woman tilted the cup to better see what floated in it.

"I don't care anymore. If you don't, I'll have your share, too. It's allowed, so make up your mind." He shrugged. And then smiled, as if apologetic.

The woman took a hesitant gulp. Evie snatched the water and drank some, before handing it back to the man. He grabbed it in both hands, swallowing the remainder, letting water roll down his chin. He chased the drops with his fingers and sucked them.

"You shouldn't do that," Evie said.

"What?" he said.

"Put your fingers in your mouth."

"I know."

Evie ran her tongue around her mouth. It tasted alright. Just stale, perhaps. But they'd know by the end of the day if it was safe. She let her eyes close again, listening to the other two settling back into their positions. She matched her breathing to the throbbing of the engine, feeling dizziness envelop her again.

The transport lurched. The sound of an explosion rattled through the vehicle. It tottered on a crumbling ridge, then pitched downwards, screeching. Evie's head smashed against the wall. She bounced. Collided with an elbow. Hot pain spread from her temple to her eyes. The other two hit the floor after Evie, crushing her feet. Someone's head smashed into the seat. They rolled over each other. Two were sick, and one began to whimper.

The door opened. The sun blinded them. They scrambled out, clutching onto each other, crawling, with their arms protecting their faces.

"You alright back there?" Evie's head shook as she tried to orient herself. The direction of the driver's voice was hard to place.

"You all alright?" he asked again. Evie felt herself being led. Her eyes still stung from the light. The air cooled suddenly. She'd been placed in the shadow of the vehicle. The young man coughed next to her.

"What happened?" he asked.

"Obstruction," the driver said.

Slowly, her eyes began to work again. She fumbled with her clothes and managed to wrap her muslin back around her face. Even in shadows she could burn. She rubbed gritty sand from her eyes, feeling it scratch down her cheeks, and watched the man doing the same. But the woman sat motionless, slumped oddly by the wall of the transporter. Evie crawled over to her, put her hands out to cover her, and saw blood crawling out of her ear. She shook the woman gently. "Hey. Wake up." Her body shuddered. "Help," Evie murmured, torn between the obligation to help and fear that she might be blamed.

The man crawled over. "She's injured?"

"There's blood, from her ear," Evie said.

"Oh." His hand hovered over the woman's shoulder.

"Get the driver."

"He's fixing the transport," he said.

"She needs help," Evie said.

"But we don't want to do something we'll be blamed for later."

Evie's eyes locked with his. She wrapped the woman's muslin around her face, pulling it tight around her ear. The blood would show, soon. The man nodded. "Let's go to the driver."

The two of them crawled around the vehicle, hugging the shade. They watched the driver banging the handle of the communicator against a broken wheel. They saw the reason for their crash—the front wheels had become stuck in a hole. It was a small but deep crater, exactly the width of the wheels. The concrete around the hole had cracked and buckled. The back wheels had spun off the road, and still turned slowly over the sand. The sand and small scrubby bushes spread out to the horizon in every direction. Occasional shards of metal stuck out of the ground, like limbs hoping for rescue. The Southern Desert hadn't been scavenged.

"Of all the places for this to happen ..." The driver swore. The communicator crackled. "Yes, hello! Finally." He kicked the sand. "About five miles ... no ... They seem alright. They got out fine ..."

The young man nudged Evie, with a pointed look. She nudged him back. He nudged her again. Evie grabbed his elbow and heaved them both to their feet. He coughed loudly. The driver looked at them.

"We're alright. But the other one seems ... asleep," Evie said.

"Yes, I understand," the driver said, "yes ... we'll be fine till then ... I'll tell them." He put down the receiver and pushed the communicator through the open hatch. "What's that?"

"The other woman," the man said. Evie thought she could feel his body shaking next to hers. The two of them sat back down and let the driver go around to the other side by himself.

He came back after a few minutes. "We're going to wait here until another transport picks us up. It should only be an hour. They'll be coming from there." He pointed towards the road ahead. It was only just visible in the dust and haze. "So just wait, don't move from here."

Evie nodded, trying to look behind him. Was she alive?

She tried to catch the eye of the young man, but he looked fixedly ahead. She tried to form words for her mouth to speak, until the driver spoke again.

"I have been ordered to disclose something to you before they arrive."

Evie looked directly at him. The young man stared at his feet.

"The other transport has a cargo of Listed."

For a moment, only the dust moved, rising in swirls over the desert and settling gently on the transporter. Evie closed her eyes.

The Listed. She had never seen them, but children dreaded that they might return to kill them.

"We should take a share of water," the man said.

The driver nodded. "Yes. Now, and again every half an hour. Three shares. I'll find a cup."

Evie and the young man sat at the side of the transport for two and a half hours, inching their feet closer to its side as the shade retreated. Their shallow breathing hardly moved the muslin draped over their faces. The driver lay at the back, as if guarding the door, though it was now mangled and unusable. Every half an hour the driver delivered water to the three of them. The communicator crackled. And that was the only sound.

Evie had tired of watching the horizon. She didn't notice the new, larger, more regular swirls of dust, growing and approaching. Eventually the throbbing of the motor embedded itself inside her brain.

This new transport was bigger than any she'd ever seen. The leading vehicle was all engine, throbbing, growling, bursting the air with its noise. Attached to it, three pods, long, black, with small ventilation holes. It stopped just before the hole. The drivers talked for a while. One of them attached a pipe to the stricken transport to drain the hydrogen from the tanks. Then they drained the water. They removed the communicator and other equipment. Then they took out the bundles with their spare sets of clothes and tablets. Evie overheard, not because she was listening, but because their conversation washed over her and she did nothing to stop it.

"Did you see anything on the road?"

"No, it was clear."

"Obstruction then?"

"Yes. Seems so to me."

"They took out the Great North Road last week, I heard."

"Really?"

"I heard. They'll no doubt catch them soon."

Evie's eyelids flickered. She looked across at the young man. He seemed asleep.

"So where are these being dropped?" the new driver said.

"The male in Bristol 2, the female needs a new transport in Bristol for the out-country."

"Damn, that's a long way."

Evie dug her nails into her palms.

"Isn't there another one?"

"No, drop her off with the rest of yours."

Evie pulled her feet closer to her body, leaning into the metal. It burned through her clothes.

We are all expendable in the great scheme of life.

Evie shuddered, and closed her eyes.

"OK, you two. In the second door, please."

They ran, crouched, across the sunny patch between the transports. They flew through the door. Evie grabbed sharp metal as she jumped up the steps, but didn't hesitate. The metal dug in deeper as she hauled herself up. Inside was hotter, but there was no sun. They found spaces on the benches running down either side. Only once seated did Evie notice the others. Next to her sat two guards, each with a gun. Other guards sat opposite. But next to them … next to them … all the way back, were the Listed.

Evie fixed her eyes straight ahead. As if afraid that their errors, their malignancy, might spread. What if they attacked? Were there enough guns? She gripped the bench. Could they stand up? Could they reach her? Surely not. She peered around the guard's body. No, they couldn't reach her. She saw the ropes. The obviously tight ropes. She had never seen the Listed. But the teachers were right: they were different. They had tight, pinched faces. Cheeks not pillows, but ridges. Eyes not pools, but empty caverns. Hair not silk, but string. And skin not skin, but grey mottled scales.

Evie sat back and breathed more easily.

What had the man done to be allowed to stay in Bristol? He looked no different to her. Was his inheritance better? But instead of Bristol, she would go to the end of the world.

The transporter rumbled on for hours, it seemed. Evie clutched her bench, rocking, jolting, half-closing her eyes.

"It's lucky they picked us up." The man's voice echoed, and yet was lost in the metal cavern. Evie's eyelids scraped her eyes as she tried to look at him more closely.

"We are very grateful," she said to the guards. The guards appeared to ignore them.

"You're going to the out-country then?" he said.

Evie frowned. Why did they all torment her? "I've been sent to check that all policies are being implemented properly. I'm grateful for the opportunity."

"I have to learn to make communicators in Bristol." He moved his feet across the floor, scraping across debris and sand. "When were you confirmed?"

"Only last month."

"Me too."

One of the guards turned to look at them. "You're lucky to be so young. Everything ahead of you." His eyes took Evie in. Her willowy form, her eyes glistening out of the dark.

"I want to be an elite guard when I've finished my First Task," the young man said. Evie's eyes opened wide. The guard flinched. "I mean, if they choose me for that. I'll do whatever they judge is best for me, of course. But …" Evie's shoulders relaxed.

The guard chuckled. "You mean, like every boy, you'd like a gun?"

The young man smiled. Evie hadn't seen him smile properly before. It seemed to wrinkle up his face. Make a child of him. "Yes, I'd really like a gun. But I'm no longer a boy."

"It's not all fun, being a guard."

"I know," he said, his eyes running up and down the weapon, "but it's quite a bit of fun, I think."

"Well, if that's what you want to do, do you want to help me feed them?" The guard nodded towards the Listed.

"Yes." The young man stood up eagerly.

The guard pulled out a metal chest. He removed neatly tied packages and threw one of them to each of the other guards and handed one to Evie. For a moment she could smell the bread and protein paste. Flavoured protein paste. Her fingers twitched on the string. She felt suddenly sick, like you do when it's been a while between meals. Underneath where the packages had been were lumps, brown lumps of dried paste, shaped into balls. The guard pointed at them. The young man picked one up in each hand, his nose wrinkling.

"Give one to each. I'll walk behind you."

Two other guards held either end of the chest, and the young man walked along the rows of Listed, dropping the lumps into their trembling hands. One of them didn't manage to keep hold of it and dropped it, sending it rolling across the floor. The man seemed about to give them another one. "Keep going," a guard said. They made quite a noise, eating. Like animals. Sucking and slobbering at the food. Picking at it with their fingers, loosening pieces with their nails.

Evie chewed slowly on her bread, taking small bites, feeling saliva filling her mouth, getting rid of the dust and taste of metal. She watched the young man, and the guards, walking along. Just a boy, trying out a man's life. His walk an exaggeration of the guard behind him, his face grim and hostile. Then she saw … something. Something didn't fit. Perhaps it was the way the woman raised her hands. Perhaps the look on her face. It brought back the smell of home, the smell of her community, the feeling of resting her eyes on familiar things. That woman. Evie sat back with a jolt. Could it be? No. She looked again, although now the woman was partly hidden in shadow. But the line of her shoulders. Her silhouette. Just like it had been in the shadows behind the air conditioner. Isabel. But Isabel was young. Isabel went for training. She wasn't Listed.

Evie couldn't swallow her food. It stuck to her tongue. It would choke her if she swallowed. She coughed, spat it into her hand and hid it in her pocket. She closed up the packet again, tying the string around it with shaking fingers.

Never stop using your mind. Never be totally certain. That was what the letter had said, but what did it mean?

Could it really be Isabel? What were the chances of meeting someone from your dome in a transport? Surely it couldn't be.

Evie breathed more quickly. Pressed her head against the wall until she felt the rivets digging in.

She asked herself questions, but knew it was just to obscure that she knew it was her. It was Isabel.

Isabel must have deserved it; she had shouted at the Porter once, Evie remembered. Only the guilty were punished; everyone knew that. Isabel had to learn how to put the good of the community at the centre of her life. She had to learn to be good.

But now she's not Isabel anymore, Evie thought. *She's something different.*

Evie checked that no one noticed her shaking.

Her heart leapt, choking her.

The young man sat back down. Opened his food packet and launched himself at his bread. Pushed it into his mouth, coughing as he chewed. He smiled at Evie. "This is good."

"Yes," she said, "it's good."

Evie saw the man for the last time at Bristol. She changed transports twice more before reaching the out-country. All in all, it had taken five days. The last transport was small, just a two-person solar vehicle. She sat with the driver, watching out the window. She saw the dust slowly conquered by scrub, by small twigs with tiny leaves. Then by tiny, dark green bushes. No one had told her it was green in the out-country. The green spread slowly, from the odd speck, to little clumps, to a green, patchy carpet. Evie itched to get out, to feel it.

They carried on. Further away from everyone else. The road was barely concrete anymore. A rusty weather-beaten sign stuck at an angle from the road. *A38.* One of the old roads then. The only way in or out, someone in Bristol had said. Why hadn't it been recycled yet?

The transport struggled up a hill, and then rolled slowly down the other side. Evie clutched her seat. In the distance, below, were living-pods. Small pods, no central dome. And something else. Evie stared. The hazy sky appeared to fade away before it joined the land.

A different colour, becoming denser as they approached. It twinkled, sparkled.

"Can you see the sea?" the driver said.

"See the 'see'?"

"The sea. Water. The edge of the land."

"The sea!" Evie gasped. Of course. The out-country. The end. The edge. Of course there was sea. *Use your mind!* "I never imagined … I thought it'd be dark."

"I'll drop you here," he said.

"Why not closer?"

"I'll bring you here, but I won't run the risk of sickness," the driver said.

Evie struggled with the latch on the door. She wanted it to remain closed, shielding her from the clogged and oozing sea, which would surely kill her. The driver reached over and opened it for her. Evie stumbled out and fell to the ground.

Evie hardly noticed her surroundings as she knelt there, clutching her spare set of clothes and tablet, too afraid to look up. The driver closed the door behind her. Then she noticed the absence of heat. It didn't weigh as heavily as at home. She held her arms out, letting the breeze filter through her clothes. It touched her skin. Cleaning it, caressing it. Cool. Unimaginably cool. Not harsh, like an air conditioner. Cool. Actually cool. She breathed it in. Light air. It seemed to bring life. Was everyone mistaken? Or was this just the sickness?

Evie only heard the footsteps once they were close beside her. She turned around hesitantly.

"Welcome to the out-country." A woman's voice.

Evie didn't move. She didn't speak. She couldn't speak for a while. "Is it always so cool here?"

"Yes."

"I didn't know it could feel like this."

Evie pulled at her muslin, beginning to unwind it.

The woman held up her hand. "Stop. It feels cool to you now, but you'll still burn if you take it off. You must stay covered, just like elsewhere."

Evie stood up and looked at the woman. Her eyes looked old, peeping out from between the folds of her muslin, older than those of most women. But she stood solidly on the ground. Like a post. The woman led Evie to the perimeter fence and showed her where to scan her wrist. Evie hesitated. The woman stared at her.

"Is there sickness here? Is everyone sick?" Evie said.

The woman pulled Evie's arm and held her wristband under the scanner. Evie let herself be led. Once she was within the perimeter the woman turned to her.

"Welcome. I'm Mary. And our village is Eden."

"Thank you. I'm Evie."

"You'll be spending the next few days with me."

Evie looked around the village, which was no more than a semicircle of small pods, with a larger pod at the edge of the circle.

"You don't have a living-dome?"

"No, things are different here. But it's getting late. Let me get you settled, and I'll show you around tomorrow."

Evie followed her into one of the small pods. The front door opened onto a round room with two bright blue straw mats. A cooker sat in between the mats, with a bowl and spoon arranged neatly next to it. Two curtains at the back opened onto two smaller pods, each with another mat and a pillow.

"You don't have air conditioning?" Evie said.

"All the pods open towards the sea. We keep the doors open. Also, we use the water. Life is different here."

"And I get my own sleeping pod?"

"Yes, for now."

A room of my own, Evie thought, sinking down on her new mat.

Later, as she slept, Evie was unaware of Mary watching her, trying to read her character in her folded limbs. Mary stood up and went outside, where she met a man. They walked a short distance away before sitting down in the doorway of his pod. He held Mary's hand in his lap.

"So, they sent another spy then?" he said.

"Yes."

"Do you think we can turn her?"

"We'll have to."

"What's she like?"

"I don't know," she said. "She's hard to read. But a fanatic, like all of them."

Chapter 5

EVIE AWOKE TO A SMELL. A sharp, heavy smell. A smell that burned a hole in her stomach. She opened her eyes and looked through the opening in her sleeping pod to see Mary's back hunched over the cooker, her arm moving rhythmically as she hummed to herself. As if by instinct, Mary stopped as soon as Evie sat up.

"Breakfast," Mary said. Neither an invitation nor a request.

"Thank you," Evie said, shuffling out of her pod and sitting down on one of the blue mats. "What is it? It smells good."

"Fish."

"Fish?"

"Fish."

"Can you eat fish?" Evie peered at the white lumps sizzling in the pan.

"Of course."

"I never did."

"Things are different here."

Mary spooned some into a bowl and handed it to Evie. Then she passed her a lump of bread. Evie used the bread to pick up the fish, and crammed it into her mouth. She chewed. And stopped. Her mouth exploded with taste. This wasn't food. This couldn't just be food. She chewed slowly, rolling the fish around her teeth. She ate methodically, scraping up every bit of fish, every crumb of bread.

"Would you like more?"

"Is it allowed?"

"If you're hungry, yes."

Evie ate another bowl of fish, and asked for more. But Mary wouldn't let her. She said it would make her stomach hurt, and then she might be sick, which would be a waste.

Evie put down her bowl, watching Mary disassemble the cooker. A breeze came in through the front door, and through a sodden sheet that dripped water into a trough. Some of it dripped on the floor. Water! How hadn't she noticed? Sweat gathered on her neck. And she'd eaten two bowls of fish! She gasped, and tried to control her breath. They'd warned her. *Why hadn't she listened?*

She fumbled with her sleeves, her eyes darting around the cream walls of the pod. She scratched her arm with her nails, pinching the skin. How to make it right? Her heart pounded, interfering with her thoughts. Suddenly, she lunged back into her sleeping pod and fumbled with her tablet.

"Evie?" Mary looked at her calmly.

"I'm in error. I didn't have the community at the centre of my heart. I shouldn't have eaten it. And water … It's not allowed! I have to confess. Now. Don't worry. I won't …"

Mary's eyes narrowed, and hardened. Slate-like, they stared at her. Evie saw no pity in them, but Mary's voice was gentle. "Things are different here. Leave that." She tried to take the tablet out of Evie's hand.

Evie clutched it tightly. Another test? "I have to confess. Everyone knows that. Don't stop me. It's not allowed."

Mary let go, but kept her hand raised above Evie's arm, ready to pounce. "We don't have a permanent connection anyway. We only communicate in the evening. Do it then."

Evie crouched on the edge of her mat with her arms clasped tightly around her legs. Another test? So many ways to be in error. The teacher hadn't prepared her for this. At home, there was struc-ture. You knew what was right. *How do you keep doing the right thing in the out-country?* she wondered. Evie closed her eyes, rocking back and forth. She dug her knees into her eye sockets, before looking directly at Mary. She thought Mary flinched and moved backwards ever so slightly.

"Why do you have fish?" Evie said.

"We get it from the sea." Mary watched Evie, calmly.

"Why don't you share it? We don't have it. Ever. You should send it to the living-domes, not keep it for yourselves, eating two bowls of food for breakfast. And you shouldn't eat alone anyway. Meals should be communal. You're in error, and I'm going to say so."

Mary didn't move. Mary didn't flinch again. Mary breathed slowly, running her eyes up and down Evie's scrawny body.

"And you shouldn't waste water. It's dripping on the floor! That's in error, too. I'm going to report that as well." Evie's voice rose to a screech. She clasped her knees even more tightly.

"You must do what you think right, Evie."

Evie frowned. "Don't you know? We can all die, just like that. The future depends on us. You want a better future, don't you?"

Mary continued staring.

"I've seen. I've seen what they do," Evie hissed, speaking though a half-closed mouth, her eyes wrinkled shut, her nails digging through her clothes into her legs. "I've seen what happens. It'll happen to you, if you don't confess."

"Would you like me to show you around?" Mary asked. Evie gasped. Another test? Who would say that? No one would say that. Evie realised her words dripped off this woman like the water onto the floor. The words flowed through her, and she remained the same. Evie's eyes filled with tears. She screamed into a scrunched-up ball of clothes, stuffing it into her mouth.

"I want to go home," she cried.

"You can't. Do you think we want you here?"

Evie remained motionless.

"Well, if you're not coming out, I'll show you around from here." Mary waited for a response, but received none. "Alright. As you so cleverly noticed, we're by the sea. There's lots of water, but it's salt water. You can't drink it. But you can get wet sheets and hang them up in the wind. It keeps you cool, and it's better for the environment than air conditioning. So, we aren't in error on that front. And fish live in the sea. We catch them, and we eat them. We can't send them inland because they'd go off. In return, we don't get central supplies. So, we aren't in error on that point either." Mary waited, noticing that Evie's shoulders no longer shook. "So, will you come out now? Whatever they told you, I'm sure they told you to be of use to us. Not sit in here like a snivelling baby."

"And the sickness?" Evie said.

"There's been no sickness here for a long time."

Evie shoved the clothes further into her mouth until they choked her.

"Get up. Come with me."

Evie pulled the clothes out of her mouth. She put her tablet neatly at the top of her mattress and crawled out of her pod. Then she followed Mary out into the village.

The pods encircled a ring of stones, which looked about the right height for sitting on. Evie counted. Twenty-five living-pods, all identically sized except for one much bigger pod. Mary was right, all the pods opened onto the sea, and had wet sheets across the doorways. Evie thought they were made of the same material as the living-domes, silvery grey, designed to reflect heat. The ground inside the circle was barren and rocky, but outside it, small scrubby bushes grew.

Curiosity led her towards the sea. Mary followed. Evie stopped when the ground fell away. Water launched itself against the rocks below. Evie leant into the wind, feeling it supporting her weight. She moved her hand to her face to pull her muslin off. What would it be like to feel wind on her face? Mary put a hand out to stop her.

"Don't let it fool you. You can still get burned in minutes."

Evie peered over the edge, imagining the feel of the spray. Once, when she was small, she'd run outside, naked. They'd poured water on her burning skin. The freshness of it still tingled in her memory.

Ropes showed the way down to the water, a worn path marking out the route people usually took. Evie watched the sea, the waves growing as they approached the land, as if roused to anger. Could the sea be angry? There was something on the sea, too. Small figures. Evie pointed.

"They're fishing," Mary said.

"How?"

"On boats, with nets."

"Boats?" Evie remembered pictures of boats. Some with sails, which came from the time before the errors began. Ships with funnels, choking the air, from the bad times. None of the pictures matched these small, unstable boats. Each had two people, bobbing and bouncing along.

"Boats. We make them from things the sea gives us."

"What does the sea give you?"

"Wood, plastic, other things from the olden days. The sea cleans them and gives them back when it's ready."

"The earth gives us things at home."

"It's the same," Mary said.

Evie watched the waves. "You can't dig in the sea."

"No."

"So how does the sea give you things?"

"When the storms come. And the water falls away. There used to be a town down there." Mary waved at the sea below their feet.

"A town?"

"Yes. But people have always lived up here. Lived a better way. The earth told us."

"But how do you receive the things the sea gives?"

"We go down. We look. When the water is lower. We can't fish then, because the boats would wreck."

"When does it happen?" Evie asked.

"Every now and again. We watch the moon. And listen for the storms."

Evie replayed the howling sandstorms of home in her mind. When people would huddle together, so close they almost touched. The storms were sent to bring them together. *To remind us we cannot stand alone.* But here? Everyone lived in their own pod. Evie looked at the shape of Mary, covered in her muslin. Would she huddle with Mary in a storm?

"Why don't you have a living-dome?" Evie asked.

"Smaller ones work better here."

"Do you all live alone? That's not allowed."

"Evie," Mary's shoulders rose and fell, "we do what we need to survive. People don't live alone; they live with their families."

"Families?"

Families used to live in houses, one for each family.

Another test?

"Families divide society, they made us selfish. It wasn't friendly. And they squander resources," Evie said.

"I'll leave you to make up your own mind about that. It's just how it is, here."

The calmness of Mary's voice stopped Evie's objection.

"Come on. You should meet the others," Mary said.

Evie turned towards the village, and took an involuntary step backwards. People. Lots of people, enveloped in cloth, staring at her. They waited for her to walk towards them with Mary. Mary stopped by the stones, looked around at the crowd, and spoke, her voice mingling with the wind, chasing around the village and disappearing into the landscape.

"This is Evie. We welcome her to our village. She's here to learn about life in the out-country. This is her First Task since confirmation, and we should help her with it." Murmurs filled the air. "Come and greet her before you go off to your tasks."

Evie stood still as eyes in cloth-covered forms walked towards her. "Welcome to Eden," they said. Evie looked into each of their eyes. One man paused in front of her. His eyes roved over her face. "You shouldn't have come," he said. Evie stared back at him.

"They gave me this task and I will do it."

"You may wish they hadn't, before long."

"Oh John, not now, it's only her first day," Mary said. "Let her find her feet." She placed her hand on his arm, and Evie stared. "Evie, this is John. He's our best farmer. Can grow anything, anywhere."

"Welcome, Evie," John said.

Evie watched Mary's hand until she took it off John's arm.

"Why don't you take her with you today?" Mary said. "Show her around the farm."

Evie followed his broad shape towards a solar vehicle. He sat in the driver's seat and patted the seat next to him. Evie climbed in, waiting for the whirring of the motor. They set off, bumping and bouncing over the ground. She watched John, whose eyes watched only the ground ahead, occasionally swinging the steering wheel violently to miss rocks. Evie hadn't noticed how steeply the ground rose up behind the village. Gravity pulled her backwards as they climbed. She gripped her seat, trying to sway in time with the vehicle, but it kept jolting her.

After about half an hour they reached the top. Three rows of wind turbines stood there, and underneath them a blanket of solar panels stretched across the top of the hill.

"We're here," John said.

"I thought you were farming," Evie said.

John got out of the vehicle and walked around to Evie's side. He appeared not to have heard her. "So, what can you do?" he said.

Evie blinked up at the turbines, two of which weren't moving properly. Evie could see that immediately. Their blades were turning out of sync. "The pitch is off on those blades. I can fix that," she said.

"I know the pitch is off."

"Why haven't you fixed it then?" Evie got out of the vehicle and found herself eye to eye with him. John's hands turned to fists inside his gloves.

"We've tried," he said.

"We?" Evie glanced around.

"Now, listen here. If you think you can show up here and tell us how to live, you've got—" Evie took a step away from him. She could see his muslin moving in time with his breath.

"No one tells anyone anything," she said. "We fulfil our obligations to our community to the best of our abilities."

"Is that so?"

Evie glared at him, her heart racing. Another test? No one would say that. Not if they had sense. Not if they had the good of their community in the centre of their heart. Not if they really cared about the future. She looked around the hill. They appeared to be alone. The dust-heavy air gathered speed up the hill, charging into the turbines, whistling over their wire anchors.

"That's so," she said.

"Well, why don't you try to fix it then?"

Evie walked towards the first turbine, conscious of his eyes at her back. She found the open door at the base of the turbine and placed her foot on the ladder. She gripped the handrail tightly and tried to step confidently upwards. They'd only ever looked at motors like this in the classroom. It should be the same though, surely? What difference did height make? None. She stepped slowly up and around the inside of the turbine.

As she climbed higher the turbine swayed gently. The wind found gaps around the rivets and whistled through the stairwell. Evie clutched rails on either side of the steps. But the steps swayed, too. She felt the distance below her, calling, dragging her down. It hadn't looked like that in the pictures. She forced herself upwards, waiting until she was sure her feet were stable before moving on.

She found the tool container attached to the ladder near the top, just as it should be. Her mind flipped to the next image she'd seen on the communicator screen. She took the box with her and opened the service hatch, which gave access to the motor and turbines. She slid herself along gently, pictures flicking through her mind. Don't get caught here, don't stop here, don't touch this. Turn this off.

Her shaking fingers roved around the components, her lips whispering to them as she touched them. She traced the wires. 'This is fixed to this, and this is fixed to that,' she chanted to herself. 'And this goes here, and that goes there, and this should go around here ... it does, good.' The sound of her voice calmed her. She unwound her muslin and took off her gloves, stuffing them into the tool container. She smiled. It looked exactly like it should.

She carried on looking, searching for something out of place. Her fingers rubbed around the metal strands. They felt a brittle, sandy thing. She rubbed her fingers together and examined them. Rust. She took out the tools and began to loosen screws, which whined and screamed in protest. Evie worked quickly now, confidently. She scraped and blew and rubbed and tightened and loosened screws. She hummed to herself to drown out the wind. She took out the spare oil and spread some around with her finger.

Finally, she tightened the screws for the last time, blew on the wires to clear the dust, and whispered to them: "You should work now, shouldn't you?" Then she inched her way back to the hatch. She turned the turbines back on, listening for the screeching as they turned again. She shut the hatch, replaced the tool container and climbed steadily back down. Her legs shook. Once at the bottom, she paused, holding onto the ladder to steady herself. Eventually, she replaced her muslin and gloves and stepped out into the open.

She emerged straight into John's shadow. Evie stopped. John looked at her, his eyes blank. Evie tried to read him from the angle of his shoulders, from his hands. But his hands were loose by his sides.

"I fixed it," Evie said.

"I can see."

"Shall I do the other one?"

"Yes, perhaps you won't be such a burden to us after all."

John moved aside and let her walk to the other broken turbine. "So, you'll fix that one, too?"

"Of course," Evie said. Her hand shook again when she placed it on the handrail. As she climbed the steps, she realised that she was unaccountably tired.

Coming down an hour later, she thought she could hear voices. John was waiting with another man. The other man's eyes looked younger, watching Evie through his muslin. Much younger. He blinked at her. Evie walked up to them both.

"Can I have some water?" she said.

The younger man nodded. "Follow me. We'll eat."

"You two go. Show her around. I'm going back," John said.

The two of them walked towards another solar vehicle that was parked a short distance from John's.

"So, who are you?" Evie said.

"I'm Sam."

"I'm Evie."

"I know. I saw you this morning."

"How do I know that I met you? Why don't you have a living-dome? If I only ever see you all with your muslins on, I'll never know anyone."

"You'll get used to it."

"No, I won't."

"You can visit people, in their pod. Come and see us."

"That's not allowed."

Sam laughed, throwing his head back. "'Not allowed.' Who's going to not allow it here?"

Evie opened her mouth to speak, but by then they had reached the vehicle and Sam turned his back on her to look for water. He pulled out a bottle and a packet of food. "Let's sit under a solar panel, on the other side of the hill. It's cooler there."

Evie followed him, feeling her feet dragging on the ground. It had been more tiring than she'd supposed, fixing the turbines. He led her through the solar panels to where the ground began to fall back downwards. But this wasn't like the seaside—the scrubby patches, dry earth, and occasional rocks stretched on towards the horizon. Evie lazily looked at the view, but then she frowned and scrunched up her eyes, trying to focus on something in the distance. Another dome? Something grey, and flickering in the light. She opened her mouth to ask, but Sam spoke first.

"My dad says you did a miracle on the turbines."

"Your dad?" Evie's brain raced. *Dad.* That word had been used before, somewhere. *Dad, dad.*

"Yes, he said you fixed a totally broken actuator."

"Dad?"

"Yes, my dad. John."

"What's your 'dad'?" Evie scratched her arm. How had she forgotten? Someone had told her what that meant.

"My dad looks after the farming, and things up here."

"No, what is that? A 'dad'?"

Sam's eyes narrowed. His head tilted to one side. "Really?"

"Tell me." Evie's fist pounded against her leg.

"He's my dad. My father. What's up with you?"

"How dare you talk to me like that?" she said. "I didn't know it was the same as 'father'."

"How dare you talk to *me* like that?" Sam raised himself up and looked down on her.

"Family dilutes your dedication to the community. It's not allowed," she said.

Sam laughed again and sat down under a solar panel with his back to her.

Another test? These people were so wrong, about everything. "I will have to report all the errors I see here. You should confess yourself. Learn to be better. We have to sacrifice ourselves for the future."

Sam snorted. "Maybe you should just stick to fixing things and keep your mouth shut."

They ate their bread and paste in silence. Evie thought it tasted odd, heavy somehow. But it filled her stomach in a comforting way.

Evie knew she would need to confess her rage. Loss of temper was wrong. Loss of control over emotions was wrong. She pinched the skin on her legs through her trousers. She hadn't needed to confess that for a long time. It was an error of those still learning. Those who hadn't yet learned how to behave.

In Evie's mind the sound of her chewing was loud, and disruptive. She became increasingly conscious of it. "What's that in the distance?" she said.

Sam shrugged. The silence continued for a few minutes until Sam, too, felt the silence weighing on him. "It's a village."

"Like Eden?"

"No, it's a Religious community. They're still loyal to the old religions."

"No one believes in religion anymore, do they? I thought they'd all been educated?" Evie peered more closely into the distance, trying to make out people.

"Not them. They still believe in some mixture of all the old religions. They mostly live apart, but they're useful."

"Useful?"

"They keep mammals."

"That's one of the five great evils of the olden days. You need to educate them."

"Apparently so. But we trade with them."

"Trade what?"

"Meat," he said, with a slight hesitation, as if aware of the storm he was brewing.

"Meat?" Evie's voice rose. She fumbled with the hem of her tunic.

"Yes, it's good for staying healthy."

"You mean …? Meat? Like, mammals?"

"Yes, Evie, we eat mammals." His body shifted slightly towards her.

"When? Often?"

"Yes. What do you think's on your bread?"

Evie looked down at it. It looked like brown paste. It looked like protein paste. "That's not mammal."

"It is. Not much, but it's there. Protein pods aren't enough. You need meat."

Evie pulled at her muslin to get her hands to her face. She stuck her fingers down her throat and retched. Her head spun and she put out a hand to steady herself, but it missed the edge of the solar panel and she tipped forward. Meat! It would surely kill her, one way or another. She coughed, desperate to get it out, but it had lodged firmly in her stomach and her body didn't want to let it go. She sobbed, burying her face in her hands, pressing herself into the ground, wanting to disappear into it. Wanting to melt away.

Sam chuckled to himself. He crawled and leant over her, making his shadow swallow her up. He leant in close so he could whisper in her ear. "You should go back. We don't want you."

His voice hissed through her mind, like water on heated metal.

Chapter 6

EVIE SAID VERY LITTLE FOR the rest of the day. She followed Sam around. Sat next to him in the solar vehicle, saw the fields with protein pods, tried to learn how the machine worked that took the salt out of the water. She told herself to remember not to drink salt water.

She looked around the large communal pod and found the communicator, but Sam refused to tell her where to connect her tablet. Evie didn't lose her temper. Instead, she crouched at the back of the pod, her hands around her knees, with her muslin still on and her face buried. Sam left her alone, and she was glad of the silence for a while. But her ears began to hum with the absence of sound.

"Come out, come out, it's swimming time!" A small cloth-draped infant ran in. Evie hardly raised her head to look at it. Its tunic was too long, and it stumbled around in circles, half-walking, half-jumping. "Swimming time! Woooo!"

Swimming. Another old half-remembered word. A history lesson breathed into life. Swimming, with water, or in the air? People did swim in the air, didn't they? Was it gliding? With cloth hanging over their heads, and metal tubes to hold. Or was that another word? The question distracted Evie for a while. She heard another noise and looked up to see the shape of Mary coming through the door.

"Come and swim, Evie. Have you swum before?" Mary said.

"No. I don't know what it is."

"Come with me." Mary held out her hand. Evie stood up and followed her out.

The villagers had gathered at the edge of the land. One by one they disappeared over the edge. Evie walked tentatively, her feet unsure of the ground. She stopped at the edge and watched. People made their way down the narrow path to a large flat rock at the bottom.

Once there, still fully clothed, they floated on the sea, and dragged themselves along by holding a rope that was attached to a boat. Once at the boat they let go. Evie shrieked. The sea, the person, something was wrong. They were walking. You didn't walk on water. An infant giggled and jumped up and down. Evie buried her head in her gloved hands. Mary laughed.

"There's a building out there. We stand on the old roof, so it's safe for the babies," Mary said.

Evie looked again.

"You try. You'll like it," Mary said.

Evie followed her down the path to the rock, and watched the person in front of her launch themselves into the foaming sea.

"Just hold the rope and drag yourself along. It's nice. You'll never leave the out-country once you've tried it," Mary said. Evie watched the jumping infants, clapping and shrieking. The older figures splashed themselves with water, then lay down in it, rolling over a few times before resting back on their arms, seemingly asleep.

Evie knelt and took hold of the rope. She tugged gently at it. "You have to jump," Mary said.

Evie counted out her breaths. She counted them again, and again. Each time the sea looked calm, another wave quickly followed. She jumped out of the way of each of them, avoiding the spray.

"You've got to go now. Really, there are others behind you who'll be furious if they miss out."

She must put the community before herself, she thought. She must do her share. Evie closed her eyes and hopped. The ground disappeared under her feet, and she sank into the water. Even through her tunic, it burned. It burned like the sun. She gasped from the shock and her lungs filled with water. Her hands gripped the rope and she pulled madly at it. After a couple of seconds her head broke the surface. She coughed out water. "It's burning!" Evie screamed. "It's burning."

"Breathe slowly. Calm down," someone shouted, the tremor in their voice exposing the laughter underneath their speech.

"Did you hear? She thinks it's hot!"

"Crazy!"

"Thinks she knows everything but thinks water is hot."

"It did feel hot," Evie shouted, pulling herself on the rope. The initial feeling of heat had gone, and she could tell, now, that it was cold. But they did feel the same, at first. The cold ran over her skin, seemingly sinking into it. Evie could feel it touching her insides, her lungs, her stomach, inside her bones. It felt as if a weight had gone; the weight of heat.

Evie pulled herself onto the roof of the olden-day building and lay down. The water reached halfway up her body and she relaxed into it, her front half-immersed, her back to the sun.

Mary followed and lay down next to her. "Glad you came?"

"Yes," Evie whispered, "the heat never left my body before."

"Things are different in the out-country," Mary said, while splashing water all over her body. "You will sleep so well tonight. Sleep like you've never slept before."

"This was an olden-day building?"

"Yes, we don't know what kind. After storms the sea gives us all sorts of things from inside this one, and others." Mary splashed water over her head. "We used to have a man who could swim underwater—he went down, he said he could see things."

"Like what?"

"Lots of things. It was a long time ago. He said there are a lot of buildings down there. More than we ever suspected."

Evie began to unwind her muslin from her face. "Don't do that. It's still not safe," Mary said.

"Even when you're not hot?"

"It's not being hot that does it. You'll still burn."

Evie re-tied it but dipped her nose and chin into the water. It smelt like metal, or fish. She could make out the shape of the roof stretching out ahead of her. Tiny feet stamped on it, jumped on it, making fountains of droplets.

Helicopters hovered over crowds of screaming people clinging to ruined buildings, deciding who to save. Mothers held up their wriggling babies.

Was that here?

Were these infants like the wriggling babies? she thought.

Evie watched two toddlers with their hands together, stamping. They shrieked, falling backwards onto their bottoms, clapping. Their shrillness killed all other sounds. The adults turned to face them and laughed. One figure, with the shape of a woman, clapped her hands together, splashing one of the babies with droplets. She wrapped her arms around it and put her face close to its head. Evie flinched. Was she hurting it? But the baby splashed the water again and giggled. The woman rolled it onto its back and scooped water onto its body.

A ritual?

But why the touching? It wasn't allowed.

Evie dragged herself closer.

The woman lifted the baby up, its arms and legs thrashing wildly. She moved it around in the air before half-throwing it into the water. The toddler laughed again and put out its hands to the woman's face, feeling her features under her muslin. Their faces got close and seemed to rub against each other.

Evie looked at the rest of them. None of them cared. A few even touched each other with their hands.

Evie looked away. It wasn't allowed.

She could feel a pain, a pain in her stomach. It moved into her throat and seemed to be choking her.

Joe had touched her, and that had hurt.

But the baby wasn't hurt.

The hand-touching didn't hurt them, she thought.

What was it that baby was feeling?

Why wasn't it pain?

Or did it laugh when it was in pain?

Surely not.

Evie rolled onto her back to watch the sky, her throat still choking her. She coughed. Her eyes stung.

"Time to go back, everyone." Evie realised she'd been asleep. She rolled over and looked down at her body encased in the wet cloth. She wriggled her gloved hands under the water, watching the material swirl, like sand in a storm. She blinked and stopped moving. The water billowed and swept through her clothes. The cloth around the top of her left arm looked a different colour. Evie watched it, unsure at first whether it was the water. The small patch spread, leaking through the cloth like blood. With her right arm she pulled up handfuls of cloth to cover it up. Then she sank under the water— no one would see, surely? They were all too busy splashing their final splashes before moving back towards the rope, and the shore.

Evie followed them. The weight of water pulled her back into the sea as she tried to get out. Someone held out their hand to help her. Evie staggered, and nearly fell over. Who'd have thought water was so heavy on you? The sea breeze pushed against her, moulding her clothes around her legs. Something strange happened to her skin. It stung. It felt heavy. Evie was shaking. Her lips knocked against each other, and there was nothing she could do to stop it. Her insides felt empty, light, and hungry. Had water got in and cooled her from the inside out? Evie didn't know. Could water get through your skin? Or your ears? She put her hand up to her head and rubbed her ear. And then, again, she tried to bunch up the fabric around her upper left arm.

The rest of the villagers stood, arms outstretched, in the middle of the village. The younger ones chased and stumbled around each other. "Don't worry, you'll be dry very soon. Go and change into your spare clothes if you're cold." Evie thought it was Mary who had spoken, but the figure turned away from her, and it was difficult to tell.

Evie began to walk towards Mary's pod. Her clothes felt stiff and solid.

"She's bleeding! She's bleeding!" Evie paid no attention to the shout until the patter of feet became loud all around her. Five boys or girls stared up at her, one with an arm outstretched, pointing at her. "Did you hurt yourself?" one of them asked.

"It's easy to do. You need to be careful of metal from the olden days."

Heat spread from Evie's lungs, to her heart, which beat more and more quickly. Her teeth knocked against each other.

"It's …" she said, coughing, "it's not. I haven't." She covered her upper arm with her hand. But that made it worse. Red grew between her fingers, spread outwards. Evie ran towards the pod and launched herself through the open door into her sleeping pod. Once there, she fought her clothes off and threw them in a pile by the door. She scrabbled frantically with her spare clothes, tangling herself up in them, feeling them choke her and trap her arms against her body.

"Don't worry. I'll tape it up," Mary said.

"It's OK. I'm fine," Evie said, trying to stop her voice leaping. "Don't come in."

But Mary did come in. She lifted the curtain of the sleeping pod aside and looked down at Evie. Evie was crouched on her mat, with one arm in the sleeve of her tunic, the head-hole awkwardly stretched around her neck. Mary thought she saw red in Evie's hand and moved closer. It looked like a pool of blood, gathered in her palm. But as she looked again, she realised it wasn't blood. It was some sort of cloth, scrunched up in her hand, its colour running out of it, dripping from Evie's hand onto the floor. Mary turned and walked back outside.

Chapter 7

AN HOUR LATER EVIE FINALLY emerged from Mary's pod. The red hairband was safely back on her arm. She resisted the urge to cover it with her hand. She glared at the other figures walking alongside her. They would surely take it from her, even though it had been given to her. It was partly the smell of food that had drawn her out, and partly that she knew she couldn't hide forever. She walked across the open patch at the centre of the village and into the larger pod, where she found the villagers sitting in a circle, talking quietly. The adults had made a large circle, and the smaller ones were in the middle: some lay, some sat, and some crawled around. All of them had removed their gloves and muslins and Evie stared at them, trying to match the faces to the shapes she'd seen before, and the voices she'd heard.

They stared back. The adults stopped talking. Mary was there, next to John. She knew him from his eyes. And Sam, who looked just like his father, sat further away, next to two other young men. Mary made a space for Evie between herself and another old woman. Evie unwrapped her muslin and hung it around her neck. She took off her gloves and wedged them into her waistband. She hesitated. "Thank you for welcoming me into your community," she said. Then walked quickly towards the space next to Mary. A few adults murmured, then began speaking to each other again.

Evie tried to read Mary's face, but there seemed to be nothing there. Evie had never seen a woman so old. She was probably over fifty.

After a few minutes, another woman walked over to Mary and whispered in her ear. Mary held up her hand and the villagers instantly stopped talking. "We must thank the earth for the gifts it has given us today. Tonight, we will eat well, and we must be grateful."

"We thank the earth for the gifts it has given. Our gratitude is unending," they all replied. Evie's lips moved with theirs, the only familiar sound she'd heard since her arrival. It was something to tie herself to. She wrapped the words around her, feeling their undulations, the shapes they made in her mouth, and in her mind. They tasted of home. They tasted of comfort.

The bowls were passed around, each of them different. Some made of wood, some scavenged plastic, some beaten, scavenged metal. Evie's was metal and felt warm. She watched the pot of food passing from person to person. Evie leant closer to Mary. "I can't eat mammals," she said.

She felt Mary's weight shift on her crossed legs. "Tonight, it's fish."

"Thank you," Evie said. It smelt like breakfast. Evie spooned out enough to fill half her bowl, and began to eat.

The other woman next to her didn't say a word; her eyes seemed fixed on her bowl. All around her, Evie heard the murmurs of conversation. Like a song it filled the pod, rising and falling, obeying its own rules. Rules she didn't know. Evie ate in silence.

John walked around the edge of the circle and crouched down behind Sam. He put both his hands on Sam's shoulders and leant in to talk to him. Sam's eyes closed. Did it hurt? Was it painful to have someone's hands on your shoulders? Evie watched Sam's face, but it looked content. Sam smiled and turned towards his father, who also smiled. Then Sam placed one of his hands on his father's. Evie shuddered. What were they doing? What was all this touching? Didn't it hurt? Her throat tightened. After a few moments John stood up again. Evie avoided looking at his face as he walked back to his place on the other side of the circle.

They allowed her a second bowl of food. The babies dribbled food from their faces, and remained unpunished. Eventually the circle broke up and people made their way back to their own pods. Evie waited, wanting to be the last to leave.

"You coming? You must be tired," Mary said.

"I need to do my confession. Where do I go?"

Mary sighed. "Really?"

"Yes, we all should do it before we go to sleep. It's the rules."

"OK." Mary pointed towards the back of the pod. "Behind the stove, there."

Evie walked over to where she pointed. An ancient communicator sat precariously on an olden-day table with one leg replaced with a stump of wood. "Is it on?" Evie asked.

Mary walked over and began fiddling with wires at the back of the screen. A light came on, and it began to whirr. "It is now. Tell me when you're done."

"It doesn't look like you use it often enough," Evie said.

"It gets used. Tell me when you're done." Mary walked out.

Evie waited for the confirmation message. Then she typed in her number. Her home screen came up. Evie began to type.

This whole place is much in error. I don't think I can correct it on my own. But I will try. They haven't eradicated a band of Religious. They eat mammals. They touch one another—I think they may have families. They live in separate pods—they don't have a living-dome. They have lots of food; some of it is fish. They say they don't have to send it to the megadomes because it doesn't keep, and because they don't get central supplies. But I don't know if this is true. They have more food than I've ever seen. The sea gives them much, I think. Including water. You probably don't know how much water there is, and they can take the salt out of it. They say that once the salt is gone it is used for farming. This is water we've been searching for all these years. And there isn't any sickness. You should come and claim it all. I have been shocked by them, and I have made many errors. I lost my temper when I found out about the mammal eating. I have tried to challenge them, but I haven't done enough. There is so much to do and I am disheartened, I don't know what to do. They make me sick. They threaten our whole future. With people like this we will never build a new world. Please give me guidance. Send people to take these supplies. I will prepare for their arrival. Please forgive me my errors, I will try to be better tomorrow, and every day thereafter. The good of our community is still in the centre of my heart. Please tell me what I should do.

Evie clasped her hands in her lap and reread her message. Was it the right tone? Surely, they wouldn't believe anything Mary might say about her now? Evie closed her eyes for a moment, and then typed a final sentence.

The one in charge of this is Mary. And she is helped in all this error by John and Sam.

Evie sent the message. Then wrapped her muslin around her head, put on her gloves, and walked back to Mary's pod. "Goodnight, Mary," she said, moving swiftly into her sleeping pod.

"Goodnight, Evie."

Mary waited until she was sure that Evie slept. Then she got up, wrapped herself up and walked quickly back to the communal pod. Once there she logged into the communicator. She disconnected a black box at the back from one wire, and attached it to another. And then she read Evie's message that the box had caught. She barely moved as she did so. It wasn't so different from those the others had sent, but something was strange. Mary reread the message, searching for the feeling inside the words; trying to touch Evie's mind. She closed her eyes. The others had confessed doubt. She remembered the pattern of their words. They had asked small questions. Mary's eyes opened suddenly. She stared at the message, looking at its shape. Evie had no doubts. Evie had no doubts at all. Mary's hand shook as she raised it to her mouth.

Mary typed.

> *Thank you for your message, Evie. Be assured, we appreciate the enormous task we have given you. We see the work you are doing, but for the moment, you must do it alone. Our primary requirement of you is to get to know them, get to know how they have fallen into such error. Learn their ways and tell us everything.*
>
> *Your errors have been logged, but we understand. You are free of guilt. We thank you again for your contribution to the good of our community, and wish you success.*

Mary sent it. Evie would receive it, as if it had come from them. Then she typed in another number, Evie's number, which the box had recorded for her. Mary sent a different message from Evie. She confessed fear, she confessed doubt. She wrote of the sickness of the sea. She wrote of the hunger and the water that kills. She wrote of the burial heaps, she wrote of only one baby, she wrote of deformities, and she wrote of the raiders who come from the sea to steal, and kill, and rape. She wrote of the end of the world. She begged to be taken away. She confessed that she feared she wouldn't last long. She said there wasn't enough food, and that she thought that she was sick.

Mary sent the message and erased everything on the black box.

The message flew through the sky with the wind. It was caught by a low-level transmitter, which passed it to the next one, as if machinery were playing a game. So, it bounced, from one to the next, and reached the megadome, where it stopped, and was no longer a game. The words it carried whispered through communicators, merged with other messages, mixed with rumours, picked up anecdotes. Anecdotes merged into facts. The facts spread from mouth to mouth, like sickness. "Don't go to the out-country. It's the end of the world."

Chapter 8

EVIE SETTLED INTO HER LIFE. She spent the days with John, or Sam, or Mary, mainly fixing and servicing the wind turbines and solar panels. They worked in the morning, and in the evening, when it was cooler. In the middle of the day, they hid in the shade. As soon as it was dark, they covered their lights, because lights could bring raiders, although they hadn't been seen for years. She learned how to get the salt out of water, changed fuses, replaced worn wires, and adjusted the angle of the turbines as the winds changed. She bathed in the sea whenever she could. She found herself longing for the cooling water while she worked. It was a distraction, which she confessed repeatedly. She confessed many things, but the replies were always the same. "Carry on. Keep going. We can't spare more people."

In the first few weeks she held out hope that a transport would appear on the horizon. A transport filled with others from the living-domes. A transport filled with other people who knew how to live without being in error. Some of them would have guns. Evie imagined them coming through the perimeter. They would List Mary, and John, and Sam. Now that she knew what that really meant, all the better. But perhaps they'd shoot Mary. They did shoot people. Evie had watched it once, when she was younger. A woman had been shot as a sign to everyone. The blood had sprayed out of her and made a pattern on the wall. It had been a beautiful pattern, a pattern like flowers. Evie drew strength from the image of Mary like that, slumped on the ground awkwardly. The image of Mary with blank eyes. Evie had even warned Mary that they would come, but Mary had laughed. Mary's laughter shuddered through Evie whenever she thought of it. How could someone laugh at that? *Perhaps Mary doesn't know what happens when you're Listed,* Evie thought. Perhaps Mary doesn't know what it means to be shot.

The rest of the village seemed wary of Evie. She repeatedly confessed their lack of community spirit.

One evening, Evie emerged over the bank by the sea and walked towards Mary's pod. She heard squelching footsteps behind her but paid no attention. The infants would sometimes follow her around. But the footsteps sped up. Evie didn't look round but could sense an adult body behind her.

"Evie!" The voice was quiet, but urgent.

"Yes?" Evie stopped, but didn't turn around.

"Be careful." The voice was definitely female.

"What do you mean?"

"Don't fight it. Become one of us."

Evie turned around, but the woman pulled her muslin up so it covered her whole face, even her eyes.

"You are so much in error," Evie said. "The domes need this food. Children are hungry. You're risking the future. We have to build a better world."

"I thought so too, once. But you must change."

"Why?"

"I came from a living-dome as well, a long time ago," the woman said, her head turning from side to side as if to check that no one was listening.

"You know better then, you're in error. What's your name?" Evie said, trying to make out her face through her muslin and remembering her shape so she might recognise her later.

"Stop it. Become one of us. If you don't, they'll … they'll …"

"What?"

"These people will kill you."

Evie hesitated. The woman's words shot through her head like pain. "They won't. I'm a representative of the Central Committee of Porters. They can't."

"They'll do anything to stop the domes finding out what life is like here. They've killed every person who's arrived and hasn't accepted this way of life. Most, they killed. And then they send back stories about the sickness, and starvation. It's a wonder the domes keep sending people. So I'm warning you. It isn't so bad. It's nice, once you accept this life."

"You're in error, and you know it. The future depends on all of us."

"I won't warn you again. But stop this, Evie. It's for real. They will kill you, and no one will notice. If you become one of us, you'll have a nice life. A better life."

Evie was about to speak again but the woman turned and walked away. Evie watched, to see which pod she went to, but she didn't walk into any pod. She walked back towards the sea and joined a group of figures. The people moved around each other, swapped places, and Evie could no longer pick out the woman who had spoken to her. Evie blinked and went into Mary's pod, where she changed into her other set of clothes, and prepared to go and eat.

Evie took her usual seat, next to Mary, and folded her hands in her lap. Evie smelt the fish. Her stomach longed for the food. She ate so much more now. In the beginning it had been strange, but now it felt as if she needed it.

Mary raised her hand and silenced the crowd. "We must thank the earth for the gifts it has given us today. Tonight, we will eat well, and we must be grateful."

"We thank the earth for the gifts it has given. Our gratitude is unending," they all replied.

Mary's hand remained raised. "Tonight, we must be especially grateful. Martin went to trade with the Religious, and we have meat."

People laughed, and smiled, and looked at each other. Evie stared at her hands and rubbed her fingers. The pot of food passed from hand to hand. People put their faces close to it and smelled. The smiled as they ate.

Mary handed Evie the pot. "I can't eat mammals," Evie said.

"What?" Mary spoke loudly, and most of the village paused to listen.

"I can't eat mammals. It's one of the Great Errors. Only the Religious stuck to that old error."

Voices rippled around the pod: "Oh, be quiet."

"What do you know?"

"Don't believe it."

"They talk such nonsense."

"She's very silly, isn't she?"

"Ungrateful."

The words mingled with one another and Evie couldn't make out full sentences. But the tone was clear. She looked around the pod, frowning. "You know you're in error. You will be punished."

They laughed. Mary laughed the loudest. She held out her hand to Evie. Evie shrank away from it. "I know they told you that, but it's not true. None of it. You can eat mammals. We do it in a good way." She put the pot at Evie's feet. Evie wanted to reach out and take some. It smelt like fish, but different. It smelt like it would taste good.

"I won't eat it. Can I have something else, please?"

Mary smiled at her. "Evie, this is what our community is eating tonight. You don't have to eat it, and we won't make you. But there is nothing else."

"Some bread?" Evie stared at the pot, feeling one of her hands moving closer to the ladle.

"If you don't want to join in the communal meal, you can go. But you can't partly join in," Mary said.

Evie looked at them. Those with food had begun eating again. Many whispered to one another.

"Give it to me, if you don't want it. I do," the woman sitting on the other side of her said. She took the pot. Evie watched it pass her by. Hunger, again. Hunger felt like home. Evie stood up and walked out of the pod. She didn't think anyone really watched her go.

Evie paused outside for a moment, listening to the sounds of the village. She listened to the sound of the sea. They merged together, voices and waves, crashing and laughing. She let the breeze cool her and listened.

Someone clapped their hands.

"We are expecting a communication tonight. Those who want to listen are welcome." It was a voice she didn't recognise. Evie crouched down. "It should be at eleven." Noise began again. "No, you can't stay up. Infants need to be asleep." Evie heard wails of protest from the young ones. Communications didn't normally happen at night. Normally they happened in the morning, she thought. But perhaps it was different here. Evie walked back to Mary's pod and lay down on her mat.

When Mary came back, she pretended to sleep. Nevertheless, Mary pulled her curtain aside and looked at her. "Evie."

Evie pretended to wake.

"Here." Mary held out bread.

Evie sat up. "Thank you."

"I was angry because you're so obstinate. But you should eat something."

Evie sat up and ate the bread. "What's happening tonight then?"

Mary frowned. "I thought you might have heard. We have a communication. Come if you want."

"From the Central Committee?" Evie said. This might be it. This might be the moment. Vengeance, punishment, they might all come tonight.

"Come along," Mary said, turning her back on Evie and walking into her own sleeping pod.

Evie frowned. Who else could possibly communicate? Maybe a local dome. Perhaps another village. She lay on her mat and waited until Mary got up again. It was dark when they came out, and it was difficult to see the way to the communal pod. A dim glow of a sustainable lamp seeped through the door, but whenever the door closed Evie could only see blackness. Evie followed Mary, and gradually, most of the adults from the village took their places. They seemed excited, and happy. But Evie wondered whether that was possibly the mammal meat. She had heard that it affected people oddly.

They took their places and waited. One of the men put a piece of equipment in the centre of the ring. He began to turn a handle. The machine crackled and coughed. Then he turned a round knob. It screeched, then went silent, then whined. Evie shrank backwards. A voice. There was a voice coming out of it. But the voice disappeared. Evie put her hand over her mouth. There it was again—a man's voice. A strange voice that sounded as if it were floating in the air, hanging between them.

The man in the centre of the circle put his face close to the machine. "Eden calling. Eden calling. Can you hear me?" The villagers sat still, leaning forward, anticipating.

"Eden calling," he repeated, "can you hear me?"

"Hallo. Paris calling. We hear you." The villagers clapped their hands, and touched each other's arms. Evie stared at them. *Paris?*

"Is that Jean? It's Michael here." Michael smiled at them all.

"Hallo Michael. How are you?"

"We are good. How are you?"

"Also good."

Evie turned to Mary, pointing at the machine. "What is it?"

Without looking at her, Mary leant closer. "Sometimes the old ways are best. We can communicate with people far away across the sea."

Mary's face looked younger, like an infant about to eat.

"We have news for you," the voice in the machine said. "We have made contact with Sydney. They are still living."

"Sydney. Incredible. How did you find them?" Michael said.

"Ahh. It's just a matter of time. We are setting up permanent communication with them. Things are not so bad there."

"Things are still the same here," Michael said. "There have been obstructions, but nothing has changed. Is there any news on that?"

"Our government has visited New Britain. But there isn't much we can do. They refuse to listen."

Across the sea? There were no people across the sea, apart from raiders who lived on rocks. There were no governments. Governments were in the bad days. Governments caused disasters.

Evie put her hands to her head. It must be a game. It must be meant for infants. No one could talk through a machine like that. You needed a communicator to communicate, not a thing that whistled and hissed.

"We have messages to relay," the voice said. "Alana?"

"Thank you, Jean," a female voice whispered around the pod. "A message for Benjamin in Wales 2. Amanda says she's sending him the items. Let her know when they've arrived. A message for Caroline, in Oxford 1: her father is leaving Paris. He will send a message when settled ..." The woman read through the list, her voice settling into a rhythm, like a chant. One of the female villagers typed the messages onto an old tablet, one of the ones they'd used before the Green Tablets were distributed.

"We also have messages to relay," Michael said, and began to read from the tablet. "A message for Johannes the engineer, in Berlin. Joanna, in London South, has had a healthy baby girl, they are both doing fine. Debbie, also in London South, is trying to find her grandmother Cassandra, known as English Cassandra, believed to be moving to Paris. Please reply if found." Michael read on. The words flowed over Evie like wind. This couldn't be true, surely? There weren't people in these places. The only world was New Britain now.

Michael finished speaking and put the tablet down. As soon as he did so, one of the women ran up, leaning into the machine. "This is Grace. I'm still trying to get news of my boy. It's been two months now. Have you heard anything yet?" Grace wrapped the cloth of her clothes around her hands and raised them to her mouth. She whimpered.

"No definite news yet." It was the woman who answered. "But Normandy told us that a sailor did arrive from Britain. He was lost. He is recovering. He is weak, but they think he will be well. He is a young man, tall and has brown hair and blue eyes. We will ask again and tell you when we know more."

Grace collapsed and sank her head into the floor. "Thank you, thank you. Tell him I love him." She sobbed, like an infant.

"We must go," Michael said. "Our time is up. We can't risk longer. Until next time."

"Au revoir," the voices in the machine said.

"Au revoir," the villagers chanted.

Michael pulled a wire out of the machine and it fell silent. Evie looked at the villagers—most of the women had tears in their eyes. They held each other's hands. The men put their arms around them. Evie flinched. What was this?

Mary picked Grace off the floor and rested her head on her shoulder. "That's good, isn't it? It sounds like he made it," Mary said.

Grace's body shook. When she lifted her face, she was smiling.

Evie followed Mary back to her pod, her feet stumbling over the ground. "What was that?" she asked.

"We communicate with other people, that's all."

"I didn't think there were people in other countries. There aren't even other countries."

"That's not true, Evie. There are lots of people."

But that's what they'd taught them. All the teachers had said there was no one else. The drought killed them all, after the Great Flood. The Porter always said that they were alone. *We are alone because we're the only ones who paid our debt to the earth. We are the only ones making sacrifices to secure the future,* he'd said.

"How do you know? Maybe they're just raiders, tricking you," Evie said.

"They're not raiders. The raiders make sailing the sea very dangerous, but nothing else. The machine is a radio, Evie. From the olden days. We fixed it, and we found them."

"They must be terrible people."

"Did they sound terrible?"

Evie stumbled again. "You can't tell from how they sound."

"They help us. They tell us what's really going on."

"Really going on?"

"They lied to you. Your whole life—they lied to you," Mary said.

Use your mind.

That couldn't be true.

These people can't even fix a wind turbine properly, she thought.

"I don't believe they lied. You're in error. You're keeping all this food and all this water for yourselves. Don't you know how much the rest of New Britain needs it? In my dome, sometimes our mouths get shrivelled with thirst. Babies and old people die every summer."

They had reached Mary's pod. Mary held open the cloth for Evie. "If we were sure they'd treat us well, we'd share our food. But they didn't, and they won't. Just as you wouldn't."

Mary didn't follow Evie inside. She walked to another pod. She vanished in the dark. Mary sat down and Grace handed her a cup of water.

"Thank you for visiting," Grace said.

"I thought you might want to talk."

"My baby." Grace stopped. She turned on the light and let the dim glow reflect around the pod. Her eyes were red. Grace sat down, and Mary held her hand.

"He was brave to try, you know," Mary said.

"I know."

"He was our best sailor. He'll have a better life now."

"I know."

Mary felt the pressure on her hand increase. Tears rolled down Grace's cheeks.

"I'm so happy to think he made it, but I'll never see him again," Grace said.

"You don't know that. Things might change." Mary stroked Grace's hand gently, watching the skin wrinkle as she rubbed her hand across it. Grace was old. "And you'll almost certainly speak to him."

Grace sniffed. "I remember when he first tried to speak."

Mary patted her hand.

The two women sat in silence for a while. After a time, Grace's tears stopped, and she leant against Mary's shoulder.

"Evie seems odd," Grace said.

"How so?"

"She seems," Grace said, then paused, her eyes scanning the floor for help, "tough."

"Tough?"

"Like a rock that no one can move," Grace said.

"John thinks she can't be turned."

"I think John is right."

"Have you spoken to him about her?"

"No."

Mary heard a tiny tremor in her voice.

"We should give her a fair chance," Mary said.

"We are."

"Yes," Mary said. "But she seems, I don't know. Injured. We shouldn't rush to condemn her."

"No, but the good of our community comes first."

"Of course."

The following evening, Mary had a similar discussion with John. She sensed patience running out. The community was restless. Evie had shown no signs of changing. She hadn't befriended anyone. She hadn't eaten mammal. She still berated them for their errors. And her confessions; Mary hadn't disclosed the full vitriol of her confessions.

Chapter 9

EVIE EMERGED FROM HER POD to find the villagers standing still, their faces turned towards the sea. The usual morning activity was absent.

"What's going on?" Evie asked Mary. Mary ignored the question, and pushed past her towards the ring of stones. She raised her arms to the sky. The grey sea crashed more loudly than usual. Foam gathered on the surface of the water as it swirled around. The wind pushed against Evie—it wasn't swirling, or rising and falling like it usually did. It pushed her, back towards the pod, like guards managing a crowd.

"What's going on?" Evie shouted at the villagers. "What's wrong?"

Still, no one answered. They all watched Mary, who now turned slowly, with her eyes fixed on the sky. Then Evie noticed that the sky was darker than usual. Where was the sun? Evie searched for it, nervous of burning her eyes. But nothing burned them, a grey blanket had spread itself over the village and as far as she could see. Where was the sun? Was this the end? Evie spun around, her eyes frantically searching for an edge, an end to the grey. What made this wind, this wind that felt like a herd of people? *The sea is angry,* she thought. *Perhaps it is wrong to swim in it. Perhaps swimming pollutes it, just like other things pollute it.*

The clouds pressed the heat down on her. Sweat gathered on her skin. She rubbed her tunic against her arms, but it just spread the dampness around. It was like being back home. Evie looked at the sky, grey, like an enormous dome above her. Her body felt saturated with heat, heavy with it. Even the air had turned against them now—it no longer cooled them but pressed the heat against them. It felt like it might almost crush them.

"See what you've done? You should have helped to build the future. You're destroying us …" Evie heard her voice carried off behind her. The people in front of her paid no attention. Evie put her hands to her head and screamed. But even that, they ignored.

Evie felt someone removing her hands from her head and clamping them to her sides. "Quieten yourself, will you? The last thing we need is a hysterical woman."

"You don't understand. It's the end!" Evie's voice rose and fell as it died out.

A man laughed in her ear. "You're ridiculous."

"You don't know."

"It's a storm, you idiot. It's just a storm," he said.

"No, I've seen storms, they aren't like this. The sky isn't grey. The wind doesn't feel like this, it swirls, it doesn't push."

"You're an idiot. Get in your pod and keep quiet."

Evie clenched her fists. Her heart beat faster. During a storm, there had always been Annie. She and Annie had their corner, their safe corner, where the sound of sand beating against the dome had been less vicious. They had each clutched their tablets, had each felt as if the pressure of their hands were communicating through them, keeping them safe. Annie always sang a song, the storm song, over and over, until it was finished. Sometimes she'd carried on after it had finished, to cover the sounds that always followed. The wailing, the shouts, the hurried bundling of bodies, and the strange language of the medics.

"I'm afraid," Evie said.

"Get into your pod," the man said, letting go of her hands. "I don't want to hear from you until it's over."

Evie's whole body shook as she walked back into the pod. Her hands fumbled with the sheet across the door, unable to open it. In the end she pushed through it, feeling the heavy, wet material clinging to her. She crouched on her mat with her legs pulled up and her arms clasped around them. She pushed herself as far back as she could get, hiding in the walls of the pod. The wind had become even more angry. It pounded the pod. It pushed against the material, and Evie thought she could feel the fastenings at the base shifting in the earth. *What if it blows away with me in it? It's only a small pod,* she thought.

Evie didn't hear Mary come in, but she noticed a change, a lightening in the atmosphere, a slight fall in the wind. Mary walked calmly through the pod. She removed the sheet from the doorway and fixed the door in place with straps and knots. Then she sat down next to Evie. She sat closer to Evie than she had ever done before. She sat so close to her that their clothes overlapped. Mary took off her muslin and gloves and folded them neatly in front of her.

"Well, Evie, it's going to be a long couple of days."

"Couple of days?" Evie's wide eyes stared at her.

"It's usually a couple of days. But we'll sit it out here."

"Sit it out?"

"It's a storm, Evie. And after the storm the sea will give us things. We will find them, and we will recycle them, and we will turn them into useful things. And life will be as it was yesterday."

"I thought—I thought it was the end."

"No. It's not the end."

"But I never saw a storm like this."

"I know, but storms are different too, in the out-country."

"Yes. Why don't you all shelter together, communally, like you should?"

Evie thought she felt Mary moving away from her, although she didn't see any obvious movement.

"We use this time to talk to one another. To share our lives with our families. To rest." Mary smiled. "And to make babies. Babies always follow storms."

"You make babies outside the breeding programs?"

Evie thought she heard Mary laugh quietly, but didn't see her lips move.

"So, Evie, that is what we will do. We will sit it out, and when it's over, we will understand each other better." Mary watched Evie's face, and Evie turned away from her.

"Are you scared?" Mary said.

"Yes. We used to get through it differently, at home."

"Well, why don't you tell me about your home? Or about your fa … about the people you miss. Or about your community. Or anything. We have all the time in the world."

Evie didn't speak for some time. Mary turned on the cooker and made them some breakfast. It was a simpler breakfast than normal, just heated protein paste and bread. Mary also poured out water for them both and placed it all on the floor in front of Evie. Evie drank, and ate. Only half an hour had passed. But the howling wind stretched time. It loaded the seconds with noise and fear so that each one felt heavy and ponderous.

"I only ever lived in the same dome," Evie said. She liked the sound of her voice as it wove itself in and out of the sound of the wind, sometimes cancelling it out, sometimes softening it, and sometimes distracting her mind so that it no longer mattered. Evie thought her voice reminded her of Annie's song.

"I was really good at learning things. When I was young, I remember the others hated calculating turbine speeds, and rotor angles, and learning how to fix solar panels. I liked it. It was always like they spoke to me."

"What spoke to you?"

"I don't know. The components. I know where they go. I know how to fix things by touching them. Or by looking at pictures of them."

Mary frowned. "When did you notice this?"

"Have other people come to you from the domes?"

Mary's frown shifted in her face. "Why do you ask?"

"I just don't think I can be the first."

"We've had others."

"Didn't they manage to change how you all behave?"

"No."

"Don't you understand that the future of us all depends on our sacrifices? We have to build a better world. A sustainable world. And we have to share what we have."

"I understand that." Mary sipped some water.

"Then why are you so much in error?" Evie said. Mary handed her the bowl of water. Evie took it. In doing so the tips of their fingers touched. Evie flinched.

"Is there one way to get to a sustainable future, Evie?"

"Yes, there's only one way. The right way."

"And how do you know that your way is the right way?"

"Because everyone agrees. Everyone knows. It's what we're taught." Evie put the bowl down in front of her.

"Some ways might have too high a cost," Mary said.

"Cost?" Evie blinked, and shuddered as the flimsy wall shook against her back.

"Yes, cost. The price, the things lost, the things given up."

"Like what?"

"Freedom, happiness, lives …" Mary hesitated, unsure whether her meaning was clear. But Evie had been prepared for doubts about costs. She had received many lessons about death.

"You can't change the world without sacrifice. People do die, people do go hungry. But it's not for nothing. Their blood is the foundation on which we build a better world. You can't change things without sacrifice."

"And how would you feel if someone you loved were sacrificed? Imagine if you had a baby. What then? Would it still be worth it?" Mary leant closer to Evie. She watched the veins at Evie's temple keeping time with her breathing. Evie's lips stayed still, fixed in a red line across her face. Mary tried to catch her eye, but Evie stared straight ahead.

"But that's exactly why we don't have families," Evie said, almost without moving. "Everyone in the community is equal, to us.

We can work for the good of all, unencumbered by olden-day prejudices. We can do what's right. And that's why you can't."

Mary stretched out her hand, as if to touch Evie's sleeve. Evie shrank into her clothes. "Evie," Mary whispered. "Evie, do you know who your parents even are?"

"Yes, of course. We all need to know our biological inheritance."

"Who are they?"

Evie took a large breath and began the familiar chant of identification. "My paternal great-grandfather was one of the founders of New Britain. He worked tirelessly after the Great Flood to build the world. I am very proud of him and try to follow his example. His wife, my great-grandmother helped and supported him in everything he did, until she slipped into error, and paid the cost."

Mary thought a look of pain flashed across Evie's face.

"My maternal grandparents and great-grandparents were insignificant. They have been removed from the record of lives, although nothing has been said against them. My father still lives. He is a mechanic, although he was injured during a storm, when he fell off the dome. He was trying to fix a communicator and the Porter said we are grateful for his sacrifice. He is undergoing re-education for unnatural attachment to possessions. My mother was in error. She was taken for training and re-education. I was too young to have met her, and I never give her any thought. I have worked hard to overcome any negative effects she may have had on me."

Mary gasped and clamped her hand across her mouth. Her eyes didn't blink.

"Are you feeling sick?" Evie asked.

"Maybe I had too much water," Mary said. She shook her head. "My mother had me when she was old, thirty-five. She thought I wouldn't live. There wasn't enough food and times were hard. You will have learned about those times. My first memory is of her holding me against her chest, stroking my hair and singing a song to me. I was afraid of something, I don't know what, and she calmed me. She gave up her food for me. She listened to my stories. She answered my questions. She would have died for me. Her death was the saddest moment of my life. I had two babies, a girl and a boy, and I love them, and I would die for them. My mother loved me, and I would die for my family."

"Where are the girl and the boy now?"

"That's your question? Evie, that's what you want to know?"

"Yes. I want to know where they are."

"The girl died. The boy sailed across the sea, and now he lives in Paris."

"That can't be true."

"It is, my daughter did die."

Evie clenched her fists. "You know that's not what I meant. I meant this pretend outside world."

"It's real. People escape from New Britain all the time. They escape any way they can."

"Escape? Why?"

"Because it's an evil, nasty, perverted, fearsome country."

Evie gasped. They would come for her, they would surely come for her, despite the storm. "No, no, no, no, no. It's not true. Everyone else is dead." Evie put her hands over her ears. "Everyone else is dead, dead, dead, gone, killed, this is all there is and they're going to kill you, and everyone else, you're all going to die, you're all going to die, and I'm …" Evie screamed. Mary touched her lightly on the arm. Evie screamed again.

"No one will hear. The storm's too loud." Mary's voice sounded as if it were inside Evie's own head.

"Shut up," Mary said, pulling Evie's arm back and forth, shaking her.

Evie quietened. "You're hurting me."

"Really? Concentrate. Am I really hurting you?"

Evie felt the pressure on her arm. Mary's hand was heavy; it pressed down on her sleeve. She could feel its pressure like a patch of heat.

"Am I really hurting you?" Mary said.

"Touching is forbidden."

"But am I hurting you?"

"It has to hurt."

"But am I hurting you?"

Mary released the pressure slightly and moved her hand slowly down Evie's arm. Evie tasted bread in her saliva. She felt her arm shaking, as if it didn't belong to her, and then the rest of her body shook.

Mary's hand slowed down even more as it reached the edge of her sleeve. She let her thumb hang in the air over Evie's bare hand. Evie could feel its pressure, although it wasn't actually touching her. She could sense its closeness. She could feel its invasion.

And then Mary actually touched her, with her bare hand, on Evie's skin. Evie pulled her arm away, but Mary's hand stayed with it, and landed on it again. Her fingers gently moved down Evie's hand, and when they reached the tips of her fingers, they moved up to her wrist again.

Evie whimpered. "It hurts," she said.

"It doesn't hurt, Evie. You aren't used to it. You've been told it's wrong. But it doesn't hurt."

Evie gasped and closed her eyes. Her hand tingled. The sound of the wind rushed through her mind. *This is wrong.* Another thing to confess. Would they tire of her endless errors?

"How does it feel, Evie?"

Evie opened her eyes to find Mary's close to hers, peering into them. She could see nothing other than Mary's eyes.

"It … it doesn't hurt."

Mary smiled, and took her hand away from Evie's. Evie's heart slowed and she closed her eyes again. It was over.

But then, then, something else. Something on her head. She felt pressure on the side of her head, moving down her hair, finishing below her ear. And then Mary did it again. Evie felt the same choking, gasping feeling, the jumping in her chest that she'd felt when her father had touched her. Her breath came in gasps. Her head tingled. It felt alive, as if it were moving on its own. Her scalp felt soft, as if it could be scraped away. Evie's eyes grew hot, and itchy. She put her hand up to her eyes and felt tears escaping. This must be stopped.

But Mary carried on. Evie's mouth opened to speak, and she said nothing. Tears ran down her cheeks and dripped off her chin. She felt them hitting her hands. Evie's whole head tingled, like it did when she went into the sea, but this tingling was warm, it made her sleepy. It silenced the storm.

Evie lay down on her mat, and Mary sat next to her, stroking her hair. Evie curled up and fell asleep with tears running down her face.

Evie awoke sensing that she'd been imprisoned. Something crushed her. Something tied her down. She moved sideways on her mat, and felt the weight move with her. In between the howling wind she heard breathing close to her ear. Evie opened her eyes. She rolled over to find Mary's closed eyes a few centimetres from her own. Mary's eyes twitched and moved under their eyelids. Evie followed the creases in her face joining her eyes to her cheeks, and her cheeks to her mouth. She looked down at Mary's hand, similarly creased, resting across her waist. Evie shifted her body to try to dislodge it. Mary's hand grasped Evie's tunic, as if afraid that it would run away. And then Mary woke. Her eyes opened, and stared at Evie, disorientated, but the look soon passed. Evie looked down at Mary's arm, still around her waist.

"Does it hurt?" Mary said.

It must hurt. Evie looked at Mary. "No, it can't hurt, otherwise I wouldn't have fallen asleep."

"No." Mary sat up. "We could probably both do with the sleep. Shall I get some lunch? I think we slept most of the morning."

"Yes, shall I help?"

"Yes, why don't you turn the cooker on?"

Neither Evie nor Mary spoke for some time. Evie flinched, and scampered away from Mary, avoiding touching her. Mary made no more attempts to hold her arm, or touch her hair. Lunch didn't take long to make. They chewed the bread in time with the wind. Evie only noticed it now when the pattern changed. The steady howl had faded into the background.

"Will the village be OK?" Evie said.

"Of course. These storms happen quite often."

"Does anyone check on people?"

"Yes. Some do."

Once they had eaten, Evie turned the cooker off, and Mary washed the bowls and placed them back neatly on the mat.

"So, what shall we do now?" Mary said.

"Is there anything we can do?"

"Is there anything you want to ask me, or is there anything you want to tell me?"

Evie's eyes searched around the pod. But no answers appeared on the walls. She sighed. "Thank you for feeding me and accepting me into your community."

"It's our duty to do that."

"Yes. But I'm grateful for it."

"How have you expressed your gratitude?"

"I've just said it," Evie said.

"Yes. But have you behaved gratefully?"

"I have tried to fulfil the obligations they placed on me when they sent me here."

"Evie …" Mary sighed. "There must be a human being in there somewhere. But you're so hard to reach."

"What do you mean?"

"You seem to have no feeling."

"Like what?"

"Love, sympathy."

"I love our community and always have it at the centre of my heart."

Evie watched Mary's eyes darken. Evie saw her right hand clench around the material of her sleeve. Mary pounded the floor with her fist. "Evie, what must I do to wake you up?"

"I am awake."

"No, you're not, you're dead!"

Evie shrank back against the wall and crawled into her sleeping pod.

"You're cruel!" Mary shouted. The air crackled and the wind howled around the pod. "And you want such terrible things to happen."

Evie frowned. "What things?"

"The things you write. Evil things. You want us to die."

"I don't write evil things."

"Don't lie. You know you do."

"I've not written anything. Where would I write?"

"You know what I mean."

"But the tablets don't work here."

Evie knelt at the entrance to her sleeping pod, and Mary sat cross-legged on one of the blue mats by the cooker. They stared at each other. Evie rolled the sleeves of her tunic up and clasped her arms. Mary breathed calmly and half-closed her eyes. The wind whistled under the door and, as it swirled around the pod, the hem of Mary's tunic fluttered.

"What have you read?" Evie said. The wind caught her words and they whipped around the pod until they escaped out the door.

"I've read everything, Evie." Mary's hands rested lightly on her knees. She stared at Evie without blinking. Mary watched every twitch and spasm in Evie's body.

Evie looked as if the wind had stolen her breath. Her hand grasped her throat. Evie looked at the space between Mary and the door.

"You read my confessions?" Evie struggled even to form the words.

"Yes, I read them."

"How?"

"Communicators are different here. I read them."

Evie threw herself on the ground, pulling at her hair. "You aren't allowed, they'll know, and they'll kill you!" Evie trembled. The walls of the pod pressed down on her. The air felt heavy. She scrambled towards the door of the pod, half-crawling, half-sliding, but Mary grabbed her arm and held her back.

"You can't go out there," Mary said.

"I hate you."

"There's nowhere to go."

Evie fumbled with the straps on the door. As she loosened them the wind wound them around her fingers. The door flapped angrily, fighting her. The wind seemed to howl more loudly as the material of the door whipped back and forth. She clumsily wound her muslin round her head and crawled out of the small opening she'd made.

Evie flung herself on the ground, covering her head with her hands. The wind flung earth, sand, and stones into her, stinging her eyes and hurting her skin through her clothes. She tried to crawl away, but the wind pushed her back. The debris in the air made it hard to make anything out. The whole village might have been swept away. Evie pulled her muslin over her eyes and tried to peer out from under it. Where could she go? She couldn't even see the edge of the land. What if she fell into the sea? She could hear it crash and roar, hungrily, as if willing her to dare to come closer.

She felt pressure on her ankle. Mary pulled her back and shouted something, but Evie couldn't hear properly. She let herself be dragged back into the pod. Once Mary had retied the door, she took Evie's muslin off and saw that she was crying. Mary pulled Evie towards her and wrapped her in her arms. Evie recognised the feeling from when her father had done it. It was sure to hurt again, and it did. She coughed. Her throat closed up and her eyes stung.

"Evie, I'm not trying to hurt you. Join us. You will be happier."

Evie let her head sink against Mary. "How long until the storm stops?"

"Tomorrow, hopefully."

Mary filled a bowl with water and wiped Evie's face, gently washing the sand out of her eyes. Then Mary washed Evie's arms. They both watched the streaks of sand running off her fingers and onto the floor. Mary lightly brushed Evie's hair with her hands.

"You'll need a good soak in the sea after this; your hair is full of dirt."

"I'm never going near the sea again," Evie said.

"But the sea gives us things. It brings us life. You'll see."

Evie changed into her spare set of clothes and sat in her pod as Mary prepared food for them.

They sat side by side, their knees almost touching, lifting the food to their mouths in time with one another. "I'm not hurting you, Evie," Mary said.

"It feels like hurting."

"Really?"

"Yes."

"Your father or mother never washed you? Or cleaned your hair, or …" Mary looked at the wall of the pod, watching it sinking and rising with the wind.

"Families are a remnant of the—"

"Yes, I know. Don't say it again."

"Only Medics and Designated Carers are allowed to touch people, or if you've been approved for breeding."

"Or guards," Mary said.

"Yes, guards, of course."

"Evie, I don't think you've ever been loved. I think they've done you a great harm, the way they brought you up. If you could love someone, you might feel differently."

"But I do feel love. I feel love for my community, and for our mission, and for the future we're trying to build."

"What future is that, then?"

"A future where we live as one with our environment. Where everyone has enough to eat, where everyone is healthy, where we don't need to work all the time, where people don't keep water to themselves."

"And how do we get there?"

"We have to undo the damage we've done. We have to make up for our errors. We have to do penance. And we have to rebuild."

"Do you think we'll ever get to your perfect future?"

"Yes, eventually we will. But everyone has to do the right thing. A single mistake can ruin it."

"Evie, I don't think everything they've told you is true."

"What do you mean?" Evie placed the piece of bread that she'd been about to eat back in her bowl. The air in the pod felt heavy again.

"We heard things. From our friends abroad."

"But they aren't real."

"They are real. They said …" Mary paused and turned towards Evie. She touched Evie's leg lightly with her hand. "They said the flooding was terrible everywhere, but the New Britainers made it worse here. They destroyed the flood defences so people would let them take over. So people would believe their promise of salvation. It wasn't like that abroad. Many people died, cities were destroyed, and the drought killed more. But they managed to rebuild without forgetting what it is to be human."

Mary felt Evie's leg shaking, and frowned, peering into Evie's eyes, watching them darting around the pod as if seeking an escape.

"That isn't true. They'd never lie to us."

Mary shrugged. "I don't know. It's just what we heard. But you shouldn't trust them."

Evie's eyes flickered back and forth over her bed. Mary followed her gaze and noticed the corner of her tablet escaping from under her mat.

"You don't need to confess everything, you know," Mary said.

Evie looked towards the door of the pod. Then she let her head hang. "I'm tired. I want to sleep," she said.

"Alone? Or shall I stay with you?"

"Yes. I'll be fine alone."

Evie listened until she was sure Mary slept. She tried to make out the sound of her breathing, but it was difficult to disentangle it from the wind. Evie reached under her mat and pulled out her tablet. She opened it and hid it under her blanket, crouching over it. Her hand shook as she fumbled with the back of the tablet. She ran her fingers down the thin metal. She had to do it twice because her nails kept coming out of the groove. Tears came to Evie's eyes, and she blinked them away. The wind seemed to be taunting her, whipping her heart into a pounding, bursting rhythm. It must still be here. Each breath seemed to bring less and less oxygen into her lungs. Her throat sealed up. She blinked repeatedly, hoping it would stop her head spinning. She fumbled with the screw at the back of the tablet, feeling for it through her misty eyes. The back panel came off. Evie held it gently. It must still be here. She turned the tablet over, almost afraid to look.

Evie smiled. Almost laughed with relief. Mary hadn't found it. Of course Mary hadn't found it. There, neatly folded, behind the solar panel of her tablet, was the piece of beautiful olden-day paper. Still exactly as she'd left it, on the day she'd handed over the plastic box.

Calmer now, Evie replaced the panel, forcing it down and fixing it back into place, just as she'd done the first time, behind the air conditioning vent. She put it back under her mat and lay on her back. *Mary hasn't found it,* she thought, *but how strange that Mary and the letter both spoke the same lies.* Mary was guessing, fishing for information on the basis of vague doubts and suppositions.

Evie wiped her face with her sleeve and tried to fall asleep. She pushed her hair away from her face and rolled onto her side. Her eyes stayed open. She put her hand up to her hair again, and touched it, running her fingers from the top of her head to just below her ear. It didn't feel the same. Her head didn't tingle. Did Mary know how it felt?

Evie touched the skin on her arm with her hand, gently running her nails up and down her skin. She felt the patch of her arm on which Mary's hand had rested. She put her own hand on the same place and lay still, listening to the pod creaking, and straining, the sea in the distance, and the howling of the wind. She closed her eyes and fell asleep. The wind kept waking her, and each time she rested her hands where Mary's had rested, and fell back asleep.

Chapter 10

EVIE AWOKE LATE THE NEXT morning. She thought the air felt different; it sat less heavily in her lungs. Her ears seemed empty, her breathing loud. When she pulled her blanket aside, she heard it rustle. The wind had gone. She looked around the pod, and saw that Mary had left. She scrambled out of the sleeping pod and through the front door, which was open now. The wet cloth hung in its usual place. Outside, the rest of the village was visible again. The pods had sustained minor damage—rips in their sides, and doors hanging limply. Evie wrapped her muslin around her head and pulled on her gloves. The villagers stood at the edge of the cliff, facing the sea. A few infants chased each other around the stones.

Evie ran towards the sea. "What's going—" She stopped. The adults stood silently, watching. Waves still crashed angrily against the rocks. The rope leading to the sea had been shredded. It hung limply, its strands tumbling over the rocks like hair. At the bottom of the slope, shapes and colours mingled with the foam, flowing back and forth, pushing against the cliff and then pulling away. Further out to sea were other shapes. Something tall and pointed sat, or floated, near the roof of the old building.

"Shall we go now?" one of the men said.

"I'm not sure it's safe just yet," another man said.

"We should at least get the boats ready." Evie thought it might have been Sam who spoke.

A few villagers moved off to fetch the boats.

"Let's get some food on," one of the men said.

"Evie, stay here and watch if you want. But then, come and help with the cooking. We also need to check the turbines and the fields. Make yourself useful."

"Yes." The figure moving away looked like John, but the voice sounded muffled beneath layers of fabric.

Evie watched villagers carrying the boats down the narrow path. A few times someone stumbled and seemed to slip, but they kept their footing. *They must be used to it,* Evie thought. The small boats launched into the waves. Instead of throwing nets over the sides, the villagers hauled up whatever the sea had given. They piled the things up on the boats and rowed them to shore. There, a line of villagers formed, passing things from one to another up the slope and back to the centre of the village. In the middle of the ring of stones, the pile grew, and people sorted it into smaller piles. Evie listened to their shouts.

"A plastic container. No holes."

"Look, an olden-day gun. But it's totally rusty."

"Give it to the little ones to play with."

"I can't open this box. Help me."

"Bowls and plates. Hardly broken."

"We can use those tonight."

"There's lots of plastic rope here. If you can help me untie it."

"See here, there's lots of wood this time. It should last for ages."

Evie sat on one of the stones, and observed the piles growing, and ebbing, and shifting. Some things were carried to the communal pod straight away. Others went for washing. Still others were given to the infants, who shrieked, and scampered, and called out to one another. Evie piled up some of the wood, but her arms dangled heavily, and she cut herself on a piece of metal. The heat seeped into her once again, and she wandered back towards the sea.

"Help if you want," a man said. "Come in my boat."

Evie peered at him, noticing the sharp angle of his shoulders and the feet pointing inwards towards each other. "Sam?"

"Of course, who else? Help fetch things. Sorting is boring."

Sam scrambled down the slope and Evie followed. Once at the bottom, Sam sat on the side of a boat and levered himself in. "Hey Dad, I brought her with me," he said.

John held out his hand to help her in. Evie tried to manage it on her own, but the boat wobbled as soon as she touched it, so she took his hand. She felt its pressure on hers as he guided her over the side. "Sit there," he said, pointing to the back of the boat. "Sam, grab the oar, you're letting it drift off."

Sam pulled the oar into the boat and the two of them manoeuvred it slowly down the channel towards the rooftop. Above the roofs of the olden-day buildings, things floated. John took the boat to each in turn and Evie helped Sam to get them onboard. They mainly found blue and red plastic containers. Evie pulled them out of the water, thinking they looked like new. They still shone and glinted in the sun. They also found pieces of round wood; some had pieces of metal attached.

"We'll have to salvage the metal," John said.

"It's such a boring job," Sam said. "Don't make me do it again."

"You'll do what needs doing."

Sam laughed. "Yes, Dad. You're grumpy this morning."

John lifted his hand and raised it above Sam's head. Evie expected him to hit Sam, but he didn't. He brought it down gently on his head, and patted him. Sam leant back against his father. "I'm tired," Sam said.

"We could all do with some proper sleep tonight."

Evie put her hand into the sea, feeling the water soaking through her gloves and onto her skin. The cold tingled, a bit like Mary's hand had tingled on her head. Evie could tell from the angle of Sam's body that he was leaning against his father, letting him take his weight. John steered the boat with one oar and kept his other arm around Sam's shoulders.

What does that feel like? It doesn't hurt, I know that now. Does it feel the same as Mary's hand? Or does everyone's have their own feeling? Evie sank more of her arm into the water. She watched the sea in front of them, and the glinting on the top of the waves. Every now and again a brighter flash caught her eye.

"Look, there's something over there," Evie said, pointing up ahead.

"It's too shallow for the boat there," John said. "I can't see anything."

Sam moved ahead and stared. "No, she's right. We can get out and find it."

John kept the boat steady by the edge of a roof. "Be careful, no one's walked on these for a long time."

"Stop worrying. We'll be alright. Come on, Evie."

Evie and Sam wobbled out of the boat. Sam stood on the roof just below their feet. The water came up to his waist. Evie stood right behind him and, when he began moving, tried to put her feet in exactly the same places as him. Sam kept looking up to check where they were heading.

"There's definitely something there," he said.

"I know, I saw it first."

The two of them waded carefully, Sam feeling his way with his feet. The waves pushed against them and Evie leaned as she walked. They got into a rhythm and Evie's eyelids sagged.

Then Sam disappeared.

Evie shrieked.

Someone shouted behind her. The water just in front of her swirled and circled around the fading patch of cloth that was all she could now see of Sam.

Evie heard splashing in the distance, and a shout. She put her hands into the water, but Sam was too far down. She bent down and tried to put her face in the water, but it felt cold, it felt like it sucked at her chin, and she stood up again.

Slowly, the shape of Sam's clothes changed, it swirled, it jerked. Evie peered through the water. Was he dying?

Sam's hand burst from the surface like a fish, and Evie grabbed it. His gloves almost came off in her hand, but she held on tight, leaning backwards to stop him pulling her in. He pulled on her, but just as she thought she would have to let go, his head appeared. He coughed, spun around, disorientated, before holding onto her with both arms as he found his footing again.

"I told you to be careful," John said, panting with the effort of having waded across the roof.

"I was careful," Sam said, wiping his eyes and rearranging his muslin. "I'm fine. Thanks, Evie."

"I think we should leave it and go back," John said.

"We can't leave it. It might be amazing," Sam said.

"Sam, I nearly lost you."

"Come off it. It wasn't that bad."

"It looked that bad."

"I'm going. It'll be fine."

"Well, I'm waiting here. Don't be long, and be careful. We can always come back later."

"Alright." Sam moved forward again, but more slowly this time. Evie followed, leaving extra distance between the two of them.

The glinting thing moved as the sea pulled and pushed it. Sam found it difficult to walk straight towards it. He looked back at his father, and forward again. Evie followed his gaze. It shone more brightly now. The two of them carried on wading.

"It's not so deep here," Sam said.

Evie looked down, noticing that the water only reached her thighs now.

They moved more quickly, but even when they'd almost reached it, they couldn't tell what it was.

They took the final few paces and paused. A white skull stared up at them, with water-filled eyes. Seaweed streamed from a hole in its head like hair.

I watched my neighbour beat a woman to death with a saucepan to steal a dining table she used as a raft.

Evie swayed with the waves and put her hand to her head, feeling the position where the hole would be. She flinched.

As the sea oozed around the head, she noticed it still had other bones attached. The current made a hand sway through the waves, its fingers pointing at the sky. On one of the fingers a gold ring glinted. It glinted so brightly that Sam and Evie flinched. Sam pulled at the head. The bones cracked. He pulled again and the head, the arms, and part of the spine came loose.

As it did so, the pressure of the water forced another head to the surface. A smaller head. And then another. Like mushrooms, they grew around them.

"Great, we can salvage these," Sam said.

"What for?"

"We grind them up for the earth. It helps things grow, and it returns things to their natural place. You didn't do this where you came from?"

"Yes. We found the bones helped grow the protein pods. We burned them before grinding. I didn't know if it was different here."

Sam grunted.

"We can't carry all of them by ourselves," Evie said.

"No. But we should take some and get help with the rest."

Sam turned around and waved at his father. He pulled at as many hands and arms as he could reach and held onto them. Evie did the same, but found that she couldn't gather up as many as Sam. She reached for one more. Evie blinked. This hand had a large golden band around its wrist. The arm rattled inside it. She paused momentarily. The arm must have filled that gap, once. That would be quite a large arm. As she pulled it closer, she slipped the gold bracelet off the hand and pushed it inside her tunic, wedging it between her skin and her waistband.

"What are you doing?" Sam said.

"I'm getting one last body."

"You took something."

"I didn't. My tunic was loose."

"I saw you."

"You didn't."

"I know what I saw."

"Everything we are given must be shared by the community. I know that. You're the ones who ignore the rules."

Sam stared at her. Evie stared back. Eventually Sam shrugged and turned towards his father. The two of them moved much more slowly on the way back, weighed down by the bodies they dragged.

"What was it?" John shouted.

"Loads of bones," Sam said.

"Good. Did you get them all?"

"No, we'll have to go back," Sam said.

"Good. Let's see how many we can take now."

Using bits of rope, they tied the bones to the side of the boat. "There's room for more," John said. "I'll come with you."

The three of them made their way back to where they'd found the bodies. Sam led the way again, more confident of his footing now. This time, the bodies they found were mostly intact, but small. Evie wondered how old they had been. What might the errors have been, of people so small?

"I think we've got them all now," Sam said.

"They must have been washed out of this building," Evie said.

"I wonder how many more are down there," Sam said. "We could try to swim down?"

"Don't even think about it. It's too dangerous."

"Mark used to."

"Mark swam better than anyone. Anyway, he said there's lots of things floating around and banging into each other down there. We should wait until the sea decides to give them to us."

John turned back towards the boat, and the others followed. They moved slowly, weighed down by the bones floating and swaying around them. Every now and again they had to stop to re-tie an arm, or catch a leg floating off.

When they reached the boat, they piled the bones up in the hull. John rowed slowly back to shore. Once at the shore, he shouted to the figures moving up and down the cliff: "Hey, we need help!"

The villagers re-formed a line from the rocks to the top of the cliff. John, Sam and Evie pulled out their cargo and threw it to the other villagers.

Eventually, the job was done, and Evie panted up the hill. The villagers had formed a pile of bones. They had fetched large grinding stones and had already set to work. Evie sat down at the edge of the pile.

"You did well," the woman sitting next to her said.

"Are you grinding them?" Evie said.

"We break them up first, so they'll fit in a cooker. After that we grind them and mix them with the soil. They help things grow."

"We did that at home. But doesn't it matter that they've been in the sea?"

"No, we have to wash it, and mix it with seaweed, once it's ground. But it still helps," the woman said. "Sort them, will you?"

Evie pulled a ribcage out and began separating the bones. "So, I don't need to take seaweed off?"

"No, leave it on."

Evie closed her eyes. It seemed that in the distance she could hear Annie crying, as she always did. And the small boys humming to themselves. And then the same boys squabbling. There was always squabbling. Evie remembered how it used to irritate her, but now her ears pleaded to hear it, sought it out in the voices around her, tried to turn these unfamiliar voices into ones that soothed her ears, like music.

But at least she knew the work. She felt the stones in front of her, weighed them carefully, feeling the edges with her thumb. It was hard work breaking up a hip bone. But with the right tool, in the right place, at the right angle, it was easy.

"Good work, Evie," the woman said.

"I've done it before."

"I can see. I'm Martha."

Evie splintered a skull. And then reached for an arm. She picked at a corroded ring still attached to a finger. "What do I do with metal? Do you melt it down?"

"Yes, unless it's gold. That goes in the pile over there." Martha pointed towards a small heap of rings on a flat stone on the other side of the stone circle.

"What do you do with the gold?"

"What did you used to do?"

"We sent it to the megadome," Evie said.

"We swap it for things."

"Swap it?"

"You'll find out."

Sometime later a boy brought around bread and protein paste. They all carried on working as they ate. As the heat seeped out of the ground, the villagers moved piles of bones back to their pods and carried on working there. Some of them moved into the communal pod. Evie followed them and sat down near the entrance, where the breeze drifted through the dripping sheet.

The sheet opened a little and she felt someone close. She looked up. Sam unwound his muslin from his head and stared down at her pile of bones. He kicked gently at the two rings and the lump of corroded metal next to her.

"So, that all you found then?" he said.

"Yes. Not much."

Sam looked around the pod. "Are you sure?"

"Yes." Evie brought her heaviest stone down on a small skull, but her hand shook, and she caught the side of her thumb. It dripped blood onto the head bleached white by the sea.

Sam passed her a small piece of cloth from one of his pockets. "Tie that around it. You'll be fine. I always hurt myself when I'm not careful."

Evie stared up at him. What had he seen? Nothing, surely. She'd been careful. She'd been very careful.

"You know where everything goes?" Sam said.

"Yes."

"I mean with the metal." He ground his foot into the floor. "All the gold goes over there." Sam pointed to a pile next to a woman on the other side of the pod.

"I know where everything goes," Evie said.

"Good. I'm off to work on the desalinator. The storms always clog it up." Sam wrapped himself up again and walked out of the pod.

Evie examined her thumb. It was mostly alright, but here and there small domes of blood seeped out of the graze. She wrapped it up in the cloth again. Surely he hadn't seen? Evie felt the lump under her waistband with her elbow, pressing into her side.

She could take it out and put it on the pile. She could do that. Evie pressed the gold band closer into her. But why? What would they do with it? They hadn't said yet. The sea had given it to her. It had called out to her, and given it just to her. A beautiful shape and a beautiful colour. A piece of light, trapped in a metal band. Her heart jumped. She could look at it, watch ripples of herself moving across it. She had seen gold before. *But we should have the good of the community at the centre of our hearts.* Evie grabbed a thigh bone and smashed it with a rock. *This isn't my community,* she thought. *They don't have the good of the community in the centre of their hearts. It should be sent to a megadome. But not by them.* Evie lied to herself. Lied that she would send it to its proper place at the proper time.

And Evie knew it was a lie.

Sam worked on a piece of pipe, shaking it. He pulled a piece of cloth through it. "I think it's clear now," he said to a man on the other side of the desalinator.

"Shall we try it again?" the man said.

"Yes."

The machine hummed. Sam and the man stayed completely still in case their inconsequential movement somehow affected the machine. The hum turned into a whine, and the two of them finally breathed again.

Sam ran out of the pod housing the desalinator and got on a transport. He raced up the hill to the wind turbines. Once there, he stopped, searching for his father. He spotted him, crouched in one of the transports, eating.

Sam drove over. "Dad."

"Yes?"

"I have to talk to you." Sam scrambled into his father's transport, settled himself into the shade, and tugged at his muslin. His father carried on eating, as if unaware of the urgency of Sam's movements.

"It's Evie," Sam said.

John stopped chewing, put his bread in his lap, and looked directly at Sam. "Yes?"

"She took something."

"What?"

"In the sea. When we went out, her and me. She took something off a bone."

"What was it?"

"It was glinting. It was something gold."

"And you saw her take it?" John said.

"Yes."

"Maybe she sorted it when we got back?"

"No, I checked. None of the piles have gold that big. It was big."

John picked at the spaces between the ends of his fingers and the end of his gloves, bending them over as if breaking fingers. "Have you asked her?"

"When I asked her about it the stones made her bleed."

"The stones?"

"She was breaking bones, and she hit her thumb. It bled."

"Alright," John said, "get on with your work. I'll deal with this."

After the communal meal Evie sat at the communicator again.

The privacy of confession isn't respected here. Mary reads my confessions. She uses them against me. The Rules say she must be punished, but they won't punish her. If you send more people, it will be worth your while—there are so many errors to correct. The sea gives things to them, more things than they tell you. They can improve the earth for growing food. And they get gold, a lot of gold and metal, more than we received. But they don't send it to the megadomes; they keep it. I told them of their errors, but they still don't listen. I'm trying to do my First Task, but it is hard. I am watched, and they grow suspicious. Sam is also one you need to catch. I'm sure he is spreading stories about me. Stories that aren't true. Stories that will stop me telling them about their errors. I am always devoted to my mission, but this mission needs more people. Please tell me when you will come.

Mary read the message later and replied to it. As usual, she replied in noncommittal terms. She preached patience and per-severance, and duty, and self-sacrifice. *Try to understand them,* she wrote. *Not everything that is different is in error.* Mary hesitated, and then deleted her last sentence. It might be what she wished they'd say, but she knew they'd never say it.

Chapter 11

MARY FOUND JOHN AFTER BREAKFAST and led him into her pod. John removed his muslin and looked around hesitantly, the mats, the stove, and the door to her sleeping pod ever present in his memory. He avoided looking into Mary's sleeping pod. He sat down by the doorway. Mary smiled at him.

"You look embarrassed," Mary said.

"That's not it."

"What then?"

"Coming in here reminds me I'm not young."

Mary sat next to him, taking his hand in her own. "Neither of us are young now. But we've kept alive. And we've kept them all alive." Mary nodded towards the door.

"That's what I wanted to talk to you about," John said.

"What's happened?"

"It's Evie. Sam saw her take something that the sea had given to all of us."

"What did he see?"

"He saw her take something gold. He asked her about it and the stones made her bleed."

"That could be an accident."

John pulled his hand away from Mary's.

"Don't you believe me?" John said.

"I believe you."

"Then we need to deal with her."

Mary sighed, and reached out to hold John's hand again. "She's never had anyone love her."

"That's not my concern."

"It's all of our concern. I feel sorry for her. Think what she might be like if someone loved her."

"We're in the business of survival, not love."

"What's one without the other?"

John picked at the edge of the mat, slowly freeing bits of cloth. "She can't stay here."

"I feel sorry for her."

"You never felt sorry for them before."

Mary sighed and placed her hand on John's knee. "She seems so broken," she said.

"You told me about her confessions. She'd destroy us all if she could. You shouldn't pity her."

"But it's people like her we're fighting for, isn't it? Those who can't even imagine a different world."

"We're fighting for ourselves. We're fighting to stay alive. That's what we're fighting for."

"Please stop destroying my mat," Mary said. John stopped pulling at the cloth and dropped a small pile of shredded blue twine on the floor.

"Sorry," he said.

"About what?"

"The mat."

"Nothing else?"

"No, nothing else. You're wrong." John stood up and kicked one of the legs of the stove. Mary turned away from him and stared at the ground. As she heard him leave, she sighed and closed her eyes.

When Mary heard shouting, she knew she had to get up.

Evie awoke to the noise and peered around the door of the communal pod.

Two long-distance transports trundled down the hill; they'd passed the wind turbines and were heading into the village. Evie blinked. *Rescue.* They'd listened; they'd come. *Salvation.* She wrapped her muslin around her head and ran out to meet them. The heat slowed her pace to a walk, but she raised her hand and waved. Inside her muslin, she smiled.

The two small vehicles stopped by the stone circle. Other villagers gathered around them. Evie imagined blood staining their clothes, pooling on the ground. She imagined the stones streaked with red.

Evie walked up to the lead vehicle and stood by the door. The door opened. Evie took a step backwards. A tall person, probably a man, got out. He was wearing colours. Evie stared. A purple tunic, and blue trousers, and a red belt. *Is this what they wear, when they come to take you away?* Evie thought. *Are these the colours of death?*

The man walked past Evie and towards Mary.

"I'm Evie," Evie said. "I'm the one who called you."

The man hesitated. As he did so, another figure got out of the transport, also dressed like him. The man looked down at Evie and shrugged. "No one called us." He held out his hand to Mary.

Mary took his hand in her own and moved it up and down. Evie blinked. This also had been in her lessons, but she couldn't remember how it fit.

"Welcome. We thought you might be visiting, after the storm. How are you?" Mary said.

"Not bad. Did you come through it alright?"

"Yes, thank you. We're all fine."

"We're here because one of our generators is broken. We'd like to trade for parts," the man said.

"Of course. Why don't you come into the pod and we can talk about it? We also have some things for you."

The two strangers followed Mary and the rest of the villagers. Evie followed last of all. Her head sank onto her chest as she walked. She felt eyes burrowing into her. She was lost, now. No one would come to save her. Evie sat at the edge of the communal pod, hiding in the shadows. She left her muslin half-wrapped around her face and peered out from under it.

Someone fetched water for the strangers and gave them bread. They sat cross-legged, with their hands in their laps. They unwrapped their heads. One was a man, one was a woman. They were young, with blue eyes.

"So, is there any news?" Martha said.

"Yes. Before the storm we disabled two more long-distance transports. They were full of Listed. We freed them but most of them died anyway. They had been broken." The man took a sip of water and lowered his head. His hands shook.

The woman spoke. "But one of the generators at Bristol 1 was disabled. We've found a new way of doing it. There will be more."

"And any news from abroad? We heard from Paris a couple weeks ago," Grace said.

"We haven't managed to contact Paris. But Dublin said they're sending men to help us, in a few months. They need to buy more equipment first."

"My son made it to Normandy, it seems," Grace said.

"Praise the Lord," the two visitors said together.

Evie covered her mouth with her hand and pulled her muslin further over her face.

Grace smiled. "Well, that's not what I said, but the feeling's the same."

"God cares about all living things, whether they believe or not." The woman leant over to Grace and put her lips on the woman's cheek.

"We might be able to help with the equipment," John said.

"Oh? What do you have?" the man asked.

"The sea gave us gold after the storm," John said.

One of the villagers carried over the small pile of rings and other jewellery and placed it in front of the visitors. The woman picked up the rings one by one, and smiled.

"Thank you. This will help. Now, about the generator, and what you want in return," she said.

"More meat," one of the villagers at the edge of the circle said.

"Meat, yes. We can trade as much meat as you want."

Evie retched. *These are devils,* she thought. *The worst devils you can get.* You know them by their colours, Teacher had said. It had never made sense. What colours? the class had asked. All colours, he'd replied. Evie looked up. These colours. These evil colours. The Religious. The ones who liked the world before, and would do anything to destroy New Britain. They'd merged all the old religions to keep them alive. They had fought the New Britainers and lured people with promises of living after death, and distracted them from the sacrifices they had to make today. Evie knew her duty. *But how do you do your duty when you are totally alone?* she wondered.

Evie watched them, hating them. As if through some evil sense, the woman's eyes found her in the shadows. "Is there someone new here?" she said.

"Yes," Mary said, "this is Evie. Come here, Evie."

Evie hid behind her clothes.

"Come here, Evie, we want to say hello," the woman said.

"Where's she from?" the man asked.

"She was sent from them," John said.

"And how's your mission going, Evie?" the woman said.

Evie looked away and pulled her muslin over her face.

"Evie, surely you must have something to say?" the woman said.

"I won't talk to you. You bringers of death. You destroyers of life. You're killing us all." Evie spoke quietly, spitting the words into her clothes.

A ripple of laughter rolled around the room.

"May the Lord open your heart and make you human again," the woman said.

"You will die," Evie whispered.

"As will we all. But then we'll be reborn into everlasting life," the woman said.

"Stop teasing her," the man said, "it must be confusing. Hopefully she'll learn to think for herself one day. We aren't what you think we are, Evie."

They talked, then, about the generator, and parts, and how the mammal infants were growing. And when to deliver things. And how much they needed. The Religious finished their water and bread, stood up, and walked back to their transports. The villagers followed them, waving as they left. Then they returned to their tasks.

Evie continued with hers, which had been cleaning the communal stove. But her hands slipped as she scrubbed. Her fingers disobeyed. Her head swayed and felt heavy. Her body prickled with sweat, and heat, and crawling.

She should have attacked them. Could she have disabled their transport? But the villagers would have stopped her.

Was it really them? Had she really seen the Religious?

The stove blurred and melted as tears filled her eyes. Evie blinked and saw drops falling onto the ground. It should have been drops of blood. Their blood.

Evie put her cloth on the ground and raised her hand to her head. She ran her fingers through her hair. It came loose from the band that tied it behind her head. Her fingers traced the contours of her scalp. It didn't feel the same as when Mary had done it. When Mary had touched her, it tingled. Was it a trick?

Small bumps grew on her arm as she touched it with her bare hand. She felt a hint, like a faint smell, of how it would feel.

Evie heard crying outside the door and wiped her face. She picked up her cloth and rubbed the inside of the stove again.

An infant ran in, wailing, its arms outstretched, its muslin in disarray around its head. "Mummy, Mummy, Mumumumum." It tripped over its feet, and lay on the ground, with red cheeks, spit dribbling out of its mouth, mingling with tears on the ground. Evie shrank behind the stove.

A woman ran in. She rushed to the infant, tearing her gloves and muslin off. "Baby. Come here. It's OK." She picked the infant up and held it close to her torso. The infant wrapped its arms around the woman's neck and clamped its legs around her waist. The woman rocked back and forth, her hand stroking the infant's head. "It's OK. I'm here now."

Her clothes muffled the infant's cries, and it grew quieter; the pauses between the wails lengthened. The tears dried.

Eventually, it raised its head and smiled. The woman smiled, too. "See, you're alright now. Shall we go back?"

She wrapped them both up again and led the infant out by the hand.

Evie put down her cloth, put on her muslin again and walked out of the pod.

She wandered around the village, looking for Mary. It was easier to tell now who everyone was. She recognised the stooping walk of Martha, the springing walk of Grace, the broad shoulders of Mary, and the way her left glove was always askew. She couldn't see her anywhere, so she went back to Mary's pod and sat by the cooker.

When Mary did return, she stepped back as she saw Evie, as if she were about to leave again. Evie looked up at her. Mary sighed, and came into the pod.

"Hello, Evie. I thought you'd be with the turbines or something now."

"No, I finished my task. So I'm allowed to rest before the communal meal."

"Yes, you are."

Mary stayed close to the walls of the pod as she walked past Evie.

"Mary?"

"Yes?"

"I think I'm sick."

Mary paused, and sat down, opposite Evie but as far away as she could be in this small space.

"Why do you think that?"

"I don't feel well."

"How?"

"I don't know," Evie said.

"I can't help you if you don't know."

Mary seemed about to get up again.

"Wait," Evie said.

"What?"

"Touching doesn't hurt, does it?"

"No."

"It makes infants feel better."

"Yes. It makes everyone feel better."

"How?"

"I don't know. It's how people show each other that they care, I suppose."

"Mothers and fathers do it, don't they?"

"Yes."

"To make the infants feel better."

"Yes."

"Is it like medicine?"

"It's better than medicine."

"Why isn't it allowed, then?"

"It is allowed. People need it. It brings them together. They lied to you. By stopping it they control you."

Evie looked at her hands, and folded her fingers together, feeling them moving against each other, the way the mothers put their fingers together with their infants.

"Mary?"

"Yes?"

"Can you … would you?"

"What?"

"During the storm, you … can you …" Evie's voice ground to a halt. The look in Mary's eyes barricaded the words inside her head. Evie couldn't let them out.

"We should go and eat," Mary said, standing up.

Evie stayed where she was, and watched Mary, hoping that she would move closer. She felt the air move as Mary's tunic brushed past her face. It felt almost like her hand, but colder, and quicker.

Mary paused at the door. "You should be very careful about what you do next. You were seen. And your behaviour today was unforgiveable."

Mary walked out the door, and away into the village.

Evie felt an emptiness inside her stomach, like hunger, but different. Bread wouldn't fill it. She hunched over, wrapping herself into a ball. *Fathers do it. Fathers do it.*

He didn't mean it to hurt. *Use your mind.*

Families hurt the community. Everyone knows that.

The infants looked so content, when they were touched. Had she looked that content, when she was small?

Evie remembered the dark, being alone, when she'd cried. Evie remembered the teachings. She remembered the Designated Carers. She remembered the shadow of her father, sometimes, in the background, watching. Evie remembered the guard waking him in the early morning. She had watched. They had let her watch from the doorway. Her reward for putting the good of the community in the centre of her heart. He had stared at her. Pride had filled her mind as the Porter smiled at her. And her father had stared, with his head high, and his hands tied, and his feet shuffling, out of the dome. The red box had lain on the floor, condemning him. That had been the day before she'd been confirmed.

But her father hadn't meant to hurt her.

Perhaps for him, it did hurt?

Evie's head rested on the floor. The floor spun like water. She closed her eyes.

I will always love you.

You are my daughter.

He knew, then, how it felt.

Evie picked up a spoon from one of the bowls by the stove and drove the handle into her thigh. It didn't hurt enough. She held the handle and smashed the end into her head, again, again, trying to hit exactly the same spot each time.

Tears ran down her cheeks. Red or clear tears? She wasn't sure.

Someone picked her up and helped her to the communal pod. They sat her on the floor and carried on, as usual.

She ate, as usual, without looking up, or speaking to anyone.

Evie followed Mary back to her pod. Mary went straight into her sleeping pod and lay down. Evie sat on her mat, staring at the door.

She heard voices outside. Familiar voices. John's voice, and Martha's voice. Evie walked out of the pod.

It was dark now, and a few villagers sat on the stones, talking, by the light of a small fire. They didn't usually do this. The villagers had said that raids were becoming rarer, but it was still a risk.

Evie walked up to the stones. As she got closer the voices died out, and hastily spoke again. Someone laughed, but it wasn't a real laugh. She sat down next to John. John appeared not to have noticed her.

"So, the desalinator is working again?" John said.

"Yes," Sam said.

"When are they delivering the mammal meat?" This voice Evie hadn't yet attached to a name.

"In a couple of days, I think."

"It depends if they've fixed the generator, probably."

"I think they'll fix it alright," Sam said.

Evie felt John looking at her. He turned away. Sam rubbed his hands and held them out towards the fire. Not too close, not so close that his gloves would singe. He wiggled his fingers, watching the shadows. John reached out and held his hand for a moment.

Evie fidgeted on her seat. Someone was talking about food, what food they'd make tomorrow, or the next day. They liked mammal meat. Evie shook her head. Her head hung down against her chest. She closed her eyes. The space between her shoulder and John's arm seemed more dense than normal air. Dense, and swirling, and cold, like the sea. But you get boats on the sea. You can overcome the swirling, and the deep. Evie moved slightly closer to John; he seemed not to notice.

Evie ached, and she didn't know why. It felt like the darkness around her sucked at her limbs, leaving them withered. The ground felt hard; it pressed on her feet. Evie stretched out her fingers, touching the shadow of John. She raised her hand and touched the edge of the shadow of Martha. She ran her finger down the edge of the shadow. It felt like touching, but without the warmth.

Evie leant in further towards John. Her tunic folded over the edge of his tunic, mingling the two. She thought she could feel heat spreading out from it. Not bad heat, not heat that the earth makes, as punishment for the bad years. It made a nice heat; the heat of shelter, the heat of safety. Evie moved her head and let it drift, slowly, towards John's arm. She hesitated.

What would he do?

But they want me to join them, to be like them, she thought. *They want me to join the village.*

He does it to Sam, and what's the difference?

Mary wouldn't anymore. Perhaps it would mend her. It wasn't right that Mary wouldn't do it.

Evie rested her head against John's arm. She could barely feel him through her muslin. His body had barely touched her hair.

"What do you think you're doing?" John grabbed her shoulders and threw her away from him. She fell over a stone and lay on the ground. Her arm hurt. "Get away from me. Don't ever come near me again. Do you hear?"

Murmurs rippled around the villagers. Murmurs like those she'd heard from her pod. Evie blinked, trying to see through the water. She pulled her clothes around herself and stood up.

"Let's see now," someone said.

"Yes, do it now."

John stood up and walked towards Evie. He reached out to her. Evie walked backwards, towards Mary's pod, but then felt hands on her shoulders. She struggled against them, but they were strong and pushed her into the middle of the circle of stones. Two people held her steady.

John stood in front of her.

"Give us what you took," he said.

"I didn't take anything," Evie said.

Murmurs rose and fell around the circle.

"Go on, Dad, do it," Sam said.

John put his hands on Evie's shoulders. Evie tried to sink towards the ground, but the others held her up. He smiled. "Are you sure, Evie?"

"Let me go," Evie said.

John shrugged and pulled his gloves more tightly on his hands. Then he put his hands around her left shoulder. He moved his hands slowly down her upper arm, pressing into her skin.

Evie whipped and wriggled.

"Keep her still," John said.

He paused over the hairband, probing it with his fingers. Then he moved on, pressing into her elbow, then her lower arm. Then he did the same on her right arm.

"Hold her feet," he said.

Evie felt hands around her ankles. They moved her legs apart. Evie tried to join them again at her knees, but they pulled at her feet.

John began at her ankles, probing and pressing her boots. He worked his way upwards, feeling her calves, her knees. Evie thrashed against the hands holding her in place. She stood on tiptoes to keep his hands away. She wriggled. She threw her head back and howled.

"It's not allowed," she cried.

Someone put their hand under her muslin and pulled her hair to keep her head still.

John's hands worked their way around her neck, where her muslin draped over her tunic.

"Is it here, Evie? Is this where you hid it?" John said, looking up at her, his eyes level with hers.

Evie didn't answer.

John's hands moved to her shoulders.

Evie pushed on the people holding her, trying to wriggle herself free. She screamed. It hurt. It hurt inside her chest. It hurt inside her lungs. It hurt inside her head.

John worked on until he reached her waistband.

"There's something here," he said.

He lifted up her tunic. Evie felt the heat scooping out her stomach. His fingers touched her bare skin. Pain ran through her.

John pressed and pulled, and then he had it. He let go of Evie and held up the golden band. It winked in the firelight, glowing bright, and red and black.

The crowd spoke as one voice, but with a voice Evie didn't understand. She pulled her clothes back into place and ran back to Mary's pod. She threw herself on the floor of her sleeping pod and wrapped herself up in her mat. She scratched at her skin with her nails, on her legs and her arms. Perhaps the marks of his hands could be rubbed off.

Chapter 12

THE NEXT MORNING EVIE WOKE up early and waited for Mary to get up. As soon as Evie saw her body moving, Evie moved closer to the entrance to Mary's sleeping pod.

"What's happening?" Evie said.

"What?" Mary rubbed her eyes.

"Last night. What's happening?"

"What do you think is happening?"

"I don't know. I'm asking you."

Mary sat up and looked at Evie. Then she got up and sat down next to her in the main pod. "Evie …"

Mary tried to hold Evie's hand. Evie squirmed away and crouched against the wall of the pod.

"Evie. You're making it hard for me to support you."

"Support?"

Mary sighed. "You haven't fit in. That's alright, but we haven't been able to change you. And then, you took something. Something that was given to all of us, to trade for things we need to live. That's unforgiveable."

"No," Evie said, staring directly at Mary.

"You can't deny it now."

"It wasn't given to you. It was given to me."

"But we must all share what is given. It will buy more meat for all of us, and possibly buy our freedom."

"It's evil to keep all this food and water for yourselves."

"You must change."

"No," Evie said.

Mary frowned and looked towards the door.

"You're selfish and you're risking the future of New Britain," Evie said. "Without sacrifice we'll never survive."

Mary blinked. "Evie, they found the gold on you. You stole from us." She traced the hem of her tunic with her finger. "We think we've given you enough time."

"For what?"

"To decide whether you will live with us, like us." Mary paused, breathing slowly and carefully a few times. Evie sensed the words forming in Mary's mind, and dissolving again, as she switched them, and altered their order, trying to settle on what to say. "You will be asked to stop writing confessions. Then we can deal with … this other thing."

"We all have a duty to reflect on our behaviour and report it."

"No, we don't. And we don't do it. You will be asked today, to make your choice."

"And if I say no?"

Mary put her hands together in her lap, and then felt each of her fingers in turn, as if measuring them, or checking them for breaks, or deformities. "I hope you'll say yes."

"And if not?"

"We have to protect our community. That's all. And we will do it."

"But all I've said is how many errors you make. It's my duty to tell you that."

"It's not your duty. If you were different, you would know it's not your duty. I feel sorry for you, but you have too much faith."

Mary moved, as if she were about to get up.

Evie grabbed her shoulders and began shaking her. "You can't do this. I'm right. I know what's right! Don't you care about the future? Imagine how it can be if we follow the rules!" Evie's shakes became more violent. Mary swayed back and forth, barely resisting. Evie's hands formed fists and she threw them at Mary's arms, and shoulders, and head.

Someone came in and stopped her. They clamped her arms to her side and hauled her out. They dragged her to the communal pod and threw her on the floor. The villagers sat in a circle around her.

When Evie looked up, she saw that Mary had come in. Mary sat down next to John.

"It's time," John said. "You have to choose. Will you live like us, or will you carry on trying to destroy us?"

"I never—"

"Just say 'yes' or 'no,'" John said.

Evie raised herself up and kneeled while she looked at them. Mary wouldn't return her gaze. The others stared, their eyes hard, hungry, and focused. Evie swayed from side to side. She gripped her knees to stop her hands shaking.

"No. You're evil. You're destroying our future," Evie said.

The villagers seemed to breathe out together, and Evie felt like she was swimming in a storm of hissing.

"Mary. Stop them," Evie said, trying to make a connection with Mary's eyes, hidden in the folds of her muslin.

"You stole from us," Mary said. "And all you've done is call destruction on our heads."

"You're hiding your food while people are hungry. It's you who need to change," Evie said.

John and Mary stared at her. The voices of the villagers swirled around them all. The sound washed through Evie and resonated in her body. She felt like she might fall apart. She closed her eyes and swayed. She imagined what she might feel if she found herself back at home.

"I want to go home," Evie said. "Please, I just want to go home."

"If you go home, you'll betray us," Mary said.

"I won't. I just want to go."

Mary and John looked at each other. They almost seemed to be speaking without words.

"We will leave you outside our boundary. You can make your way back, if you can," Mary said.

A couple of the villagers laughed; hard laughs that sounded like stones falling.

Evie closed her eyes again, feeling her legs shaking, and tasting blood in her mouth.

Someone put some bread into her hand. The crowd pressed in on her, sweeping her along. Hands wound her muslin around her head, and they took her outside. Someone put her tablet in her pocket. They bundled her into a small transport. A man got in next to her and started the motor. They drove towards the wind turbines, and the sounds of the crowd died.

Evie fixed her mind on the image of her dome disappearing into the distance. How wonderful it would be to see it appearing again, sparkling through the swirls of sand, calling to her, holding all the people she knew.

The man turned away from the wind turbines, driving around the edge of the hill. He drove out of the perimeter. The dust swirled here; there were more rocks. The area hadn't been cleared. The man drove on.

Evie looked at him staring ahead and throwing his weight into the corners to balance out the rocking and sliding of the vehicle.

"What?" Evie said.

The man didn't answer, Evie thought she heard a grunt.

"I don't have my spare set of clothes," Evie said.

The man laughed.

"Where are you taking me?"

He didn't answer. Evie looked over the edge of the transport. Could she jump? But the rocks would hurt.

The sun rose higher in the sky and the man pulled the canopy fully over the transport. The sandy wind gummed up Evie's eyes.

The heat seeped in.

"Can I have water?"

"No," the man said. But he fumbled under his seat and pulled out a water container. He drank from it and put it back.

"Please," Evie said.

The silence continued. Evie tried to catch his eye, but he never looked at her. Eventually, he stopped, in a place that looked no different to any other place they'd passed. Evie sighed, her breath drying her mouth out even further. Maybe this stop was for water. She looked at the man.

"Get out," he said.

"Why? Can I find a transport here?"

"Get out."

"What are you doing?"

"Get out."

"You can't leave me here. I can't walk from here."

"If you don't get out, I'll drag you out."

Evie stumbled as she got out of the transport. Her hand stayed wrapped around the door handle.

"Let go."

"Can I have water?"

"No. Let go."

Evie gripped tighter. The man reached across the seat and hit her hand with a piece of metal. Evie screamed, and fell backwards.

The transport whirred louder, and turned. Evie ran after it, unevenly, holding her hand.

"Please." Only the swirls of sand heard her shout. She imagined the man driving back to the village, and eating his breakfast.

Evie sank to the ground, holding her hand to her chest. But the sand seared through her clothes. She could feel the burning on her knees and her shins. She stood up. Her tongue stuck to the sides of her mouth; she thought she could feel it swelling. The sun pressed down on her like a roof, moving lower, crushing her. She put one foot in front of the other and saw it sink into the ground. She began to walk. The sand crept in through the tops of her boots and felt like it was melting her ankles. She tried to brush it away with her hand, but it was hard to stand up again.

In the distance the air flickered, like looking at the sun on gold. It hurt to look at it. Blood ran down her fingers and dripped onto the sand, and dried immediately.

Evie couldn't walk for long. She thought she heard a voice and looked around, but couldn't see anyone. She thought she saw her father, in the shimmering air. Had they taken her to him? She held out her hand, but the image flickered.

Evie's skin burned, even under her clothes. Her tongue felt too large for her mouth. She closed her eyes. Just one bit of water. One bit of water would make it alright.

When Evie could no longer stand, she fell. The ground hurt and she rolled, trying to stop it burning. But it didn't stop. The sand mingled with her clothes and cut her skin.

Then she could no longer move. She buried her head in her arms. The heat pressed her into the earth and the sand heaped around her.

"I'm sorry," Evie said. "Take me back."

Evie would have cried, if there had been water enough in her body to make tears.

Who did she talk to? Evie didn't know. She thought she felt a person near, but knew there could be none. But in her mind, she saw her father.

Evie melted into the ground. Her skin peeled; her shoulders stopped shaking. She thought she was falling asleep forever.

Chapter 13

WATER. WATER TRICKLED. WATER so cold that it hurt. Her eyes wouldn't open. The place smelled strange. It smelled sharp. It smelled of dying. Blackness swallowed her again.

The next time she heard voices. The voices spoke oddly. They lingered over the wrong parts of words, dragging them out. One voice was high, female. One was old, a man or a woman, the voice didn't say. Were they speaking to her? Her eyes wouldn't open. She moved her tongue. It hurt, like she'd eaten rocks. Her throat felt closed. She couldn't speak.

Someone put a hand on her head. It scorched her; it felt like the hand had reached all the way beneath her skull. She was lost to them, again.

Sometime, when it was dark, she managed to open her eyes. The night brought patches, patches of cloth and sheets, and a door, perhaps. Evie made a strangled noise, and heard someone shuffling towards her.

"Hello?" the voice said.

Evie tried to speak again, but couldn't.

"It's alright. Don't try. Have some water." A hand supported her head and let water trickle through her lips.

Evie felt it soaking into her. It smoothed her throat. She felt like she might be able to speak, but words still wouldn't come.

Evie slept, but this time it felt like sleep, not like drowning.

Every time she woke, people put small pieces of damp bread in her mouth. She chewed slowly and felt them scraping down the inside of her. After a few days, the bread was less painful, and so they gave her bigger pieces, and drier pieces. Her eyes stung whenever there was light, so she didn't properly see the people who helped her. But their hands felt familiar, after a while. One was a woman with cool, soft hands. The other a man, whose hands felt larger and warmer. He lifted her head with no effort at all, cradling her skull in his palm, like an infant's.

Over a week later Evie felt light on her face. She instinctively turned away from it. But then she moved her eyelids slightly and noticed that they no longer hurt so badly. Hesitantly, she opened her eyes. They stung, but the scraping, searing pain had gone. She sat up and squinted.

They had placed her in a small pod, with familiar grey sides. The mat she lay on was red, and padded with folded sheets. A couple of rolled-up sheets had been put behind her head.

There was a small water container at the end of the mat. And beyond the container was a door, with a sheet draped over it. Evie thought she could hear the murmur of voices somewhere beyond it. The smell she'd dreamt was real. It still smelled of death.

Evie tried to sit up, but her arms buckled, and she lay down again. They had left her tunic on, but underneath it, her legs were bandaged. Her feet were bare, but red, and the skin peeled off them in patches. They had made bandages for her hands that looked like gloves.

This didn't smell like Eden. But where could it be? A proper dome? Had they come, then, at the last minute, to save her? To avenge her?

"Hello." Her voice sounded like someone else's. Her mouth formed the word in an unfamiliar way. Evie shook her head. "Hello." This time it sounded more like her own. She ran her tongue around her mouth, feeling the scratches, tasting blood around the base of her teeth.

She heard rustling outside the door. A hand held the side of the sheet and pulled it aside.

Evie shrank back into her mat, her eyes wide, her mouth open. She pulled a sheet from under her and held it to her body. The bandages on her hands wouldn't let her hold it tightly. She tried to pull her legs up to her body, but they stung when she moved.

The woman smiled and walked towards Evie. She picked up the water and sat down next to her. Around her neck was cloth, of the forbidden colour.

"Praise the Lord, you've come back to us," she said.

"No! It can't be."

"It can't be what?"

"You."

"Me?" The woman smiled again and placed her cool hand on Evie's forehead. "We didn't think you'd make it."

Evie tried to turn away but wanted the water more. She lay back and let the woman help her drink. Could she hear her heart? Evie tried to calm it.

Use your mind.

There was nothing she could do now. Nothing at all. Not while she was broken.

"Where am I?" Evie said, avoiding looking at the woman.

"You are in the desert."

"Who are you?"

"I'm Rachel. We live here."

"In the desert?"

"Yes, there's nowhere left to us now."

Evie looked at the scarf.

"Yes, I think you know who we are," Rachel said.

Evie took another sip of water. She felt the beginning of hunger.

"May I have some bread, please?" Evie said.

Rachel nodded, and stood up. "I'll bring you some proper food soon. I think it will help you."

Evie looked away.

Later, she heard Rachel outside the door again. But Rachel didn't come straight in. Evie heard whispers, and then Rachel's voice. "No, she's not ready." A man said something insistent, he might have asked how much longer. Evie couldn't make it out. He pressed further. "We have to ask her. This is important."

Rachel walked in carrying a bowl. She fed Evie a lumpy, warm liquid. Evie ate all of it.

"More?" Rachel said.

"Yes, please. It felt good."

Rachel brought her two more bowls, and then Evie fell asleep again.

During the next two weeks she only saw Rachel. Rachel fed her, and cleaned her, and washed her gently with water that skimmed over her skin, leaving it slippery. It stung her burns, but made them feel better afterwards. Rachel took off the bandages from her hands. She gave her medicine that made her sleep, and she rubbed white cream on her feet. Evie watched the skin beginning to grow again, slowly.

"Someone wants to speak to you," Rachel said one morning after Evie had eaten breakfast, managing to hold the spoon by herself.

"Who?"

"Our priest."

Evie struggled to put the spoon back in the bowl without dropping it.

"What's a priest? What does he want to talk about?" Evie said.

"Who you are. Why you've been sent to us."

"I'm very tired."

Rachel took the bowl. "He's very wise, and very kind. You needn't be afraid. He said you would come, one day."

When Rachel left, Evie heard more murmuring. The sheet flicked sideways again, and a man walked in. Evie had expected him to be larger, or younger. This man was old. He sat cross-legged on the floor, and Evie reached out to grab the things he held.

The man gave them to her. Evie put the red hairband next to her on her mat and opened her tablet. As she did so, pieces of it slid out and onto her lap.

"I hope you understand. They can find us with them."

Evie picked at the fragments. She gasped, picking up the pieces again, turning them over, hoping that next time they'd look different. The back had come off, but where was the letter?

"I have it," the priest said.

Evie stared at him. "It's mine. Give it back."

"We've been waiting for you for many, many years. More years than we can count."

"What? It's mine, give it back."

"You brought it to us, didn't you?"

"I didn't know you were here."

"Everyone knows we live in the deserts. What else were you doing out here?"

"I …" Evie hesitated, her mind not working fast enough. "I didn't know I'd find you."

"But you did, praise the Lord, and your message will change the world."

Evie frowned. "They will kill me if they find it."

"They won't find it. And we will protect you. We're ready to follow you. Together we'll spread the word. And it'll spur us on, to overthrow them."

"What do you mean?" Evie said. She struggled to raise herself up and shook her head. "You don't make sense."

"The old people always said it was so. We never believed, but now you've come. The voice of truth. The word of God." The priest tried to hold her hand. Evie closed her eyes and managed to move it out of reach, despite the pain.

A trap?

Evie tried to look out of the door. This could be a megadome.

This could be a test.

And these people are evil. They eat mammals. They want to destroy the world, she thought.

"What do you mean by overthrowing them?" Evie said.

The priest laughed, and his cheeks creased like Mary's. "Britain should be run differently. This regime is evil. They kill, and torture. But you know this. Don't be afraid. You're safe. You can speak plainly, here. We're ready to do your work." The priest looked into her face, smiling, hopeful.

Evie coughed. "But we have to save the world. We have to make sacrifices for the future. So our descendants can live with plenty," she said, her voice shaking. "There is always a cost."

The priest's smile wavered. "We are loyal, I promise. You don't need to test us."

"You aren't loyal to New Britain."

The priest looked like someone had hurt him. His lips quivered, and he shook his head. Evie thought he looked like an infant who'd been told he wouldn't be fed.

The priest sighed. "Why do you have this document?" he said.

"It was given to me. I should have handed it in to my teacher."

"And what it says?"

"She was weak-willed and didn't understand the sacrifices we have to make. It's shameful to have an inheritance like that. She deserved to die. I didn't want my teacher to know the terrible things she said."

The priest held her gaze for a few moments. "Is that really what you think?"

"Yes. I've always worked hard to overcome my inheritance. I should have destroyed it, but olden-day paper is a treasure."

He nodded, and then stood up slowly. His shoulders hung as he walked out.

He left the pod. Evie thought he said, "She's not who we thought," to someone outside.

Rachel gave her more medicine, and she slept.

The priest returned once more to ask whether Evie wanted to be taken somewhere. The longing for home overwhelmed her. She asked to be taken to the closest megadome. They would take her home from there. The priest asked what she would do, once she got there, and Evie replied that she'd do whatever was needed.

Sometime later, Rachel came back into the pod. "We will always be grateful to you, Evie," she said.

"Thanks for looking after me. I will tell them that the Religious are kind to strangers."

Rachel nodded. "Even though we're evil?"

"You just need teaching. It doesn't have to be bad. But the future we're working towards is worth every sacrifice."

"Yes, it is," Rachel said. She held out a small cup of medicine to Evie. "Drink this."

"I don't normally have medicine after dinner."

"This is different. It's to help you get on your way."

"My way?"

"To your next stage in life."

Evie drank, listening for the sounds of home. She felt tired and sank back on the mat. She closed her eyes. Her limbs felt as if they no longer belonged to her. She seemed to be floating, like swimming. Somewhere, in her mind, panic flickered. But by then she could no longer move or speak. Her breaths were difficult. The air struggled to open her lungs. She gasped. Her eyes no longer opened. Her lips no longer moved.

Evie never woke again.

But the letter lived and was copied, copied many times. And it passed, from one community to the next, through the desert, along the roads, and into the domes. It was hidden in sacks of protein pods, stuck to the bottom of hydrogen tanks, slipped into wheel arches, and in the soles of boots. It was read, and believed, or disbelieved, and destroyed, or passed on. People died saving it, and every burned copy had already spawned offspring that lived and travelled the country. Some copies made it overseas, where they were added to, confirmed, and supplemented.

This was how a common story united the acts of rebellion. This was how different purposes merged. This was how the Revolution began. Their symbol was the red hairband, worn by Evie, the Prophet, the bringer of truth, who gave her life for the cause.

PART 2: PRESENT

LAURA'S STORY

Chapter 1

LAURA DIED THE INSTANT EDMOND was born, but she never realised this was what had happened. She felt them placing Edmond on her chest. She smelt blood, life, and death, mixed into one. She opened her eyes, but the things she saw no longer belonged to her.

People think memories die with the body they're attached to. But Laura's body clung to its memories; it felt their traces in its fingers, it caught their sounds and wrapped itself around them. Laura knew who this body belonged to, but it was no longer hers. She inhabited it like a sheepskin blanket. It hung about her. And then unexpectedly it would slip into place, and for an instant, become her own. Laura would gasp, and try to keep it there, but the threads connecting her to it were cut. For the rest of her life, Laura struggled to catch the words to explain what had happened. She never could, because it was impossible to describe what it was like to be dead to those who were still alive.

"Mum's sleeping." The words burrowed into her ears.

"She needs to feed him."

Laura knew there was a hand on her arm. It shook her, gently. Laura hesitated before making her body wake. The shaking became insistent. She made her eyes open.

"Hey! You fell asleep. But they say you should feed him. How are you?" the man she knew was her husband said.

"Where am I?" Laura's voice lagged behind her thoughts. Her lips moved out of synch, as if their instructions had travelled far.

"Still in hospital. I think they'll let you go home later."

"No, I mean, where am *I*?"

Her husband shrugged. "You're in hospital. But don't worry, I got a private room. How're you feeling now?"

"I'm not feeling."

"Not feeling what?"

"I'm just not feeling … at all."

"That'll be the drugs. Well done though. He's the finest boy the midwife ever saw."

And that was the first time Laura thought about *him*. Facts tumbled through her mind. A baby had come. A baby boy had come. She would have to care for him. The list of facts suppressed the absence of feelings. "Is he OK?"

"Perfectly healthy."

Laura thought she should feel happy but couldn't quite be sure what happy was. She knew she had felt it once, but the imprint of it had faded.

"That's good," she said, but, without any meaning to support her words, they tumbled out of her mouth and crashed to the floor. The door opened and a nurse carried Edmond in.

Edmond rested against her. Laura felt his body relax. His head nuzzled into her, and she fed him. It felt like her blood was draining away. Laura stroked his head gently because she knew it was what her hand was supposed to do. And then they took him away again. But as the nurse lifted him off her, Laura's manicured hands remained in place, as if she were still cradling her baby.

* * *

Darkness smothered the room and crept in at her ears. It filled her body, stuffing it up like a scarecrow. The sound of her breathing rushed through her, as if her body had disappeared. She knew that her back must hurt, although she couldn't feel it. She moved forward, almost imperceptibly, balancing the drowsy baby over the side of the cot. Her eyes stung, and the cot's bars multiplied, and divided, and merged with one another. Her feet wobbled, although she hadn't asked them to. She tensed her body and held her breath.

He snuffled. He moved his head. Laura closed her eyes and felt sleep taking advantage of the foothold it had been given. Her head fell forward. She managed to hold it up, but like a balloon attached to a stick.

He opened his mouth, horrified at the trick that she'd played on him, and cried. Laura swept him up again and fell backward onto the chair beside the cot. "Please sleep. Please just sleep," she whispered. It almost seemed possible that he would understand. "Just stop it and sleep."

The warmth of her body calmed him, and he relaxed against her again. Laura kept her eyes open. Her ears rang. Whenever she blinked, her eyelids tried to seal themselves together. Edmond slept. She lost sense of time and was about to put him in his cot again but noticed a lightening in the air. The corners of the room had appeared. Birds sang, lively, refreshed after the night. Laura imagined gluing their beaks together. Cars moved in the distance. The world mocked her.

Her husband's face appeared at the door, attached to a piece of toast. "Good night?" he said, his eyebrows raised in hopeful anticipation.

"No, I don't think I slept at all."

"Well, remember what the midwife said. Sleep when he sleeps."

"Yes, I remember," Laura said.

"Anything I can get you?"

"Food, and drink, and sleep."

"I made you tea and toast in the kitchen."

"OK?"

"Have a good day. I might be a bit late. There's drinks after work." He swallowed his toast with a smile, and left.

Laura heard his feet on the stairs, the slam of the front door, and his key in the lock. The sound of the bolts flying home reverberated up the stairs.

She stroked Edmond's head mechanically. When he opened his eyes she smiled, because she knew this was what was best for him. She fed him and washed him. She struggled to keep a grip on her mind, but it slipped loose, and seemed out of reach. She forced it to remember lists, to plan the next half an hour. Pick up clothes, pick up baby, hold his head, walk towards the kitchen, put clothes in the washing machine, go to the fridge for food. Nevertheless, she would find herself in the kitchen later, with dirty clothes in one hand, wondering why she had ever left the bedroom. As she looked around, cards shone from every flat surface, twinkling in the sunlight. 'Congratulations,' they said. And it was only because she was dead that she could bear it at all.

Half hours stitched themselves together into hours, and hours lined up to form days, and days clung to one another. Each minute felt stretched with effort even though multiple days passed by without notice. In the darker hours Laura tried to remember who she was, or who she had been. She could make pictures march in front of her, parading a sequence of events, but she could never move into them, or feel them. "I used to be Laura," she said to Edmond one night, but it felt like a lie. "I *am* Laura," she said, but that felt no more true.

* * *

Laura fell asleep in a warm patch of sun on the sofa. No part of her mind remained awake. Dark waves of sleep rolled her up. Her breathing slowed so much that a person watching her would have doubted that she breathed at all. In this state, her mind was free to travel. It floated above her, resting, and waiting.

Laura's mind began to see. It saw, but didn't feel, panic. It watched people running and dragging children as water rushed around them. The sea swelled, and waves like fists smashed them down. Water poured in through all the doors and windows in the world. It consumed houses, vehicles, farms and hills. It carried on until nothing familiar remained. Someone cried. A voice sounded in the distance; it demanded attention.

Laura gasped for air, clawing herself up the side of the sofa. It felt as if her throat was blocked. Edmond was crying. She coughed, pounding her chest with her fist. She scrambled into his room to find him hitting the air with his fists. "Oh Eddie, I'd just got to sleep," Laura said, still straining to get air into her lungs. She picked him up and fed him again. "You shouldn't need feeding this often. Don't you pay attention to what it says in the books?" She pointed at the pile of baby manuals, none of which had proven a reliable guide to Edmond the Unsatisfied.

She sat in the chair by his bed, holding him gently as he fed. She tried to hum, because she had heard that music was good for babies. But it sounded out of tune with her mind. She coughed again. Her throat hurt, and it tasted of saltwater. She shook her head. "Why don't they tell you it's really this hard?" she asked Edmond. Edmond blinked at her, and might have shrugged his shoulders. Laura frowned. No, he couldn't have shrugged his shoulders. He couldn't even have understood. But he stared at her, and Laura stared back.

Eventually, he fell asleep. Laura crouched over a cushion. She waited until his body heat warmed the cloth beneath him and then quickly covered him with a blanket. He was fooled. He stayed asleep. Laura walked backward out of his room before turning around. A cold cup of tea fermented by the bed. She walked into the bathroom, pulled her pyjamas off and stepped into the shower.

The hot water ran down her body, almost scalding the skin off her back. She held out her hand in front of her face and watched drops running down her fingers. It didn't seem part of her. Laura wondered whether they were her hands, or whether you can wake up with someone else's hands. She had never had thoughts like this before.

As she dried herself, she looked into the mirror. Her brown hair tangled across her neck and around her ears. She rubbed it with the towel, watching it flicking back and forth. She caught her eye and flinched. Someone watched her. A person in the mirror watched. Laura blinked. *Those are my eyes,* she thought. *I'm watching.* She looked away momentarily, but it felt as if the eyes in the mirror had never looked away. She peered into them, wondering whether she'd ever really noticed her eyes before. They had always been green, and they were still green now. But were they her green? The pupils expanded as she stared into them. Laura pulled away and steadied herself against the sink.

In the next room, Edmond cried. "Oh, for fuck's sake, can't I even get a shower in peace?" she said. She pulled her pyjamas on again and ran into his bedroom. He stopped crying as soon as she stood in front of him. "Can you see now?" she said, looking at the child. "Can you see Mummy now? Well, that's progress. When do you decide to sleep and wipe your own arse though, hey?" Edmond blinked and waved his fist.

Laura picked him up and kissed his cheek. "Can you let me get dressed, Eddie? Then we'll go for a nice walk and look at the ducks. And if we're in luck, I can talk to the woman at the café and feel like I'm a nice normal human being. How does that sound, Dumpling? Would you believe your mummy could negotiate contracts like a demon, but now her greatest victory is showering before lunch?" Edmond didn't believe her; he sucked at his fists. "And I must get some new toothpaste. Will you remind Mummy later? This one makes my mouth feel like I've gargled with ditch water."

Laura and Edmond did make it out. Laura fidgeted with his blanket, afraid that he might overheat, or freeze. She still wasn't used to steering a pushchair and nipped the ankles of passers-by. They frowned, and she pulled her jumper around herself. The wheels got stuck in drains and it was surprisingly difficult to get up kerbstones in a hurry. They left the main streets and went to the park. Laura breathed in the cool sunny air. It didn't feel like it reached her lungs. Edmond gurgled and kicked his blanket off.

"He's a lovely boy." Laura looked up at an old woman.

"Yes, thank you," Laura said.

"How old is he?"

"A month."

"Gracious. He'll be a big lad when he's grown."

"Yes."

The woman bent down to hold his hand. Edmond gripped her finger and shook it. The woman seemed to flinch and draw back. "Well, have a lovely day, dear," she said backing away.

Laura watched her tweed skirt swishing back and forth as she walked towards the exit. "Jesus, old people," Laura said to Edmond, peering into his pushchair. "I didn't much like her either."

Laura and Edmond walked around the pond. It took five hundred steps, unless she walked to the bin on the furthest side, then it took five hundred and twenty. She walked around the pond again, and then again, counting her steps each time. Then Laura pushed Edmond into the coffee shop and ordered a decaf latte, which she slurped while Edmond wriggled and squirmed. She picked up her phone and posted a lie about her life. She kept looking at the clock. How much longer would he last? Would he finally go two hours without food? Or would his face boil with rage the instant ninety minutes were up? And what would happen after that? Another lap around the pond, maybe two. There was milk to buy on the way home. And then what? More hours to fill with nothing and everything.

Laura overheard a fragment of conversation. They'd said Tuesday. It was one o'clock on Tuesday. She looked at her watch. They would all be sitting at the rectangular oak table, staring at the flat screen on the wall. Her boss would be bringing them to order, corralling their eyes towards him. Who would be in her seat? Would they have expanded to fill her space? Or would it still be empty, waiting for her return? Laura frowned. She couldn't remember the feel of her seat, or the smooth wood that she had run her hands over so many times. Her boss's face was a shadow. She had seen it so many times. Was it possible that she'd forgotten? *He had a nose,* she thought. *Begin with that.* But no specific nose came to mind. Eyes? She wasn't sure. Most people's were brown. He definitely had two, which were probably brown.

Edmond began with a tentative cough that turned into a cry. In the time it took her to unstrap him he'd turned into a furious wrinkled beetroot. Laura wrapped a headscarf around herself and fumbled with her clothes. "Shit, Eddie, what have you done to me?"

Chapter 2

LAURA WATCHED HER HUSBAND'S HANDS leafing through the wine list. He turned the same page back and forth, frowning.

"You know I can't have any anyway?" Laura said.

"Not even a bit?"

"No, not really. Breastfeeding."

He sighed and put the folder on the table between them. "But it's worth it, I suppose. He's growing well."

"You noticed?"

"Of course I noticed." His hand inched across the table towards Laura. Laura kept her arm still and watched his hand crawling on top of hers. "We should do this more often," he said. Laura tried to work out whether she was able to feel his hand on hers, or whether she just knew she should feel his hand.

"Yes, I suppose we should. The food's nice."

"Not just for the food. You seem to have disappeared a bit somehow."

"Disappeared?"

"Sorry, I don't know how to say it. You're still here, obviously. Just ... I suppose it's a bit all-consuming for you."

"Maybe I have disappeared," Laura said, wriggling her fingers under his. He squeezed her hand and smiled at her. Laura looked out of the window behind his head. People walked purposefully back from work, shoulders hunched, bags swinging. "Maybe I don't have a purpose."

"Eddie is a purpose and a half."

"Yes."

"Better than work, surely. That used to stress you to no end."

"I suppose." Laura watched a woman framed by the window answering her phone. The woman smiled a warm, infectious smile. Laura made her lips copy the shape.

"That's nice to see," he said.

"What?"

"You haven't smiled in ages."

"I'm not smiling. I'm trying on a smile like I try on a dress."

"What?" He looked about to say something else, but the waiter disturbed him. Laura watched him ordering wine but couldn't hear what he said. If she concentrated really hard, she thought she could hear a high-pitched buzzing in the background.

Eventually the food arrived, and Laura sliced her steak, watching the blood running out of it and drowning her plate. "So, how's work then? You seem busy at the moment." She watched her husband's face as he chewed, his food making lumps in his cheeks.

"Good, actually." He swallowed.

"Good. Anything exciting?"

"We got a new contract this week."

"Oh good. What's it for?" she said.

His eyes wandered around the restaurant and he breathed heavily. "It's for an energy company."

"Oh yes?" Laura's voice caught in her throat and she coughed.

"They've asked us to design software that tells people how much energy they use," he said, sounding as if he were reading from a presentation.

"Isn't that what gas meters are for?" Laura scooped up some potato and swallowed it. It tasted like everything else tasted now. Bland, and slightly earthy. Laura chewed and squeezed it through her teeth.

"No. Not like meters." He wiped his hands on his napkin. "It'll tell customers what they're using their electricity and gas on, and whether similar houses use the same amount for the same things, like hot water, and cooking. It'll help them be more efficient."

He looked at her with eyes open, eyebrows raised, awaiting compliments.

"That's interesting," Laura said. "Does this food taste odd to you?" She watched his face. His mouth dropped as he sighed.

"You don't seem totally focused at the moment," he said, sawing through green beans.

"I haven't slept forever."

"Not forever, exactly."

"No, not precisely." Laura let her cutlery clatter onto her plate. He stopped sawing. She watched the light flickering off the silver, the enamel, and the polish on the table. The lights outside the window cascaded into the room with long silvery tentacles. Laura blinked but they didn't leave. Lights swirled slowly in front of her, weaving in and out of one another.

"Laura." His voice knocked her backward in her chair.

"Sorry. I saw something odd."

"I think maybe you should see someone. I'm a bit worried. It's a new experience for both of us, but you seem sad, or lost, or something." His hand crept across the table again. He held her fingers gently. So gently she couldn't feel his hand.

"Someone?"

"Well, the doctor perhaps. I don't know."

"Why?" The buzzing in her head grew louder and she could no longer hear what he said. She gazed around the room as if her eyes had lost something. She looked at everything in turn, but none of the tables, chairs, flowers, or people matched what her eyes wanted to see.

Her body froze. It felt less under her control than normal. Laura felt her head turning so it faced her husband again. "That software," she said.

"Laura?" He leant in towards her and moved his hand up her arm. "Are you OK?"

Her next words flowed out of her. It felt like she'd stabbed a bag of rice. "Have you read about China? They're giving everyone social credits. It's a score to show how honest they are. You should give people a score, to show how efficient they are. For their homes. People love getting a score, like marks out of ten. Competition motivates people." Laura sighed. Her head felt heavy and her eyelids sank. For a moment the table seemed to blur.

"You're tired. But that's an awesome idea." He stroked her cheek and brushed her hair out of her face.

"Yes, I am tired."

As they walked back together Laura rested her head against her husband's shoulder, and he supported her weight. She tripped off the kerb occasionally and he half-pulled, half-lifted her up. Once he'd seen the babysitter out, he found her in Edmond's room, sitting on the chair with her head hanging over the back. She gripped Edmond tightly as he fed.

"Jesus. I thought we might have time for a cuddle," he said.

"He always needs to eat. Constantly."

"I'm going to bed then."

"OK."

"About the doctor," he said. Laura closed her eyes. "I really think you need to see someone."

Laura moved her head in a way she thought might pass for a nod, but she struggled to stop it moving. She listened to the sounds her husband made as he brushed his teeth and got undressed. She heard him pulling the duvet over himself. She waited.

And then she picked up Edmond and put him gently back in his cot. "Sorry for waking you, Eddie. 'Cuddling' isn't what Mummy wants right now. You just let me get some sleep, OK?"

Edmond wriggled in his sleep, his lips moving as if they still sucked at something. His fingers curled and uncurled themselves until he relaxed. His breathing became heavier, and then Laura knew he slept. She crept out of the room and undressed in the dark bedroom. She brushed her teeth and grimaced at the aftertaste. In the bathroom she checked her phone, and misrepresented her evening. She crept into the bed, careful not to disturb the folds in the duvet. Just as she managed to ask her mind what was going on, she fell asleep, and stayed asleep.

* * *

Laura watched the doctor closely, trying to read what her nimble eczema-scarred hands typed. Laura plaited her fingers together, then unwound them again and picked at the hem of her skirt. She noticed a ladder beginning in her tights. The doctor's fingers skipped over the keys, but then stumbled. She pursed her lips and deleted a line of text using her index finger.

"Any other symptoms?" the doctor said.

"I don't know," Laura said.

"Anything else you think is odd that you've noticed since" — the doctor waved her hand at the pushchair—"since the little one arrived?"

"It's hard to know what's normal, so I can't know what's odd."

"Well … anything other new mothers don't talk about."

Laura frowned and focused her eyes on the closest wheel of the pushchair. "I don't know any other mothers."

The doctor relaxed back in her seat. She brought her ankles together, so the rubber soles of her shoes touched. She folded her hands in her lap. Laura noticed the photo of a sizeable family on her desk. She felt the doctor's gaze on her.

"Well," she said, "that might be part of the problem, you know. It's a big adjustment and it helps to talk to people who understand. Can your family help?"

"I don't have any family."

"Friends?"

"My friends are at work."

"As is your husband, I presume?" The doctor picked up a pen and flicked it between her fingers. "Sometimes you can have hormone imbalances, too, which make it all a tad more difficult." She reached across her desk and picked up her prescription pad. "I'm going to prescribe you some mild sleeping pills. And I want you to find a mother's group or meet other mothers at a playgroup or something. You need to get out a bit more."

"We go out every day. We watch the ducks."

"Yes. A little more human contact is what I meant. It is hard but you'll get through it. We all do." The doctor pressed a key on her keyboard. It felt like a full stop. Laura watched her eyes wandering to the clock.

"And the oddness?"

"You mean, not feeling like yourself? A few nights' sleep will do wonders."

"He doesn't sleep through." Laura nodded at the pushchair with the silent, and deeply asleep Edmond.

"You need to sleep whenever he takes a nap," the doctor said.

"But he doesn't sleep." Laura felt her cheeks reddening and rubbed them with the back of her hand. "I mean, this is unusual. He never does this."

"He'll sleep more as the weeks go by." The doctor nodded and handed Laura the prescription. "You'll do OK. He looks really healthy."

"Thanks." Laura stood up, letting the arms of the chair take her weight. She paused, knowing that as soon as she left, the moment would be over. It had seemed, ten minutes ago, that help was close at hand. Laura swayed slightly, as if she were teetering on the edge of a chasm.

As she walked out, she heard the doctor typing again. Laura walked through the waiting room, curving around a coughing man. She fumbled with the door, struggling to get herself and the pushchair out. In the end she used the pushchair as a battering ram and forced her way onto the street. Waves of people rolled past. It seemed as difficult to move onto the pavement as jumping into a fast-flowing river. No one looked at her. They avoided her eyes on purpose, Laura thought. She reached out a hand, wondering whether it would hit a barrier, or a screen, or something dividing her from them. But it didn't. The buzzing in her ears grew louder. Laura shook her head as if trying to dislodge an imprisoned fly. She stepped unsteadily onto the pavement and followed the tide of people to the chemist.

Later, Laura sat on a bench holding the paper bag with her

prescription. Edmond peered out at her from under the hood of the pushchair. He waved a hand, and then looked at it, puzzled. "Yes, it's yours. You're moving it, silly," Laura said.

Edmond blinked and his tongue crept out between his lips. "Hungry again?" He looked at her.

"What are you thinking, hey?" Edmond didn't reply. He stared impassively at her face.

"When do you speak, hey? It'll be so much easier when you do." Laura picked him up, unbuttoned her jumper and hid him under her scarf while he fed. She looked at her watch. One hundred minutes. He'd managed one hundred minutes.

* * *

Laura watched the nurse picking Edmond up, his legs dangling from his nappy, his face bubbling with outrage. She placed him in the metal scale like a fresh chicken ready for stuffing. She stepped back. Laura squinted at the display, flickering in time with Edmond's kicking. The nurse pulled a pen from her top pocket and picked a precise point on the growth chart. She held it at arm's length.

"He's growing well. Well done, you."

"Thanks," Laura said, moving to pick Edmond up again.

The nurse turned towards her. "Still breastfeeding?"

"Yes. Mostly."

"Good for you. It shows." The nurse looked around her at the other mothers half-heartedly forming a queue.

Laura scrambled for Edmond's clothes and moved to the side of the room.

"At least you didn't wee on her today, Dumpling. That's something."

Laura fought him back into his Babygro, knocking the arm of a woman next to her.

"Sorry," Laura said.

"It's OK. There's never enough room on these tables," the woman said, before moving Edmond's jumper away from her own pile of miniature clothes.

Laura concentrated on buttoning Edmond's garments before she looked up. The other woman frowned down at her own child, struggling to get a hand through an arm hole.

"Come here often?" Laura said.

The woman laughed. "Well, yes, every month. You?"

"Same. Not sure why though. It's clear he's growing."

The woman sighed as she picked up a tiny pair of socks. "It gets me out the house though."

Laura rocked Edmond back and forth. The woman's child let itself be manhandled into its clothes. Laura turned and walked towards the table with tea and coffee, and leaflets about breastfeeding, and vaccinations. The other woman followed.

"I'm Sarah," she said.

"I'm Laura. Nice to meet you."

Laura sensed someone else standing next to her. She turned to face her. The woman smiled.

"And I'm Penelope," she said.

"Nice to meet you," Laura said.

Sarah quicky looked over her shoulder. "Yes. It is."

The three women stood awkwardly, looking at their babies, and scanning the leaflets. Laura gulped down some squash.

"So, do you live round here?" Sarah pointed vaguely at the window.

Laura looked at the decaying shed outside, wondering how many years it would take to die. "Yes, just up the road really. We walk here. You?"

"We're behind the high street. Not so far." Sarah fumbled with the brake on her pushchair.

"I haven't really met many other people with children." Laura looked expectantly at Penelope, but Penelope turned to put her baby in its pushchair.

"There are loads of groups you can do," Sarah said. "I can give you a list, if you want."

Edmond wriggled in Laura's arms, turning his head from side to side. "I'd better get back to feed him. But we could meet up?"

"Yes, that'd be nice." Sarah said.

Penelope nodded enthusiastically.

* * *

A week later, Laura walked up and down outside the café. She checked her phone. Definitely the right place. Definitely the right time. Her brain registered nerves but she couldn't feel her heart beating quickly. She gripped the handle of the pushchair so tightly it became hard to control. She searched the crowd, and eventually saw Penelope and Sarah.

"Laura!" Sarah waved.

"Good to see you again," Penelope said. "Sit here, next to me."

Laura sat down and busied herself adjusting Edmond's blanket. "Hello," she said, avoiding their eyes.

Laura ate a biscuit and ordered tea. She repeatedly fiddled with Edmond's blanket, and her phone. Her social media post erased the awkwardness and exaggerated the camaraderie. She desperately searched for a way into conversation. News, TV, the weather? Surely not the weather. Suddenly she remembered—baby classes! She blurted out the question.

"Baby sensory is my favourite," Sarah said.

In her relief she barely heard the reply. "Sensory?"

"They do lots of stuff, experience different sounds and smells, and touch," Sarah said. "It's good for their development, and hanging out with other mums is cool."

"Oh, I thought the world was sort of a new sensory experience for them," Laura moved her lips into the shape of a smile.

"Yes, but not enough," Penelope said. "Studies show it really helps with their brain development."

"Great." Laura noticed again that her voice lagged her instructions to speak. She took a minuscule sip of tea to make it last longer. She sat back in her chair.

Laura watched the two women. She collected details about them and wound them together into biographies. Penelope was rich. She had a nanny. She laughed too quickly, and it sounded like breaking glass. Laura watched her features tense, her lips form a taut line, and her blinks that made her mask fall back into place.

Sarah was never still, her hands fidgeted in her lap, and she brushed her hair away from her face. Her eyes rested on her child, never the person she spoke to. Laura felt Penelope's eyes on her. She seemed to ignore Sarah, but Sarah seemed not to care. She always spoke politely. *Are you alive?* Laura wondered. *Are you a person?*

"So, what did you do, before babies?" Laura said.

Penelope and Sarah looked at her with raised eyebrows. "I was a musician," Sarah said.

"Wow. That's amazing. In a band?" Laura couldn't place Sarah's new jeans and sensible boots in a band.

"No. In an orchestra. I was second violin for the London Phil."

"Wow. That's amazing," Laura said, again, as if for the first time. She looked around the café for inspiration. There must be all sorts of interesting things to ask a musician. None of those interesting things came to mind.

"I played the violin at school, but I was rubbish." Laura clenched her fist and felt her nails digging into her palm. She breathed in heavily and looked at Penelope.

"I'm not really into classical music," Penelope said.

"Oh well," Laura said. "I'm sure it's really nice when you know what's going on. I'm a lawyer."

Sarah frowned at her. "What kind of lawyer?"

"Contract law." She watched Penelope arranging her features. The cry of a baby interrupted them. Laura flinched; it was Edmond. "He eats constantly. Is that normal?" She looked up hopefully at the other women and reached for him.

"You should try bottle feeding. It fills them up more." Penelope patted Laura's knee gently.

"I think it depends if they're having a growth spurt," Sarah said.

Laura fumbled with her clothes like an inexperienced teenage boy. Edmond pounded his fists against her and then wound his fingers into the hair on her temples. He pulled hard. Laura fought to open his fist. "Shit. Anyone else find this completely shit?"

Sarah laughed again. "Breastfeeding, yes. Totally. It's so hard, but so worth it. If you can, that is."

"No, all of it. Having a baby," Laura said. She watched the other women. They both found a reason to check their babies. Like dancers, they moved together. Neither of them looked at Laura.

Eventually Sarah frowned and looked around the cafe. "It's hard, but just the most amazing thing I've ever done."

Penelope breathed in slowly. "It's important to be grateful because so many people can't have children."

"Yes, I suppose," Laura said. "But nothing prepares you for this, does it?"

Sarah reached into her pushchair and picked up a girl dressed in a pink Babygro. She rubbed her cheek against the top of the baby's head and closed her eyes. Her hands tightened gently around the tiny body, pulling it into her. Sarah's face was content, and peaceful. She reached for one of the scrunched hands and uncurled the fingers. Her daughter gripped her thumb. Sarah leant back in her chair. "This is the best thing, isn't it? Sort of like what I was always supposed to do."

Penelope smiled and nodded, looking towards her own child.

Laura bit her lip. She closed her eyes. She felt Sarah's emotion washing through her and found nothing that matched it in herself. A black chasm spread from within her, up her body and through her mind. "I need to get back."

"I'll text you about the sensory class," Sarah said.

"It's great fun, and there's lots of other mummies there," Penelope said.

"Yes, do that. Thanks." Laura fumbled with her clothes again, with the pushchair, and with Edmond. She tripped out of the coffee shop and stumbled home.

She carried Edmond into his room and laid him on the rug. She shut the door and sat on the floor. She grabbed the hair at her temples. It didn't hurt when she pulled. Edmond kicked his legs and frowned. He watched the mobile on the ceiling.

Laura wrapped her arms around her body. "I'm so sorry," she said.

Edmond seemed not to have heard.

"Why don't I feel that, Eddie?"

Edmond didn't know. He squeaked and turned his head to one side.

Laura remembered howling once, when she was a child. They had said she'd been hysterical, but she knew she hadn't been. Her crying had filled up the empty space in her body. Her mind struggled to clutch onto the memory, to grasp it, and relive it. But it couldn't. Laura felt tears on her cheeks. She crawled up to Edmond and leant over him. She closed her eyes. She saw a picture of him as a boy, alone, clutching the hand of a stuffed rabbit. His eyes searched for something in a vast empty desert. What must it be like to feel totally alone and not know why? she wondered.

"I'm so sorry. You deserve a proper mummy." She held his head between her hands, feeling the pulsing soft bones, before running her hands down the length of his body. She straightened out his legs and felt each of his toes. She heard sobbing, but didn't realise that the sound was hers. She kissed his wrinkled forehead.

"I promise ..." Tears fell on his cheeks. "I promise I'll make you feel loved."

Edmond gurgled.

Laura wiped her eyes on her sleeve and lay down next to him. She put her hand on his chest and felt it rising and falling. "I'll do the right thing for you. Always," she whispered into his ear. They lay together on the carpet and, for once, Edmond didn't cry. He breathed noisily and squeaked. Laura closed her eyes and tried to imagine what she thought she should feel. She made her features replay Sarah's expression. None of it left any imprint on her body, or her mind. The sun moved across the window until the shadows of the cot rose up the wall.

She realised, then, that she'd built herself a prison from which escape was meaningless.

Chapter 3

"You're still looking fine, Laura."

Laura watched her wine whirlpooling around her glass, seemingly given a life of its own by the small movement of her hands.

"Thanks." Her voice echoed around her head.

"But seriously, we miss you. Coming back soon?" He leaned across the table, folded his hands together, and tried to look into her eyes.

"I don't know. I want to. You think it'd work?" Laura avoided looking at him. She watched a young woman on the other side of the bar running her hands through her glossy black hair. The two men talking to her bent their heads towards her.

"Angie makes it work, doesn't she?" His fingers twitched against each other. He checked his watch.

"Yes, but Angie does admin," Laura said. "It's easier to manage. There's never any time-critical filing."

He shrugged his shoulders inside his well-fitting suit. "I was thinking you could maybe step back a bit, do more of a supporting role."

Laura's hands shook. She hid them under the table and scrunched up the hem of her shirt. "Supporting role?"

"Yes. You've always been good at the documentation side of things. Very good, in fact." Laura watched his eyes wandering towards the door.

"It's the negotiation I like best." Laura fixed her attention on the girl, who turned sideways and leaned back against the bar. Her skin glowed in the soft light. One of the men placed his arm on the rail behind her, while the other moved in front of her.

"That side of things has been pretty fine since you left."

"I didn't leave." The two men laughed at something the girl said, but Laura could see they weren't really laughing.

"Well, it is called 'maternity *leave*'." He smiled a professional smile.

"I may get a nanny. Then it wouldn't matter."

"It always matters."

"Did it matter when you had children?"

"No, but I'm not a mother."

Laura heard her intake of breath, but wasn't aware of any movement in her lungs. She frowned at the girl. The girl smiled, and the two men moved their mouths into the shapes of corresponding smiles. The girl moved her head quickly, and had trouble finding her balance again. The man with his hand on the bar moved his arm so that it touched her back.

Laura struggled to disentangle the voice of her boss from all the other voices in the bar. The sound of her breathing disappeared into the noise and she felt as if she'd lost touch with it. As if she were floating. Laura gripped her wine glass and took a large sip. She couldn't feel it in her mouth. "You do realise how monumentally unfair that is?" she said.

He frowned before finishing the dregs of his pint. "It's life. It's the way it is."

"But it shouldn't be the way it is. Why not let me come back and do the exact same things I always did, and just see how it goes?"

"You'll have the same title and pay. But you've got to be realistic." He shrugged.

"How so?"

"I can't have people dropping things because their kid is sick, or falls out of a tree, or the nanny's sick, or falls out of a tree. Trust me, it happens." He drummed his hands against the table.

"My husband can drop his things. It doesn't have to be me."

He laughed a humourless laugh. "I think we both know that's not going to happen."

"It might happen."

"Why don't you just come back, do what I ask you to, and we'll see how it goes? I can't be fairer than that."

Laura thought she should feel like crying, but there weren't any tears inside her. "OK. I'll think about it." She watched her boss stand up and thought she'd said goodbye, and that she'd promised to send him an email, but she wasn't sure.

Laura stood up too and walked towards the girl at the bar. She stood quietly by her side for some time before one of the men noticed her.

"Can I help you?" he said.

Laura looked into the girl's eyes. "You should go home. Now."

"What the fuck business is that of yours?" the girl said.

Laura shrugged. "I just know. You should go."

Whatever the girl's next words were going to be, they got no further than her lips. She stared at Laura, open-mouthed, trying to focus on her face.

"Seriously. I'm right," Laura said.

"What are you?" the girl said.

Laura shivered. She turned and left, wondering at the strange things drunk people say. She walked out of the pub, surprised that darkness had arrived in the time she'd been in there. The headlines of the evening newspapers warned of drought. She winced. Her breasts throbbed. She crossed her arms in front of her chest. Edmond needed feeding.

A few minutes later, Laura found a seat on the underground. She posted a complaint about prejudice against working mothers. Ten friends liked it immediately. She closed her eyes and swayed in time with the jolting of the carriage. The rushing and rumbling grew louder. Laura opened her eyes slightly, but the light burned. In the distance, she heard a roar. The roar grew louder, or moved closer, she couldn't tell. She made her eyes open again. The bodies in the carriage around her seemed to have grey faces. Their eyes had lost their colour. They opened and closed their mouths as they spoke, but it looked like they were gasping for air. Laura could only hear the roaring now. She gripped the seat either side of her and turned to look at the end of the carriage. The sound came from there.

Laura thought she screamed. She didn't remember standing up but found herself pressed against the door. She crouched on the floor, covering her head with her hands. She knew what was coming. She saw water bursting through the windows and forcing its way through the doors. It flung itself through the carriage, throwing everything in its path at her. She took a last gulp of air and braced herself.

Laura couldn't hear anything anymore. Until something shook her, and sounds waded through her mind. Her lungs spasmed. Laura shook her head. She gasped, and breathed in air. Her body sprang back to life.

"Are you OK?" Big brown eyes stared into her own.

Laura glanced around the carriage. People stared at her. The water had gone.

"I … I thought …" Laura coughed, tasting saltwater in her mouth. "I saw …"

"It's OK, dear. You're OK now. Shall I call a doctor?" Laura looked into the brown eyes again. The elderly woman gripped her elbow and helped her into a seat. She sat down next to Laura and patted her hand. "Do you need a doctor? We should call a doctor at the next station."

"No, thank you. I'm OK." Laura shivered uncontrollably, as if her entire body had been chilled.

"Are you sure? It's no trouble, really."

The eyes in the rest of the carriage turned away. "No, I need to get home. My baby needs feeding."

The elderly woman smiled. "If you're sure, dear. But you look after yourself."

"I will. Thank you. I don't know what happened. It's not happened before."

"I do think you should speak to your doctor." The woman patted her hand again.

The two women sat in silence until Laura reached her stop. When the old woman got off she waved at her through the window. Laura's hand felt warm where she'd been holding it.

Laura raced into the living room, pulling off her jumper and reaching for Edmond at the same time. She shook him gently. "Come on, come on, come, you've got to be hungry." Edmond opened his eyes, confused, before deciding that perhaps he could manage a snack.

"I gave him a bottle about an hour ago," Laura's husband said.

"No, no, no, he's got to eat. I feel like I'm going to burst. It bloody hurts."

"Well, there is the pump." Her husband settled back into the sofa and crossed his legs. "I only just got him to sleep."

"It doesn't work as well as him," Laura said, shaking Edmond gently to fully wake him up.

"I thought I was helping."

"Yes, yes," Laura said. Edmond began sucking urgently at her breasts. "There we go." Laura sighed and sank onto the sofa.

"How did it go?"

"Not well. They'll give me all the crappy bits to do if I go back."

"Like what?"

"Like drafting, and re-drafting, and not negotiating, or running any of the deals."

"That's not so bad, is it? It's what you used to do."

Laura switched Edmond from her left breast to her right. "I worked really, really hard to move on from that. And I—" Edmond lost his grip on her nipple and she moved him slightly until he latched on again. "I don't see why I should give it up."

"I understand why you're angry. But I suppose that's the way it is. It wouldn't be for long, I suppose."

Laura sighed. "I was thinking. Can we, you know, if something happens …? Like we have a nanny and she gets sick, can we agree to take turns having time off work? Or if he's sick and someone needs to stay home. Can we take turns?"

Her husband frowned. He massaged the back of his neck and pulled at his jumper. "I don't think it'd go down too well if I had to skip work at short notice. But I'm trying to do as much as I can."

"I know. I'm not saying it'd go well for either of us. But we should take turns. That'd be fair."

Her husband coughed. "But people won't mind so much if it's you going home for an emergency. They sort of expect it. It'd be very tricky for me."

"But that's not fair."

"I agree it's not fair. But it'll look worse for me. I will do it sometimes, of course; we're in this together. And ... emergencies are rare; I think you're fixating on something that'll hardly happen."

Laura watched his back as he walked into the kitchen.

"I did take this afternoon off, so I am here for you," he said. "Fancy some tea? In other news, I made dinner."

Laura carried Edmond into his room and sat in the chair. "This is bollocks, Eddie. Total bollocks. All of it."

Edmond opened his large dark eyes and Laura looked into them. He seemed not to need to blink often. Her head drooped and she yawned. "And what the hell was that in the underground? Is Mummy going mad, Eddie? Have you frazzled my brain, too?"

Laura closed her eyes. 'No Mummy,' Edmond seemed to say, 'you're not mad. You're not mad at all.'

Laura tried to put the incident on the underground out of her mind, but whenever she thought of it, her skin burned with cold.

Chapter 4

LAURA RUBBED SOME SICK OFF her jeans with her thumb. Penelope's hand shook as she put the two large cups of coffee on the counter. "They're so hard to carry, but I need a vat of caffeine to keep going these days," Penelope said.

"Tell me about it. Thanks."

"No, thanks for coming over."

The two women filled the silence by blowing on their coffee. Laura picked her phone up, looked at it quickly, and then put it screen down on the worktop. Penelope looked slowly around her kitchen. Her gaze stopped at the oven. She frowned.

"So, how've you been?" Laura said. She rubbed at the sick again.

"Good. Good," Penelope said, sighing. "You?"

"Good, too." Laura slurped the scalding coffee, but it didn't burn her mouth. "Been up to much?"

"No, not really. Arabella takes up any free time I have."

"They do that, don't they?"

"Yes, they really do."

"Nice coffee. Thanks."

"No problem. My husband is picky about coffee so we got a proper machine."

"Oh? Is he picky about other stuff, too?"

Penelope's eyes widened and she put her coffee down. Laura watched her slow intake of breath that raised her shoulders and inflated her chest. "I'm not sure."

"Sorry. I didn't mean anything. I'm just bad at conversation."

"It's OK."

"Yes." Laura watched the leaves swaying outside the window. "I'm thinking about going back to work. Are you?"

"Yes. Well, I haven't left really. I do a lot from home now."

"How's that working out?"

"Good actually. I'd be lost without Marta though." Penelope spoke slowly, emphasising each word equally.

"Should we check on them?" Laura said.

"On Marta? No, she's fine. It's what she does."

"But she's got Eddie too now."

"Oh, it's no trouble." Laura wondered whether Penelope's attention had wandered.

"Oh," Laura said. "I can't work from home so well. I don't know if I can go back to what I used to do."

"You should get a nanny. I'll put you in contact with the agency I used. They're really good."

"Do you worry about Arabella in the day?"

"If I'm out, you mean?"

"Yes."

"No, never. Marta knows what she's doing. The agency said she has excellent references."

"I worry about him when I can't see him. All the time."

Penelope folded her hands in front of her on the counter and leant in towards Laura. "Honestly, I did the first few times, and I don't think I want to commute every day yet, but it gets easier."

"Yes, I suppose it must," Laura said. She turned and looked into the open plan living/dining/eating/intimidating room. Plumped up cushions sat to attention on high-backed, firm sofas. Recently polished silver photo frames dominated the faces they enclosed. "Lovely house."

"Thanks. It was a mess when we bought it."

"No mess now."

"No, the baby stuff stays in the playroom."

"Good plan," Laura said. She rubbed at the sick again, but the sick had long gone. "You must entertain a lot with that table. It must be lovely being able to have half the county over."

"We host charity dinners."

"Oh, that's nice. Which charities?"

"Local ones mainly," Penelope said, picking at a loose bit of nail varnish on her thumb. "We like to support the local environment. Climate change is terrifying."

"That's a good thing to do. And the recent temperature data is terrifying. Did you see what they said about India? I worry we don't recycle enough too, but I'm so tired at the moment I can hardly tell the difference between cardboard and plastic."

"That's understandable," Penelope said. She put her hand to her head as if to check that her hair still existed. She turned away from Laura. "Do you like having a baby?"

Laura took a slow drink of coffee. Had those words really been said? She felt poised on her toes, ready to topple in any direction. "I love Eddie," she said. Laura flinched and rubbed her cheek. Was that true? "But I wasn't prepared for how it is. I find it really hard."

"You said something when I met you with Sarah. You said it was hard, and you said it like you meant it."

"I did mean it. It is hard."

"Most people don't mean it when they say it. They say it because they don't think they can say it's easy."

"It's hard for me because I don't feel like myself anymore. It's like I've disappeared," Laura said.

"I feel like that. All the time. I didn't think anyone else did."

"I'm not sure they do. Have you seen a doctor?"

"They gave me antidepressants," Penelope said. "And I see a therapist. But I can't explain to doctors and 'professionals' somehow."

Laura put her head in her hands. "My doctor said I should meet people, and get a grip, basically. I posted on a mental health forum too and all I got back were love hearts and people telling me how lucky I am to have a baby."

"I have a private doctor you can try. But he'll probably just give you drugs."

"Do they help?" Laura said.

"No. I feel even less like myself."

"So that's why you got a nanny and things."

"I want to be the person I was before. I figure if I do the things I did before I might be that person again. But then people disapprove."

"I don't disapprove."

"I didn't think you would," Penelope said.

"I guess we just muddle through and hope things turn out OK in the end."

"Do you think they will?"

"I have a horrible feeling they won't," Laura said. She paused, trying to read Penelope's face. But it gave nothing at all away. "Do you ever see things?"

"What do you mean?"

"Things that aren't there. I have dreams about drowning that I think are real, and I see water where there isn't any."

"You're probably sleep deprived. It makes you hallucinate. I had it once at university."

Laura coughed. "Really? Too much studying?"

"God, I wish." Penelope laughed. For a moment her face relaxed and a girl appeared in her features. "Too much alcohol, and too many late nights."

"Maybe it is just that then. I hope it stops."

Penelope touched Laura's hand with her fingers. "I'm glad you came over today."

"I'm glad, too."

"Are you busy on Wednesday evenings?"

"No, I don't think so."

"Come with me to the local environmental group then. It's not a big thing. We just do a newsletter and chat about things. It's more of a social thing. Second Wednesday each month."

"OK. Maybe I will. Thanks."

Laura fetched Edmond from the nursery and fed him quickly before leaving. She couldn't find Penelope downstairs when she left. After shouting goodbye, she closed the door behind her. She strapped him in the car seat and drove down the triple lane drive.

"Well, that went better than expected, didn't it, Eddie?" Laura looked in the mirror. She saw his fist waving in the air above his seat. 'No, it didn't, Mummy. I hated it,' he seemed to say. Laura turned into the main road and checked her foot on the clutch. It seemed to be slipping.

Laura gasped. Her fingers tightened around the steering wheel so that she could barely steer. Water lapped at her feet and sloshed around the bottom of the car. She stopped at the side of the road. A truck sped past, shaking the car. Laura's breath came in short gasps. "It's not real, it's not real, it's not real." She closed her eyes. The passing traffic shook her again.

Laura concentrated on breathing in and out slowly. Her feet didn't feel wet, just cold. "It's not real." She felt her legs with her hand. Her jeans were dry. Her fingers moved slowly down. Her calves were dry. She whimpered and pushed her hand downwards. Her ankles were dry. Laura opened her eyes. There was no water. She rested her head on the steering wheel. "What's going on? This can't just be tiredness, can it, Eddie?" Edmond told her no, it wasn't tiredness. "I've got to find someone to help me. Fuck, I can't be going mad. I don't have time for that." Edmond reassured her that she wasn't going mad.

Chapter 5

THE PSYCHIATRIST TOOK NOTES WITH a pencil that he had chewed almost to the point of disintegration. When he wasn't writing it barely left his mouth. Laura looked around his office. The oak framed certificates promised so much. *If he can't help me, then who?* she thought. Laura sat on her hands and looked at him expectantly.

"And what ..."—he paused to remove a bit of wood from between his teeth— "... what brings these incidents on?"

"Nothing. They just happen."

He frowned. "And it's always water?"

"Yes."

"And you say you've never been involved in a drowning incident before?"

"If I had, I'd probably have described it as a flashback, not a dream."

"Indeed." He stopped writing and put his pencil down in his notebook. His hand hovered above it. He looked up at Laura. "You aren't sleeping well?"

"No. My baby still needs feeding in the night."

"It's quite common to be depressed after the birth of a child."

"I don't think I'm depressed," Laura said. She watched his hand dropping lower. His finger twitched.

"Why not? People don't always know." He grabbed the pencil and put it back in his mouth. Laura thought he looked like Edmond, desperately sucking on a dummy.

"I've been depressed before. This doesn't feel like that."

"Was that when your parents died?"

"Yes."

"How is it different now?"

"I felt really sad then. I felt empty. I felt like I'd died, too. I didn't want to wake up, or get out of bed. I didn't want to do anything. Now I get up early and look after Eddie all day, and do lots of other stuff. I'm not depressed."

"Do you struggle to relax?"

"I have a baby—I don't know what it means to relax anymore."

"Do you worry about him?"

"Yes. Constantly."

"But I have to check again. You're sure you've never had any thoughts about harming Edmond, or yourself?"

"Of course I'm sure. I haven't ever."

"OK." He took the pencil out of his mouth. "I think we should call your husband in now. Do you want to say or ask anything before I do?"

"Do you know what's wrong?"

"Yes, I do. And we can treat it. But we should discuss it with your husband, too."

The psychiatrist picked up his phone and very quietly asked the receptionist to send Laura's husband in.

Laura's husband walked tentatively into the room. He sat on the armchair next to Laura's. He leant back, trying to find the back of the chair. When he found it, he felt too horizontal for a serious discussion. He sat up again. One hand searched out Laura's hand and held it.

"Laura has some symptoms of postpartum psychosis," the psychiatrist said. He let the words rest. "It's atypical, but we can treat it with drugs, and we can treat it in hospital. I'd prefer to begin treating you at home, unless you'd prefer to be admitted?"

"What about Eddie?" Laura said. "I can't be admitted." She pulled at the hem on the inside of her jacket. She found a hole and burrowed her finger in. Her finger stuck and she pulled it out. She heard the lining rip.

"You and Eddie would come in together."

"I think it's better they both stay at home," Laura's husband said. She squeezed his hand in gratitude.

"How has your wife bonded with … Edmond?"

"She's a great mother. She takes care of him really well. He's thriving."

"She's feeling emotionally disconnected, but doesn't appear to have had trouble bonding with Edmond. And the hallucinations seem not to involve the child, or his welfare. So, Laura, I'm going to prescribe you some antipsychotic medication. But we need to monitor this carefully. I'll book you in for an EEG and an MRI. You can continue breastfeeding. And I want to see you in three days. In the meantime, call any time. I'll give you an emergency number for out of hours, too."

The psychiatrist stood up. Her husband stood up. Laura stayed in her seat, afraid that standing up would make it real.

After they'd picked up the drugs, Laura and her husband went straight home. The babysitter greeted them cheerfully, as if they'd been on a date. Laura ignored her and lay down on the sofa with her face in the pillows. She felt her husband's hand on her shoulder.

"It'll be OK. We'll get through it," he said.

"I wish I'd never made the appointment now. He said I'm crazy. I've gone mad. They might lock me up."

"It's not the nineteenth century. No one's going to lock you up. You take the medicine. We'll find someone to come and do the cooking and cleaning and things. And I'll look after you and Eddie. I love you."

"I love you, too," Laura said. She shivered. Those words were anaemic now. She tried them again. "I really love you."

"I think Eddie needs a new nappy, and then I'll make you dinner."

Later, Laura's husband handed Edmond to her. Laura cuddled him to her. "You wouldn't have wanted to get that close to him five minutes ago. He'd done a whopper," he said.

Laura fumbled with the small bottle of pills. She put Edmond down next to her and opened it. She shook one pill into her hand

and swallowed it. After picking Eddie up again she sat him on her knee. She buried her nose in his neck and smelt his musty, sicky baby smell. 'I hope you don't think those'll do anything,' he seemed to say.

Laura pulled away from him quickly. "I know that's not you, Eddie. You don't know shit, and can talk even less." Laura kissed him on the cheek. He wrapped his fingers in her hair and pulled at it insistently.

* * *

Laura listened to pans scraping out of the grill and landing in the sink. She heard a waterfall bouncing off them. That wouldn't do the wooden worktops any good, she thought. She looked through the door, but couldn't see the mess. It grew in her imagination, conquering everything she couldn't see. As a distraction she posted pictures of Edmond online. Friends sent her hearts and smiley faces.

"Dinner is served."

Laura got up and carried Edmond into the kitchen. She put him in his bouncer before looking up. Her husband put two plates with burgers and chips on the table in the kitchen. They both sat down. Laura winced at the scraping of the chairs on the floor. She sighed; he hadn't made such a mess after all.

"I'm sorry if I haven't done enough for you," he said.

"It's OK. You've had work."

"Yes, still. We'll definitely get a cleaner or housekeeper-type person. What type of person does general things? 'Housekeeper' makes it all sound a bit nineteenth century." He squeezed a large dollop of ketchup onto the side of his plate.

"I met one of those women I told you about a few days ago. She gave me the number of an agency. I think a nanny does that sort of stuff, too."

"A nanny?" Her husband's burger hovered halfway between his plate and his mouth as he squinted at her.

"She had a nanny and she did some cleaning and other things."

Laura watched as her husband put down his food and rubbed

his hands on a baby wipe. "Do you …" He rubbed at something on his wrist. "Do you want time away from Eddie? Is that it?"

"Shit. No. I wasn't lying earlier. I want to be with him. But I don't want someone who doesn't know how to change a nappy, or thinks it's OK to park a baby in the oven or something."

"OK. Makes sense. But you must tell me if anything changes. If you feel different."

"Of course," Laura said. She ate with one eye on Edmond, who lay in his bouncer contentedly kicking his legs.

"I think I burned the chips. Sorry."

"Don't worry. It's fine." Laura chewed a crispy chip. It tasted of the same mud that everything else tasted of.

"I'll call that agency first thing tomorrow, then," he said.

"Thanks. I stuck the number on the notice board. Will you clean up, too? I'm tired."

Laura curled up to sleep in bed while her husband noisily tidied and cleaned the kitchen. She heard him speaking to a colleague. He always hid his accent at work. She heard him trying hard to be patient.

* * *

Afterwards, he paced up and down the living room, picking up books and putting them down again. He ran his hand over a picture of Laura and him at the top of a mountain. It seemed to him like a picture from a magazine. He put Edmond to bed and then walked into the kitchen.

He looked at the notice board. Sun-bleached takeaway menus surrounded cards for plumbers, electricians, handymen, and a pest remover. A blue pin attached a blank piece of paper to the middle of the board. He pulled it off and turned it over. Blank, on both sides. He scrunched it up and threw it in the bin. Then he sent himself an email: 'Urgent: find nanny who also does stuff.'

He checked Edmond one last time before going into the bedroom, where he sat on the side of the bed, watching Laura sleep.

Chapter 6

LAURA WAVED AT PENELOPE WHEN she saw her walking towards her down the road. Penelope walked stiffly, as if breaking in new shoes. The two women turned down a small overgrown path that led to the church hall.

Laura hesitated in the doorway. She had never been there before, but her body felt as if it knew the space. The musty smell of a leaky roof, or damp absorbing walls. A kitchen with white cupboards turned cream with use. A water heater over the sink, and draughty toilets. Radiators that smelt of burning in the winter. For an instant she felt small, as her body dissolved into her senses. She felt herself a child again. Sounds that were not there replayed themselves. Shouts, and laughs, and the clatter of Mary Jane shoes scuffing on the floor. Laura half-expected to see small friends as she pushed open the swing door.

Instead, at two rectangular tables arranged into a square, six other women sat, all within reaching distance of a plate of biscuits. One held a folder and a pen, poised to write. They smiled at Laura.

"Welcome. It's always wonderful to find a new member."

"Hello," Laura said, sitting down on one of the empty sides. Penelope sat down next to her and smiled encouragingly.

The ladies of Friends of the Earth introduced themselves. Laura gave them a few details about herself. "Penelope said I should come. I'm trying to get out more after having my baby."

The lady with the pen frowned. "Penelope?"

One of the other women interrupted her. "How old's your baby?"

"Four months. I'm sort of getting it together."

"Lovely, dear. Well, you'll find us very welcoming. Most of us have grandchildren though, not children, so it's good to get some young people in."

Laura took a biscuit from the plate. It felt like damp sand, as if it had been in a cupboard for a while. She sat back and listened.

Blanket weed had spread in the pond in the park. It needed treating. One of the ladies offered to drop some barley straw in it. Another doubted the efficacy of this tried and tested treatment. A walk was arranged to patrol the riverbank. Reports of unusual amounts of rubbish had flooded the communal email. The ladies fixed a date for the following week. Laura felt obliged to finish her biscuit. Someone made a pot of strong tea and put a bowl with tea-stained, hardened sugar on the table. Laura watched Penelope, who didn't take any tea, sit with her hands in her lap and her head on one side, smiling absentmindedly at whoever spoke.

They handed Laura a newsletter. "This is what we do every quarter," one of the women said.

Laura flicked through the pages. Rubbish collection dates, development plans to be opposed, requests for help clearing roadsides, advice for saving water, and an article about disposable nappies. Laura paused to read the article.

"People can write whatever they want; it's for discussion. Personally, my daughter-in-law wouldn't have coped without disposable nappies." Laura thought she heard a collective intake of breath.

"But it's important to remember the long-term costs," one of the women said.

Laura smiled. "My aunt had a bucket of nappies with, what was it called? Milton? Like some sort of fetid putrid stew in the kitchen. Disposable nappies are awesome." Laura thought she saw Penelope frown, but the others laughed.

"Do you fancy writing something?" The woman leant in towards her, hands clasped, eyes fixed on Laura's face.

"I don't know. I don't know anything to say right now."

"Oh, we wouldn't need it straight away. It can be anything."

"Can I think about it?"

"Of course. Keep that one, and my email is on the back." The woman underlined her name with a blunt pencil that scratched the paper.

Half an hour later Laura and Penelope left. They walked down the road together. Penelope looked from side to side, as if searching for something, or trying to find her way.

"So, did you like my little soldiers?" Penelope said.

Laura laughed. "They are quite sweet. Very well-intentioned, but utterly ineffectual, I'd assume."

"Don't underestimate them. When they set their minds on something there's no stopping them. They stopped the council opening a Starbucks all by themselves. Pretty much everyone else failed."

"Wow. I guess when you have little else to do you can devote all your energy to things like that."

"Exactly. And were I to invade France, I'd have them organise it."

They'd arrived back on the high street. Laura assumed Penelope had parked her car somewhere close. "I guess this is where we go our own ways," Laura said.

"Yes. If you get bored, come over."

"I will. It was nice to see you again. Be nice to do something in an evening, but it sort of depends when I can get baby cover."

"Yes." Penelope turned to walk away, but hesitated. With the forced casualness of someone pretending to make a chance remark, she turned back to Laura. "I think you should write an article for that thing, you know. I think it'd be good."

Laura smiled. "Thanks for your vote. I'll think about it." For a moment she had the sensation of Penelope's eyes burrowing into her mind. Laura shook her head quickly and the sensation passed. Laura and Penelope said goodbye.

Laura felt she was floating as she walked home. Her feet couldn't feel the pavement, and her hands couldn't feel the strap of her handbag. Her head swayed with a seasickness and she tried to force her mind back into its body. Nevertheless, the lightness made her body tingle. *Maybe it's the drugs,* she thought. She paused. She hadn't had a dream or seen water for three days. *Perhaps I'm better,* she thought. *Perhaps this is it.*

* * *

The psychiatrist smiled at her, with his pencil still in his mouth. "That's good. I wasn't sure they'd work so quickly."

Laura sighed. "They seem to, which is good."

"Well, in a few weeks we can think about weaning you off. But don't expect never to use them again. So, I'd like to work on some strategies with you."

"Strategies?"

"Ways to control the hallucinations."

Laura settled back into her seat. The psychiatrist's voice soothed her. He told her to slow down her breathing. "I want you to recognise when you're seeing something that shouldn't be there, and try to stay calm."

"It's a bit hard when I think I'm going to die."

"I know. But you can try to distance yourself slightly from the experience. Try to talk to yourself."

"I did that last time."

"Did it work?"

"I suppose. I told myself it wasn't real. And I felt down my legs and they were dry. Then, when I opened my eyes again, it was gone."

"Good. That's a good thing to do. Staying calm, or as calm as you can be, is the main thing."

Laura's breath rushed through her body.

"When you feel panic, close your eyes, breathe slowly, and tell yourself that you know what's real. If you can, stop what you're doing, sit down, or be still, and wait for it to pass."

"I'll try." Laura frowned. "In the moment I think it's totally real, though."

"I'm not saying this'll come easily, but it's something to work towards. You can reason with yourself. Like with the incident on the tube. No one else was panicking—if you notice things that don't fit with the hallucination, reason with yourself."

"They weren't scared because they were dead already."

"But they couldn't have been dead; you'd just seen them alive."

"I suppose. It seemed like something had just suddenly turned them dead."

"Turned them dead?" The psychiatrist took his pencil out of his mouth and wrote something in his notebook.

Laura giggled. "I know people don't 'turn dead.' Of course. But it didn't seem like they'd died. It was more like a change of state, like ice into water. And then they were gulping like fish."

The psychiatrist nodded and took a slow breath that expanded his chest. He coughed. "Yes. But if you notice things that can't be true, try to turn your attention to them, and use them to bring yourself back."

Laura nodded. "I'll try."

"OK." He wrote out another prescription. "I'll see you in a few days. Call me, or the out-of-hours line if you need anything, anything at all."

Laura nodded and stood up eagerly, her eyes grasping for the door. She shook the psychiatrist's clammy hand and escaped.

* * *

Laura spread out her fingers to grasp the tunnels of wind buffeting down the escalator from the station. She recognised it from August commutes. She smiled and closed her eyes. The person she used to be seemed within reach of her fingertips. Her hands twitched to grasp at it. With a lurch, the escalator tipped her off as it came to an end. Laura stumbled and fell against a grumpy man. She pulled her bag against her chest and walked outside.

She hesitated, her eyes searching the people outside. They settled on a woman sitting on a bench, in a posture she used to know well. "Hey, Becky," Laura raised her hand, and Becky turned towards her.

Becky gave her an enthusiastic hug before pulling her out of the crowd. "Look at you! You haven't changed a bit, you know. It's been way too long."

"It has, hasn't it? How are you?"

"I'm really good. Shall we get food?"

They walked up the high street. Laura watched their feet. They must have trod on exactly the same paving slabs, together, many times before. If they had left imprints, they could have followed them. She looked up occasionally and the unfamiliar shops jarred in her mind like early morning alarms. Her gaze lingered on the things that hadn't changed, as if staring at memories might turn back time.

Becky led her into a vegetarian café. "This OK?"

"Of course."

They sat opposite each other, watching each other's faces for signs of change. Laura rubbed her hands together, and then did it again. Becky reached out and held her hand.

"So, how've you been? How's Eddie?"

"Eddie's good, thanks. He's growing loads. It's *such* hard work and I'm not so good at it. But it's OK. You?"

"It's OK?" Becky's eyes widened. "In your email you said, well, you didn't say, but I read that it perhaps wasn't OK?"

Laura's body relaxed and slumped towards the table. "This is why I miss you. It's not OK. It's properly fucked me up. I have hallucinations, and I think I'm going mad."

"Have you seen a doctor?"

"Yes, I'm on loads of drugs. I could probably sell them round here and pay for dinner."

Becky laughed. "Are they helping? The drugs."

"I think so."

"So, what caused it?"

"I dunno. Lack of sleep, general feeble-mindedness." Laura smiled.

"It must be tricky without any family. From what I hear most people have mothers and other assorted relatives who help." Becky bit her lip. "I'm so sorry. You should have called me."

"It's OK. But thanks. I didn't really know what was going on."

"No." Becky ran her fingers through the hair curling around her face "I should have called you, properly checked up on you. I'm sorry."

"Don't feel bad. I sort of didn't want anyone to see me either."

"But that's why I should have come. There's no way you wouldn't want to see me unless something bad was going on."

"It's OK. I know why you didn't."

Becky looked out of the window and into the distance. Her eyes grew heavy. "Is that why you didn't bring him?"

"No, I want you all to myself! I want to have a proper conversation and not get covered in sick and bogies. I want to be myself again."

Becky blinked and shook her head. "Thanks. But I do want to meet him, you know. Who's he with? Some homeless guy you met on the way to the station?"

"We have a girl who comes over a few days a week. She's got him."

"You have staff? Oh my God. Laura has staff."

"Not really. Indentured servants perhaps."

"Let's get food. I'm vegetarian now. Had you guessed?"

They ordered food and Laura felt that time had evaporated, or shrunk. She almost thought they might be going home together, to the clean but untidy flat, to the barely used kitchen, and the Sunday morning discoveries of strange men's shoes in the hall. And the hungover breakfasts where the owners of the shoes would be discussed, and dissected, and usually discarded. But Becky didn't live there anymore either. Laura wondered whether two other girls had moved in and taken over their lives.

"I can't believe that when we lived here, we were so keen to pair off and get married," Laura said. "And now I look back and think how happy we were."

"And now I'm divorced, and you have a baby. It's supposed to be a different kind of happy."

"Yes. And if we did go back to how we were, it wouldn't be the same."

Becky stabbed at a falafel as if it were in danger of escaping her plate. "Also, I was a bit dim back then. I'm glad not to be working for a crappy wage and taking orders from dickheads."

"Well, there is that. We did spend a lot of time complaining," Laura said.

"So how are you filling your time? Except for Eddie, of course?"

"Time sort of just runs out. I'll see if I can do some sort of work. But arranging anything is like planning an expedition. It's OK for the men, they just carry on like before."

"Bastards," Becky said, scooping up the last of the falafel.

"Yes, bastards. So, we'll see. I might do some local things."

"Like flower arranging and the WI?"

"Shit, no. If I join the WI, shoot me."

"You never know. They're probably off bungee jumping and white-water rafting or something."

Laura smiled contentedly. Her body felt still, as if it had settled into itself and no longer needed to flutter around. She watched the other people eating their vegetarian food. Becky took a selfie of them both. Laura smiled into the camera; her fists clenched under the table. "What's the issue with meat then?"

"What do you mean? The usual issue. Cows, methane, climate change, animal welfare. Haven't you seen the news?"

"I do know all of that. Do you have to not eat all meat? Chickens and cows aren't the same, are they?"

Becky almost choked on a sweet potato chip. "Good thing you never wanted to be a biologist."

"I'd have been an awesome biologist—I look great in khaki."

Later, they sat in a small bar sipping cocktails, more slowly than they used to. They made a vague arrangement for Becky to visit. Laura watched the young single people mingling, watching each other, trying not to watch each other. Girls leant in towards each other, whispering secrets. The men, speaking too loudly, their arms mobile, drawing attention to themselves. Laura thought how stressful it had been, waiting for calls and texts, and worrying about when she could text without seeming desperate.

Laura and Becky hugged tightly at the entrance to the station. Becky put her hand on Laura's cheek.

"Call me, yes? Anytime," Becky said.

"Yes, I will. Look after yourself, and see you soon, OK?"

Laura sat on the train looking sideways at the end of the carriage. Would the vision come? It didn't. The other passengers looked normal. The underground rattled and banged like it usually did. Laura smiled and sat contentedly in her seat.

* * *

The flat was dark and quiet when she got home. Her husband had left the hall light on so she could see. She tiptoed into the living room and turned on her computer. Her hands felt heavy and her fingers unresponsive, but something flowed through her; she knew she wouldn't be able to sleep. Perhaps it was the alcohol—they'd told her not to drink. Laura closed her eyes for a second and felt the pressure of the keys on her fingertips. She began to type.

She wrote about climate change, and the benefits of vegetarianism for the planet. She wrote about compromise, and the importance of small steps. She distinguished between mammals and birds. "If we just stopped eating mammals," she wrote, "we could get most of the benefits for very little change in our diets. And it's easy to do with children."

Laura sent it to the woman from Friends of the Earth. The next morning, she could barely remember that she'd written it.

Laura thought she'd never made an impression on the world the way she had wanted to when she was young. She'd not become the star barrister of her dreams; she'd not stepped into the vision that had made her study so hard. She'd compromised, and tried, and failed, and consoled herself with other things. It would have shocked her younger self to know that of all the things she did, this forgotten article was the thing that changed the world.

Chapter 7

Her cheerfulness infected Edmond the next morning, who blew bubbles and thrashed his arms and legs. Laura hummed and Edmond tried to join in, with a dribbly smile.

"You're singing—that's so cute, Dumpling. I should record you and play it back when you're older." Laura buried her face in his neck.

She walked around the flat putting back all the things the nanny had left out of place. She straightened the mugs on the shelf, so the handles all pointed straight out. She alternated the colours of the cushions on the sofa. In Edmond's room, she folded up his clothes neatly and put them in colour coordinated piles by the changing mat. She matched his socks. And Edmond watched her, following her every move.

"It's good to have things tidy, Eddie. I hate mess."

Laura turned the radio on loudly and sang along to the songs she knew. She wrote a list of things they needed to buy.

"Sometimes I think your dad just hoovers up milk. Hey?"

She looked at Edmond. He turned his face from side to side. He sucked on his tongue. His cheeks reddened.

"Talk about hoovering up milk. Hungry again?"

She sat on the sofa with him. He stared up at her as he fed and she stroked his hair.

"Remember how hard it was at the beginning? Now we've both got this sorted, and then you'll be on proper food soon."

'Thank God,' Edmond seemed to say.

"Cheeky." Laura stroked his spongy head. "Won't it be funny when you can actually talk?"

"But I am talking to you, Mummy."

Laura carried on stroking his head, brushing the wispy hairs back with her fingers. She frowned and breathed slowly in and out. She watched a bird walking down a branch outside the window.

"You aren't, Eddie. You're just my brain. Babies can't talk." Laura wondered why she'd spoken out loud. She carried on taking to herself silently, soothingly. 'Babies can't talk, babies can't talk, babies can't talk.'

"But I'm not a baby, Mummy."

Laura's arms shook. She closed her eyes. 'Babies can't talk. Babies can't talk. Babies can't talk. Babies can't talk.' Her mouth found the rhythm in the words and sped them up, hurtling them through her mind.

"I'm not a baby, Mummy."

Laura sat still and looked at Edmond. "You clearly are a baby. A small baby who cries and eats and definitely can't talk. You're in my mind."

"If I tell you something you don't know, will you believe me?" Edmond said.

Laura frowned at him. "You can't know anything I don't know."

"Bet you I do."

"What?" Laura giggled like she giggled at horror films. Had she forgotten to take her drugs that morning?

"In the second drawer down, under the bathroom sink you'll find a toothbrush, a red one, and toothpaste, and a spare pair of pants, and some socks, blue socks."

"What?" Laura said.

"The girl left them, for when she doesn't go home before coming to take care of me."

Laura clutched him to her. 'Babies don't talk. Babies don't talk. Babies don't talk. Babies don't talk.' She paused to breathe, noticing that her chest shook as she did so.

"Go and look, Mummy." Edmond stared up at her with his unblinking eyes. He looked at her expectantly.

Laura laid him gently on the carpet and walked into the bathroom. She sat looking at the drawers under the sink for some time before reaching out to open the second one down. She touched the white handle with her fingers and pulled at it gently. As it opened, she avoided looking in, until she could no longer hide from what it held. A red toothbrush, and a tube of Colgate whitening toothpaste, and blue socks, and white underwear. Laura pushed the drawer closed and sat on the floor. 'Babies can't talk,' she whispered over and over again. And then she stopped. She raised her head and smiled.

She walked back into the living room and knelt beside Edmond. "You didn't tell me, you know. I must have known. I must have seen them before, just not noticed. That's what happened. Or maybe Daddy told me."

"For fuck's sake." Edmond waved his fist in the air.

"Babies definitely don't talk like that. I talk like that."

Laura inched away from Edmond, keeping her eyes fixed on him. She pushed her hands into the carpet, feeling it swallowing her fingers. It felt like a carpet should feel. She leant against the wall and felt her body shaking. A faint ringing reverberated in her head. When she shook it, her mouth tasted of mud and the room swayed back and forth. Laura rested her head on her knees, soaking up her tears with her jeans.

Cold spread from the wall into her back and seemed to freeze her insides. Her breath caught in her throat.

"I am going mad, Eddie. It's true."

She crawled across the floor and picked up her phone. Her fingers fumbled with her password. She called her husband.

"Hey," he said in his busy voice.

"Hey. How are you?"

"Good. You OK? Anything happened?" he said.

"No. Well. Sort of."

"What?" The patter of his fingers on the keyboard stopped. She heard his breath.

"Did you tell me the girl had left a toothbrush and things in the bathroom drawer, under the sink?"

"No. Has she?"

"Yes."

"Is it a problem?"

"No, not really, but I didn't think she was that sort, and she should have asked. But I thought Eddie told me."

"What?"

"I thought he was speaking to me. He told me, then I looked and he was right."

"But he can't speak."

"I know. Obviously. I must have known before somehow." Her phone shook against her cheek. She listened to the silence, the silence that precedes the discovery of a lie.

"I'm going to call the psychiatrist," she said.

"You do that. I'll come home as soon as I can."

"OK. I'm really scared."

"It's going to be OK. But whatever you think he's saying, he isn't."

"No, I know. Thank you."

Laura looked down at Edmond, who frowned up at her. She made sure he was safe, then turned her back on him and called the psychiatrist.

The psychiatrist came to the phone quickly. Laura told him that Edmond had told her to check a cupboard. She listened to the silence on the end of the phone. He spoke quietly to someone else. Her heart rate slowed. She breathed more slowly. He would make it stop. Just stop.

"What exactly was he saying to you?" he said.

Laura looked at Edmond, kicking his legs on the carpet. He gurgled and mumbled happily to himself.

"Laura. Did you do what he asked?" The psychiatrist spoke quickly, urgently, as if springing into action. Laura winced.

She frowned. She walked over to Edmond and sat down next to him. She put her hand on his chest, and he smiled at her. She wedged her phone under her chin and picked him up.

"It was nothing really. He just said he can talk," she said.

"He just told you he can talk." The psychiatrist's voice leapt with the desire to make her do something.

"Yes, but maybe I was dreaming or something."

"When you called you said … Look, you need to come in tomorrow, as early as you can."

"Why?" Laura said, pressing Edmond into her chest. "What will you do to me?"

"We should discuss it tomorrow."

Laura hesitated. Discuss 'it'? What might he be thinking? What might he be planning?

"I'm the expert about me. I'm not going to do anything bad. I just want it to stop," she said.

"I'm sure you're not." Laura sensed doubt flowing through her phone.

She agreed to see him, but closed herself off from his words. She hung up and threw the phone onto the sofa.

"I don't like him at all, Dumpling. I think he's planning something bad for us."

She crawled into the corner of the room, and laid Edmond at her feet. "I just want it to stop. I need it to stop. Why can't anyone help me, Eddie?"

"I'll help you," Edmond said, rolling from side to side and waving his fists in the air.

"Stop it. Please. This isn't real."

She covered her ears with her hands, but his voice slipped through her fingers and into her mind. Her earrings pressed so tightly into her head that blood trickled down her neck.

Her husband came home to find her like that. He peeled her hands away from her head and cleaned her neck. He fed Edmond and put him to bed. He tried to get Laura to eat, and then put her into bed with a dose of medicine.

Later, he stood in the kitchen, watching the lights from the traffic in the distance. He did what he always did in an emergency: he called his mother. He didn't filter the desperation out of his voice as he had with the psychiatrist.

His mother told him to put Edmond first. To do what was necessary.

"She seems OK most of the time, but then sometimes I'm so afraid for her," he said.

"Afraid of what?"

"I don't know. She loves Eddie, but you do hear things about what women do. I don't know what to do."

He cooled his forehead on the windowpane while his mother talked and talked. He wished she were close, so that it might be her shoulder he leant against.

"She's going to see him first thing. I'll call him straight after and we'll talk about it. We're hoping she suggests going to hospital herself. If not, I'll see."

He could hear a soap opera theme tune in the background, and was, for a moment, transported to the chequered carpet, homework, and the scorching electric fire. Contentment.

"I think she's more likely to make the decision if she goes by herself. I'll feel happier if she does it," he said. "OK. Thank you. I'll let you know." He hung up. The silence that followed cut him off from the world.

* * *

That night, Laura slept deeply with the help of her sedatives. Sleep bundled her up like a blanket, cocooning her from the world. She floated above herself, then drew away and left her sleeping body. She saw the roofs of flats and, further away, the small peaked tops of terraced houses, and big open spaces. Wisps of cloud tangled themselves in the skyscrapers. Everything slept and the silence muffled her ears.

Slowly, she sensed someone next to her, but every time she turned to look, they were gone.

"You can't see me yet," the voice said, although it didn't come from next to her, but all around her.

"Who are you?"

"I think you know."

Laura's brain had prepared to say that she had no idea, but knew this was wrong. "Eddie?"

Laura spun around as if to catch him, but didn't see him.

"Don't do that," he said.

"Don't tell me what to do. I'm your mother."

"Well, technically. But watch. I brought you here to show you."

Laura watched, and nothing happened. Nothing happened for a long time. A breeze chilled her cheeks, and her fingertips went numb. Nervousness crept through her as she looked at the ground and remembered that she couldn't fly.

A street began to glisten in the dull light. She noticed another, as if it were a mirage, or polished stone, or, or … water. Laura gasped.

"It's the future," Edmond said.

"What do you mean? This isn't happening now?"

"No, it's what's going to happen. It's what we're trying to stop."

The water spread. It began as puddles after an April shower, thin and slight, and smelling of spring. It turned into the aftermath of a summer downpour, pooling in hollows in the roads, collecting on low-lying drives, and running into underground car parks. The water ran and ran, the puddles grew, the smaller roads evolved into canals, and the bigger roads filled and spilled into buildings. Laura watched the lower bricks of houses slowly drowning.

"Make it stop," Laura said.

"We're trying. That's why I'm here. We needed your help."

"I don't understand."

"In the future, we found you. We found you in the data, and we contacted your mind."

"I'm dead in the future, surely?"

"Yes, but you left so much behind. All your documents from work, all your pictures, your music, the stories you like, the places you want to see, the food you didn't like. Your friends, your family, all your hopes and fears, and thoughts about everything—your husband and his job. It's all stored. It lives on for us to reconstruct."

"But that isn't me."

"But it is you. You are your data. And we remade you, as you are now. When you gave birth, your mind became disconnected from your body somehow. The trauma of it, we supposed. And now I've managed to contact you."

"I don't understand."

"Just watch," Edmond said.

The water lapped gently at windowsills. No roads remained. The branches of trees quivered with panic, stretching their leaves out of the water, waving at her, bracing themselves against the flood. The water rose higher. It rose silently, peacefully, almost beautifully. Edmond directed her attention further away. Laura watched a huge wave rolling through the city. It must be on the Thames. She put out a hand to stop it. It pulled apart the Dartford Crossing as if it were made of string.

Laura felt nauseous as she fell downwards. Edmond helped her find her balance.

"I don't want to see," she said.

Laura flew over a giant lake, or sea, or whatever this water was. Edmond led her to where her house had been. Laura's heart bounced around her chest.

"How do I get home?"

"Just go down," Edmond said.

Laura hovered. She couldn't fly forever, but neither could she touch the cold dark water. As if he'd read her mind, she felt herself floating downwards.

"Just let yourself fall. It'll be fine. But Laura?" He coughed. "Mummy?"

"Yes."

"You must do exactly what I say tomorrow. OK? I'm not a baby, and I can talk. And I am going to take care of you."

"What's going on?" Laura said, again trying to turn around to see him.

"We're trying to stop this happening. It's difficult to change the past, but we can affect it. The future is so terrible that I'll never give up."

"Are you really from the future?"

"No, I'm in the future. But part of me is here and part of you is there. We thought if you did something, it might help."

"What?"

"You planted an idea about monitoring people's energy use. And you wrote about not eating mammals."

"I did what? Those are tiny things, surely?"

"People used to study the big things in history. But we worked out that it's the small things that can make the difference."

"So, what difference have I made?"

"We don't know yet. We plant ideas as early in the timeline as we can, and hope they change things."

"What changes?"

She sensed Edmond hesitating.

"You wrote an article. Do you remember? For the magazine. Small things, unnoticed at the time sometimes have the biggest effect."

Laura shook her head. "None of this makes sense, and time travel is nonsense, really."

"People travelling through time is impossible. Information can travel through time, though. Our consciousness is just information. My body stays in the future, but my mind is here. But it can't go just anywhere, we need a 'pull,' a connection to the past. Usually this happens when people have gone through trauma of some sort. Their minds fracture a little. We reconstruct their data and make a connection with that. It's like a touching of hands through time."

"That's what you're doing with me? It sounds crazy,"

"But it's true. You're here at a pivotal point for the world. If we normalise ideas now, we can rob them of their power in the future. Stop them being used against people."

"What are you then? What have you done to my baby?" Laura spun round again, trying to see him. "What have you done to us?"

The silence grew between them. Laura sobbed.

"Your baby is too small to be anything yet. He's fine. I'm just here for now."

"What else isn't real?"

"What do you mean? All of this is real."

"You've taken over my baby. You make me do things I wouldn't have done. What else isn't real?" Laura wiped the tears from her face as she tried once again to look at him.

She heard Edmond sigh. "Penelope," he said.

Laura screamed, hammering her fists against her legs. "I knew. I knew she was wrong. And I thought I was crazy. I thought it was me. I thought I was losing my mind. How dare you? Go away and leave us …"

"Remember tomorrow. I'm trying to help you."

The air rushed past her. She raised her arms. Her feet hit the water first, but it wasn't cold. She sank down through the muddy water. She thought about breathing, and began to struggle, her arms and legs thrashing against bits of debris. Her lungs exploded and she screamed, expecting to die.

Laura sat up in bed. Her husband jumped up and placed his hand on her back.

"It's OK. You had a nightmare," he said.

"It's not OK. I saw what's going to happen. Eddie showed me."

Laura breathed in jerkily and coughed. She tasted the muddy water and wiped her tongue on her pyjama sleeve. Her husband brought her a glass of water and she gulped it greedily.

"It was real," she said.

"OK. Go back to sleep. You'll feel better in the morning."

Laura lay awake, listening to the distant traffic. *Traffic can't drive in a flood.* Eventually she fell asleep again and dreamt nothing. The next morning, she tried to remember the details of the dream, but it had faded. She knew Edmond had been there. Edmond had shown her a terrible future. She opened the curtains and saw the sun, and dry ground, and people walking like they always did, and cars repeating their daily journeys. Laura rested her head against the window. It could be a play she was watching, or a series on TV. How do you tell what's real? The pictures outside, or the pictures inside? Laura massaged her temples. *There's no way to tell*, she thought. She frowned, searching her brain for the name of a man who'd believed something like that.

She walked into Edmond's room and found him awake with a frown creasing his forehead.

"Morning, Dumpling. Sleep well?"

He kicked rhythmically at his blanket. As she picked him up, she felt a wave of revulsion. He grabbed at her hair and tugged insistently until Laura gave in and held him close. She whispered in his ear: "I haven't forgotten."

Edmond stopped pulling at her hair and relaxed against her. She patted his nappy and laid him on the changing mat. She undressed him and stroked his chubby legs.

Her husband watched her for a while before coming into the nursery.

"You seem better today?" he said.

"Maybe I just needed a good sleep," Laura said.

"Maybe. You'll still go today though?"

"Of course." Laura smiled at him but felt her lips moving oddly.

"I'll have my phone with me the whole time. And I'm coming home after lunch."

Laura frowned at his back as he left.

Chapter 8

LAURA AVOIDED LOOKING AT THE psychiatrist. His gaze locked onto her face.

"You don't seem totally focused on our session this morning," he said.

"I'm sorry. I didn't sleep much."

"Your husband confirmed you've been having hallucinations involving Edmond."

"He called you?" Laura watched a delivery van failing to do a three-point turn in the tiny car park.

"Yes, I think he was concerned."

"But I said I'd call you. And I did." Laura winced; had the driver scraped the blue car?

"Does it make you angry, that he called?"

"Yes." She held her breath as the van inched out the exit.

"Why?"

Laura folded and refolded her hands in her lap. "Because I can handle this."

"He has an obligation though. Sometimes people don't realise what's in their best interests. He's only trying to help."

"Yes." Laura rubbed her palms down her jeans.

The psychiatrist raised an eyebrow. "Yes?"

"Yes." Laura watched another car inching through the narrow gates.

"Do you have anything to add?"

"Why don't you widen those stupid gates? Just trying to park must drive people to the edge of sanity."

"Laura, we're here to talk about you, not the car park."

"I hate the car park, so it is about me."

The psychiatrist shrugged his shoulders. "So, tell me about the hallucinations with Eddie."

"I haven't had hallucinations with Eddie."

He placed his elbows on his desk. "Your husband, and you, said you were convinced he was talking to you. Telling you to check in a cupboard."

"No, it was a dream where he told me things. It seemed real when I woke up. But it was a dream."

"That's not what you said yesterday."

Laura squinted, and tilted her head to one side. "I'd had a nap in the day. It was a dream. You know how you sometimes wake up but aren't quite awake yet? It was like that. I called my husband, but it was a dream."

The psychiatrist scribbled in his notebook. Laura watched him underlining something repeatedly. "What sorts of things does Eddie tell you, in your dreams?"

"He tells me the world is going to flood. And that people will drown. And that we can't stop it."

"And how do you feel about Edmond?"

"I don't know. He thinks he's trying to help me, in my dreams."

"Do you ever feel that he's going to harm you?"

Laura laughed. "He's a baby, what could he ever do to harm me?"

"Quite. But I don't mean literally. Are you afraid of him?"

"I'm never afraid of him, in my dreams, or in real life."

The psychiatrist wrote carefully this time, spending time on each word. Laura watched a car trying to leave the car park. 'Go, go, go,' she told it silently, 'there's someone going to pull in in a minute; then you'll be trapped.' Sure enough, the two cars stopped bumper to bumper at the gate, one desperate not to back out onto a busy road, the other panicking about reversing into the cramped rows of cars.

"It's important to trust me, Laura," the psychiatrist said.

"I do trust you."

He leant back in his chair and put his pencil in his mouth. She could hear it clicking around his teeth.

"Can you come in again tomorrow? I'll ask if your husband can join us."

"I don't want my husband to join us. Also, tomorrow I'll have Eddie all day, so that's not so good. Monday, maybe?"

"I'd rather not leave it until after the weekend."

"Why does my husband need to be here?"

"He doesn't need to be here. But it'd be helpful if we all reach an agreement about your treatment together."

"Oh. What do you have in mind about my treatment?"

The pencil clicked against his teeth again. He sucked at it as he pulled it from his mouth. "It's just good to review all the options periodically."

"Like admitting me?"

"No one is going to do anything you aren't happy with."

"'Happy' meaning 'what I've been coerced into agreeing with'."

"You seem much more combative today, Laura. Is there anything you want to talk about?"

"No. I'd like to go home. I'm tired."

Laura could just see the bumper of her own car, straddling the white lines in an ungainly position. Now that the car next to hers had left, it looked like her fault, but the other car had taken up part of her space. She planned out her route to the gates. Better to approach from the left; then she might see anyone coming in before they got there. And then turn left and go the long way around.

She became aware of expectation in the air.

"Yes?" she said.

"OK then. I'll see you tomorrow."

Laura left, unaware of what she had agreed to.

* * *

She returned home to find her husband sitting on the sofa, cradling Edmond in his arms. He fussed over him, readjusting his blanket, stroking his fingers.

"Hello?" Laura said.

"Hello." He carried on folding the blanket around Edmond's sleeping body.

"I wasn't expecting you just yet."

"I told you I was coming home early. Also, I got a call."

"From the girl? Maybe we should get rid of her."

"No. From the doctor."

Laura hesitated in the doorway. She placed her handbag gently on the floor and leant down to unzip her boots. She walked slowly towards the sofa and bent over her husband's shoulder. She touched Edmond's wispy hair.

"What did he say?"

Her husband turned his head. His eyes looked into hers from a few inches away. Laura moved closer to him.

"What did he say?" Laura said again.

"He's worried about your hallucinations. About Edmond."

"I told him, it was a dream. He wants to lock me up. I'm not seeing him again."

"I'm worried, too," he said, moving away from her.

"I'm not going to hospital."

"No one's going to put you away. But they might be able to help you get better there." He tightened his arms around Edmond and shuffled down the sofa. "It's not OK that you think he's talking to you."

"It was a dream."

"You phoned me. It wasn't a dream."

"I'm not going to do anything bad. Can't you hear me?"

"Laura, please sit down."

Laura walked over to the window and looked out. The drizzle stuck to the glass. People with umbrellas shuffled outside. The rain gathered in puddles on the pavement.

"Everyone's going to die," Laura said.

"What?"

"Everyone's going to die. Maybe today, maybe tomorrow, maybe in a decade …"

"This is crazy. Sit down. We need to talk."

Laura looked at Edmond and closed her eyes. "Wake up," she said to him. "Wake up." She sat on the windowsill, knocking their wedding picture to the floor with a clatter. Edmond wriggled under his blanket until a bare foot appeared.

"It's not crazy, and I'm not crazy, and I'm not going to hospital."

"We just want to understand what's going on and work out what we should do. Maybe he'll just change your drugs."

"He doesn't need you there to do that."

"But I'm your husband. Of course I'll be there. I love you."

"You love me like a pet."

"What's got into you? This is …" He hesitated, the words hanging between them.

"Crazy? Insane? Mad? Is that what this is?"

He turned away from her and walked towards his phone on the coffee table. Laura ran after him and put her hands on Edmond. Edmond opened his eyes.

"Give him to me. He'll be hungry."

Her husband hesitated. Edmond opened his eyes and, as if he were on his mother's side, began to cry. Laura took him and sat on the sofa. 'Run, Mummy,' he seemed to say. 'Run while you have the chance.' Laura fed Edmond calmly, smiling at him. She felt her husband near.

"What's this?" he said, placing the pill bottle on the seat next to her.

"It's my drugs."

"I know."

"Why did you ask then?"

"It seems very full."

Laura held Edmond firmly. A bird pecked at a twig on the branch outside the window.

"Maybe we have a nest?" she said, nodding towards it.

"Laura. Have you been taking them?"

"Of course. I'm bad with names. What kind is it? It'd be nice if it's a nest."

Her husband opened the bottle and turned it over on his palm, fiddling with the small pills that hid in the cracks between his fingers as he tried to count them.

"I don't think you have, you know."

"I think I have, you know."

The bird picked at something on the branch, hopping from side to side.

"I suppose birds'll do better in a flood. How long do you think they can stay in the air for?" Laura said.

"There's no flood, and I don't give a crap about the birds. When was the last time you took one of these?"

Laura let Edmond wrap his fingers around her thumb. She jiggled his arm gently, watching the vibrations roll through his body.

"It says, 'Take one a day, in the morning, with food.' I took one this morning, with toast. OK?"

"Where's your prescription? When did you get these?"

"The nice people at the chemist keep it, so they can order more." She smiled at her husband with her head tilted to one side. She watched him pick up his phone again, walk into the kitchen, and close the door. His voice seeped through the gaps around it.

"Can you hear what he's saying?" Laura said to Edmond.

"I don't need to," Edmond said. "He's dobbing you in."

"Eddie, really. If you want me to believe you're talking to me, it's not a good idea to sound exactly like me."

Edmond shrugged. His face settled into a disgruntled frown.

Her husband's voice grew louder.

Laura wrapped Edmond up in his blanket, hurriedly stuffed him in his pushchair, grabbed the nappy bag, pulled her boots on, and wheeled him out of the front door. She didn't close it for fear of making a noise. She scampered down the damp street and into the main road, where she paused momentarily and laughed.

"I feel good, Eddie. I feel free."

Edmond said nothing.

Laura pulled her hoodie over her head to keep out the drizzle and walked to the park. She sat down on the sodden bench and turned Edmond towards the ducks.

"Even a flood only reaches halfway up a duck," she said.

Edmond kicked out a foot.

Laura closed her eyes. Her ears buzzed and she rubbed them. She looked at the pond again. The ducks circled their duck house, pulling at weeds. Under the water she thought she saw a goldfish. The water lapped gently at the stones around the edge, and at the path. She watched the small ripples, counting the intervals between them. Three, always three. But … Laura frowned. The pond seemed to swell, and sink, as if it breathed.

"Did they reach that far up before?" Laura asked Eddie, pointing at the water covering the path. She looked around, but everyone else seemed to have left.

Laura felt her heart beating and placed a hand over her chest. It didn't feel like her heart. She breathed in slowly and heard her breath rushing past her.

"Eddie?"

Laura picked him out of his pushchair. She sat him on her lap, holding both his hands. He nestled in towards her. "It's OK," he said.

Laura glanced at the pond again, and gasped. It had swallowed the stones around the edge. It had drowned a bush. Laura breathed in and out slowly. 'It's not raining that much, this can't be real, this can't be real.' She moved her feet further under the bench.

"Don't be scared," Eddie said, "do you want me to take you with me?"

The water swelled and expanded and breathed its way towards her. Laura watched it. 'It's not real,' she muttered to herself. 'It's not real, it's not real.'

"I can, and I will. What do you think they'll do if you stay?"

"I'm scared."

"I can take you with me. But you have to choose. Stay and deal with this, or come with me."

"Come where?"

"To the future. I can bring your mind with me. You can live with us. But these bodies will stay behind and live out this life as best they can. We can't bring them."

Laura shivered. "Just my mind? What about my real baby?"

"Yes. Your consciousness will be with me and you'll be safe. Your body and the child will carry on here."

Laura pulled her legs up and huddled on the bench. She reached for the nappy bag and put that beside her. She looked behind her. Her hands lay so lightly on her knees that she barely felt them.

"I haven't felt completely in my body for a long time."

"So, let me bring you to the future. Let me save you."

The park glistened with standing water. The grass oozed dirt and mud as it drowned.

"I'll never know my real baby."

"I'm *your* real baby."

"Take me with you. I don't want them to think I'm crazy. I don't want them to lock me up."

"But it's forever. You can't come back."

"I don't want to be here anymore."

Laura breathed in carefully, and out carefully. She counted her breaths. She reasoned with herself. But every time she opened her eyes, she saw only water. Silent, creeping water. She smelt the scent of rivers, and mud.

"Close your eyes. Hold onto me. It'll feel strange, but I'm taking you with me."

Laura buried her face in Edmond's small body and held her breath. She sensed the water, creeping closer. She scrunched her eyes closed. The air seemed to dry out. The damp and the smell receded. Edmond's blanket rubbed her face, as if she had never felt it before. The smell of it exploded in her head. The warm air she breathed sank into her body, rather than rushing through it. Her thoughts felt attached and under control. Her skin tingled, as if awakened, or reborn. Laura smiled.

"I'm alive," she said.

A voice came from all around her. It sounded like Eddie's, but more distinct.

In front of her sat a semi-circle of figures dressed in long robes. They sat on the floor in a yellowish room. She felt herself in the midst of them, but her vision was fixed ahead. She tried to move. There seemed nothing for her to move. One of the figures came towards her, his face excited and happy.

PART 3: FUTURE

BERTRAM'S STORY

Chapter 1

BERTRAM CLAPPED HIS HANDS.

"Flood!" He raised his voice to make it heard above the scuffles and shouts of the children chasing around the pod.

The small bodies in front of him squirmed and wriggled onto the desks and chairs. Bertram turned away and counted.

"Ten, nine, eight …"

Furniture crashed to the floor. He held his breath, waiting for a cry, which never came. The children laughed, and he waited.

"Who's drowned in the flood?" Bertram spun round.

Except for three, all the children stood on the desks in the middle of the room, perched precariously, some with arms held out for balance, others with only a toehold on the furniture. One boy had wedged himself in the door of the pod, his feet flat against one of the supports, his fingers whitening around a door post. The three drowned ones looked downcast. Bertram smiled.

"Well done, children. Now you've used up some energy, can we get back to the lesson?"

The children clambered down and rearranged the classroom. It took some time before they all faced him again, tablets ready, their breath coming in quick gasps and the smell of little unwashed bodies enveloping him.

"The Revolution. Who can tell me what you read about that yesterday?"

The class watched him silently. He saw answers flickering through their eyes, and then fading away as doubt gained the upper hand. Others avoided looking up, suddenly preoccupied with their tablets, or their tunics, or the position of their seats.

Bertram sighed. The smell of roasting meat swept in with the breeze.

"The sooner we get through this, the sooner we get a break. Come on now. Help me out. The Revolution?"

One hand waved at him from the back.

"Yes."

"Evie brought the truth to our community. We had been hiding in the desert and were called the Religious in those days. New Britain persecuted us, but our communities lived on. Then everyone got to know about what Evie said, and there was Revolution. We defeated New Britain. And now there's a government made up of people from all the places in the country. Things are voted on, not dictated. Life is better." Her voice floated through the pod like dust on the breeze, dispersing before it reached him.

Bertram sighed, wondering whether she understood half of what she'd said.

"Yes. That's right. What was the truth that Evie brought?"

Another child spoke: "The New Britainers had lied to everyone. They caused the Great Flood and made everyone scared so they'd let them take over."

"Good." Bertram nodded. "And our community. What were we doing?"

"New Britain persecuted anyone who believed in religion. So, all the religions decided on the Great Amalgam ... Amaglama ..." Bertram watched the child's lips contorting and twisting with the newly learned word. He smiled.

"Yes, that's right. The Great Amalgamation. There used to be many religions, but they joined together, as one, to fight against New Britain."

The child sighed, and continued. "And after that we just had one religion. But all the Religious hid in the desert, so they wouldn't be persecuted." The child ran out of breath and stopped abruptly, looking around the class for someone to share the burden.

"That's right. New Britain tried to eradicate belief in God so people would put all their faith in them. The main religions put their differences aside and joined together for survival. They formed the Amalgamated Religion. Arguing that their common faith in God overrode any differences between them, they started to worship together, in secret. They called God by different names, but the underlying thoughts were the same. And then Evie came. So—" Bertram nodded at a girl, whom he often relied on.

"Evie brought them the truth, in a letter, so everyone had to believe it. They knew the New Britainers were bad people. So, we had Revolution, and we got rid of them. And we live in their homes. They were bad people."

Bertram flinched. "They weren't all bad people. People often believe what they're taught, and they do what they're told. We set them free."

The girl frowned. "New Britain was bad though."

"Yes, *it* was bad. That doesn't mean everyone in it was bad."

"But we burned them all. We wouldn't have done that if they hadn't been bad."

Bertram's blush spread from his neck to his cheeks. He closed his eyes with the effort of stopping it.

A few of the children shifted in their seats as if their surfaces had become rough and painful. One blinked to contain the water in his eyes. Another picked at the hem of his tunic. Bertram watched them, wishing he could reach out and hold them close.

"Children," he said, "no shame or blame attaches to any of us because of the actions of our parents or ancestors. We make our own way in the world."

The children looked at each other, twitching, glancing at particular people and then looking away.

Bertram paused. "Children, I too was an orphan like you. My parents remained loyal to New Britain. But they died, and then the Brothers took me in. It's nothing to be ashamed of. You will grow up here, and do good work."

He sensed he'd lost their attention. The now overwhelming

smell of food burned a hole in their concentration and brought them back to everyday concerns. They looked towards the door, listening to the sounds of bowls and spoons clattering on tables.

"And that's why we celebrate Evie in the Autumn festival. What are we planning to do then?" Bertram said, his voice like a net dragging them back to the lesson.

"We wear red hairbands, and we sing songs about her. And we think about how we can try to be like her. Brave, and strong, and ..." The child ran out of words.

"And we eat honey cake. Lots of honey cake. Do you remember last year Paul ate so much he was sick all over?" a boy said. The others looked at him, and burst out into laughter.

"Alright. We're hungry. Let's call it a day. But tonight, I want you to read the next two pages. You'll find them ready on your tablets."

The children stood up and ran out into the communal pod where they sat at long trestle tables and waited for the servers to hand out the steaming bowls of food, and cups of water. They grasped the cups and poured the water into their mouths, as if they hadn't drunk in days.

Bertram listened to their voices disintegrating as they merged with the sounds of the meal, the hum of the air conditioners, and the wind thumping against the edge of the pod. He picked up his tablet to set the evening's work, flicking through last year's exercises. He opened the letter. The letter that had begun it all. The summary of it was so familiar that it seemed almost to be one of his own thoughts, not a thought he'd been given.

> *They made it worse; they broke the Thames Barriers. They flooded us. They killed us, and left us to kill each other, because it was the only way we'd give them such power.*

Bertram looked quickly at the door, and then opened the full letter, not the abridged one the children learned. He followed the familiar lines, pausing at the ones that almost stopped his heart.

I hope you are loved ... Mothers held up their wriggling babies. And people elbowed them out of the way.

Bertram closed his eyes and imagined the noise, like the worst storm he'd ever experienced, and swelling masses of water, perhaps like the material they covered the domes in, he thought, grey and billowing, overwhelming. He tried to imagine the bond between a parent and child. What would it feel like, to be so attached to a small person? Or to be that person, and feel that longing from your parent? What would it be like? He pulled the purple sleeves of his tunic down and wrapped his arms across his body.

He read on, to that final, puzzling section. The line that had spawned dissertations and theses since the early days. But the paradox seemed no closer to resolution.

Please, never have faith in an idea, never stop using your mind, never be totally certain.

What did she mean by faith? Over time, the meaning of words had shifted like dunes in the sand, so no one knew what faith was to her. We need faith, they'd taught him. We need faith to improve the world, but also, we should never have it. Bertram tried to let the thoughts behind the words echo through his mind. Perhaps the truth was in the flow, not the separate words. Perhaps the truth was beyond them.

The bell rang. Finally, the communal meal. Bertram turned off his tablet and went to eat. He took his place at the table with the other novices. He looked out for Percy, but couldn't see him.

"How are your students today?" the man next to him said.

"They just don't concentrate at the moment," Bertram said. "I even had them play a game before I could get anything from them."

"It's the weather."

"The weather?"

"They're like the sheep. As soon as it gets cooler, they hop and skip around and can barely keep still."

Bertram put his spoon down.

"The children are like the sheep?"

The man shrugged. "If your task was with the animals, you'd know it was true."

Bertram shrugged.

"Can't you smell it? The cooler air. It smells like cleanliness. It feels like energy," the man said.

"It isn't so cool though, is it?"

"It depends how you measure it, Brother Bertram. If you look at the thermometer, no. But I feel it. I even took off my muslin for a couple of seconds to feel it on my face."

"You shouldn't do that."

"I never burn. I know when it's safe."

The two ate their sheep meat and protein pods, and mopped up the sauce with brown bread. They both took tiny sips of their portion of water.

"What do you have to do after this?" the man asked.

"I have to see my Master. He wants to talk about my proposal."

"Oh. I remember." Bertram thought he saw derision in the man's eyes. "I hope it goes well."

"As do I," Bertram said, looking away. The irritating noise of chewing swelled around him. "And you?"

"We have another visitor from France. I have to make him welcome."

"The second in a month?"

"Indeed. Perhaps one day we can truly get to know each other again."

Chapter 2

BERTRAM CRUMPLED HIS TUNIC IN his hand. He spun sharply around and retraced his steps to the opposite side of the pod. He breathed in deeply, hoping the air would drown his heartbeat. He closed his eyes momentarily before looking sideways at the door.

A noise. He'd heard a noise. He stopped. Footsteps approached. Bertram shrugged, trying to assume an attitude of indifference as the assistant walked in.

"The Master will see you now," he said.

Bertram nodded. "Thank you." He walked into the study and waited for the assistant to leave.

The Master typed slowly on his tablet. Without raising his eyes, he waved Bertram towards a seat. Bertram sat down and smoothed out the wrinkles in his tunic. He adjusted his belt, twice. He aligned his feet so they were parallel with each other, and at right angles to the Master's desk. One of the children's songs snuck into his head where it drowned and twisted the phrases he'd practiced. '*Tum ti di dum dum*, bones and ...' Bertram frowned and placed his hands on his forehead.

"Are you alright, Bertram?" the Master said.

"Of course. I've been looking forward to this chance to discuss ..."

"It's the highlight of my day too, Bertram." The Master pushed his tablet aside and folded his hands together.

"Good." Bertram nodded, ignoring the sarcasm. "What did you think, then?" He frowned and clenched his fist. "I mean, it would be an honour to hear what you thought of my proposal."

The Master nodded. "How long have you been writing?"

"Five years, Master."

"And you remain at the proposal stage."

"Yes, Master. But it's just a matter of finding the right project."

"And this is it, I suppose?" The Master reached for his tablet.

"I believe it would be a great contribution to our knowledge."

"'The History and Development of Children's Education in New Britain'?" One of the Master's eyebrows wandered up his forehead.

"Yes, Master. I think we can learn a lot from how people taught their children. How education turns them into different people."

"You didn't think to ask first what is meant by 'education'? We have to understand the core essence of a concept before turning to practical matters."

"I want to do something useful. I know it's traditional to analyse our words, and to trace the history of our ideas. But ..." Bertram frowned. "There's no point to studying words when we could be improving the world."

"In order to pursue practical knowledge, we must first understand the structure of our thoughts. What's the use of a survey of ..."—the Master waved his hands—"... of what teachers said and did, without understanding what we even mean by 'education'? There are numerous theories about the nature of education, and how it is to be understood in the abstract. These have nothing to do with the tedious practicalities of teaching. You should have begun there."

"Perhaps there isn't a nature of education. Perhaps what we do is all there is."

For the first time since he'd arrived at the Institution for the Education of the Orphans of the Revolution, Bertram watched the Master struggle to find a word. His mouth formed an 'O' before collapsing into a quivering line.

"Have we taught you nothing?" he said, the words straggling out of his mouth like string.

"Everything I know, I know because of you. I will always be grateful."

"But this is unacceptable."

Bertram looked at his feet. He watched his toes disappearing underneath the hem of his tunic. He fumbled with the knot at his waist. It had really come to this, then. For a moment Bertram struggled to force the words out, but eventually the sentence he'd practiced spilled out of him in a voice that didn't sound like his. "I did think that I should perhaps spend some time with a more practical order, and finish my project there."

The Master sank back in his seat and placed his hands on the table in front of him. He turned his tablet on and off repeatedly. Bertram watched his shoulders rising and falling and wished he could pause time. Would they let him go? Did he want to go?

"You are disinclined to study knowledge. No matter how hard we try ..."—the Master paused to search out Bertram's eyes with his own—"... you're always drawn to people. Which 'more practical order' do you have in mind?"

Bertram wriggled back in his seat. "The Historians. I fear they are misunderstood ..."

"You know of them?" The Master's eyebrows fled up his forehead again.

"Yes, their records are still here. I read them."

"Not everything about them is in our records. They thought they could contact people who had lived in the past, do you know that?"

Bertram paused, weighing up how much to admit. "People who are dead?" Bertram feared his voice betrayed him.

"Yes. They thought they might speak with people who are dead. This is heresy, of course. Once we die we go to heaven, or hell. The dead can't communicate with the living. So the Historians were sent away. It was hoped they'd disappear. But they didn't, and we've lost touch with what they're doing. Why would you want to spend time with them?"

"Because I like history. I didn't know about their heresy, exactly. But they seem to gather data, find out everything they can about the old world. I think this knowledge is useful. And it's useful for understanding what we do with the children."

"That word again. Useful. We must understand concepts and the essence of things. We must work out what we really mean when we use our words. Any move towards practical implementation is dangerous and must be done under the closest supervision. It's exactly when people believed they could change the world that they caused its near destruction." The Master stared at Bertram, his eyes unwavering.

Bertram fumbled with his belt again. "The Historians are reviving knowledge of old technologies. And the way people back then understood the world. Not everything they did in the old days led to disaster."

The Master turned to look at a spot on the wall above Bertram's head. He frowned, then turned his tablet on and read something.

Bertram could hear their breaths mingling together, their rhythms out of sync. Should he speak? Eventually the Master looked up again.

"There may be something you can do. Spend time with them. Learn what they do. But also find out about their heresies. It's time we came to grips with them."

"What do you mean?"

"I will give you permission to finish your project with them. But that won't be your task—watch them. Tell me of their heresy."

Bertram clenched his fists together. He breathed rapidly, heat spreading through his body.

"I don't investigate heretics. I'll be there to learn."

"Yes, but gain their confidence. They'll only tell us if they're approached with understanding. Heresy is particularly dangerous now."

Bertram fidgeted on his seat, conscious that he must look like one of his students.

"Yes. I know the Amalgamation is at risk. To avoid a splintering of the faithful we must stay focused."

The Master nodded. "It doesn't help that in other countries there never was an Amalgamation. The more people travel, the more they want to divide back into the old religions. We must root out heresy because it will tear us apart. I have decided."

"And is that my project, or can I get credit for the work I intend to do on education?" Bertram said, twisting the sleeves of his tunic around his hands.

His Master sighed. "Nothing will ever come of what you find out about education. But if you do well, and report back information that is useful for eradicating the heretics, I will see to it that you're granted a doctorate *in lieu*."

Bertram nodded. His image of himself dissolved in his stomach. He felt his body slumping even as he tried to support it. He watched the Master's eyes roam around his pod. A doctorate *in lieu*? They thought he'd never write anything important. That he would forever understand the world through other people's words. That he would never contribute to knowledge. His Master's hand reached for the gavel. The Master raised it uncertainly before smashing it into the table. The vibration rocked Bertram back in his seat. Almost immediately the door opened.

Bertram became aware of himself a few minutes later as he walked down the dark tunnel to the living-dome. The air conditioners resonated through his head. The sound hurt as he listened to it; he felt it turning parts of his brain to jelly. He paused before entering and buried his eyes in the palms of his hands. He knew that if he looked up, he would cry. It might fill the void in his soul. He would never do the job of an Enforcer. Never. To think of his certainty that visiting the Historians would get him what he wanted. He saw himself, and his naivete, as if from afar, and looked at himself with the scorn and pity he'd receive from the others.

'I'm not stupid. I'm not stupid. I'll make it work,' he told himself. One of the other novices rang the bell in the centre of the dome. Bertram wiped his eyes, breathed in deeply, and stepped inside.

He walked towards the long tables that stretched across the middle of the dome. He ignored the cooks and the food, and sat down in his usual place. The voices around him sounded happy. The bell rang twice for the formal second meal, and the novices hurried to their places. They sat in silence, hands folded in their laps, eyes turned towards the entrance.

The bell rang three times. The Masters walked in, two by two. Their black, stiff robes dragged on the floor. Bertram and the others rose to their feet and looked at the ground. The Masters walked to their table, gathered their robes in their hands, and sat down together like a many-bodied insect. By some signal that Bertram had never discovered, their voices joined together: "We must thank God, and the earth, for the gifts we've been given. Tonight, we will eat well, and we must be grateful. Help us continue the Revolution, and the work of the Prophets." The students turned to face the screens above the Masters' table. Bertram blinked at the faces, blurred, or out of focus, or pixelated from the great Data Purge. He frowned at the black spots of Evie's eyes.

"So, how'd it go, Bertie?" The man leant across the narrow table, his eyes fixed on Bertram's face.

Bertram made his lips smile. "Really good." He watched disappointment creep across the face opposite him.

"That's great! So, he approved your project?"

"Yes." Bertram could feel the insincerity seeping through his being. "I told him that there's a difference between us and that I should go and study something more practical. There is merit in it that isn't understood here."

"Oh yes? Where are you going then?"

"I've decided I'll visit the Historians."

"Oh. I thought there'd been some sort of disagreement between us and them?"

Bertram sighed, "Yes. If you'd read their records you'd know— they're all still in the archives."

"That's what you're for. To read the things no one else has any use for." The man smiled, his lips curling.

Bertram leant back. "They're historians. They study the past, they search for records, and piece together how the old world was."

Another man turned towards them. "They didn't just do that, though, did they? I heard they think they can contact the dead." He watched Bertram. Bertram smiled.

"That's what we've heard. Perhaps my project has other aspects to it … ones I can't discuss …" Bertram paused. He looked down the table, wondering how many listened in. He was sure that even the Masters could hear. "Perhaps there's more to my project than just history." Bertram smoothed his hair away from his face. "Perhaps I'm doing important work, while you sit here tending sheep, and washing children, and thinking about thinking about other people's thoughts."

The man opposite recoiled slightly before recovering himself.

"Bertie!" he said. Bertram smiled at the others at the table, while tightly gripping the edge of his bench. He thought even the Masters stared, or shrugged at what he'd said. He felt their eyes gleaming at him, although their awareness of their exalted status prevented them indulging in the curiosity shown by the novices.

Bertram finished his bowl of protein pods and sheep meat and waited. Surely something else must have happened today, something else for people to talk about. No one had failed to control the students? No one had been attacked by a sheep? No. The day had passed entirely uneventfully, except for Bertram and his mysterious project.

Bertram's dinner formed a lump in his stomach. His shoulders slumped towards the table. He waited.

Eventually, the bell rang once, and he stood up. He walked slowly into the dormitories and sank down on his sleeping mat. He picked up his tablet and turned it on. After flicking through a few messages, he opened his students' work. He closed that file and opened his pictures. He lay flat on his back and held the tablet close to his eyes so he could see nothing else. His fingers traced the outline of her face. He imagined what she might say, and because he couldn't remember her, this was easy. She'd tell him how clever he was. How, eventually, everyone else would see what she saw. And then she would hug him. He'd seen it. That's what mothers did.

The following morning, Bertram awoke cradled by the wellbeing of a happy dream. He opened his eyes. The Historians. His heart leapt, his breath caught in his throat, and he scrambled out from under his blanket. He brushed his hair away from his face and rubbed his beard, trying to hold onto the calmness that had enveloped his sleep. It had leaked from his mind, which now raced away from him as he stared at his fellow novices.

They rose silently, winking and nodding at one another. They filed into the cleansing pod, where they turned on the pump that measured out equal rations of water into wooden bowls. Bertram splashed it over his face, and turned away before washing himself under his tunic. He poured the used water into a tub, where it was sent for irrigation.

Bertram hurried his breakfast, ignoring the whispers and murmurs of the others. The bell rang twice, and he jumped up from the bench and scuttled towards the tunnel.

He swore he could hear the children's shouts before the sound-proof, explosion-proof doors opened. The sound raced down the tunnel like waves of water. Bertram smiled. Inside the children's pod, small bodies leapt and danced on beds, tunics lying crumpled on the floor.

"Brother Bertram."

"Head Carer." Bertram nodded at the elderly woman. "How was the night?"

"Good. As you can see, they've woken fully refreshed and ready for the day."

"Indeed."

"We do have a new arrival."

Bertram's smile faded. "You wouldn't think forty years after the Revolution we'd still be taking in orphans."

"Brother Bertram," the woman said, sighing. "You know …"

"I know. Where are they?"

The woman pointed to a small boy sitting on his bed at the far end of the pod.

"Does he have a name?" Bertram said.

"Not yet."

Bertram clapped his hands together. The children quietened, the last shouts and giggles dying out as his eyes scanned from right to left. "Single file, into the dining pod. Hurry now, you've a lot to learn today."

Bertram tried to deepen the tone of his voice. He'd schooled his eyes in sternness. But the children smiled at him as they passed. "Morning, Brother Bertram. I like it when it's your day." Bertram nodded, biting his cheeks to prevent a smile escaping.

He stopped the new boy and led him to a bed. He patted it gently. "Sit down."

The boy wavered, looked for the exit, picked at the rope around his waist.

"Stand up if you want. I just want you to feel comfortable."

The boy nodded but remained standing.

"What's your name?" Bertram said.

The boy shrugged.

"Where have you come from?"

The boy shrugged again and looked at his feet.

Bertram smiled at him. "Well, you don't have to say anything. I assume they found you hiding out somewhere? Scavenging? But you'll be taken care of here. We'll feed you, clothe you, and educate you. And when you're older, you can go out and serve the community or you can stay here and devote your life to knowledge. We'll give you a home, and …"—Bertram looked into the boy's eyes—"… and we will love you."

The boy frowned and scratched his leg.

"When you're ready to talk, we'll listen. But now, are you hungry?"

The boy's eyes opened, and he looked greedily around the room. Bertram stood up and placed his hand momentarily on the boy's shoulder. He flinched as he felt the sharpness of his bones. The boy followed him to the dining pod. Bertram led him up to the cook.

"Give this boy extra helpings, as much as he wants, until he fills out a bit."

He patted the boy on the back, trying to infuse his touch with the feelings he had no words for.

A hand rested gently on Bertram's shoulder. He spun round. "Percy!" he said.

"I've been looking for you. I forgot it was your turn for breakfast."

"I looked for you last night. Have you heard?" Bertram said.

"About your project? Everyone's heard."

The two men walked slowly towards the edge of the pod where the dim lights left shadows in which to hide. "So, did you stick to your plan?" Percy said, his head inclined towards Bertram, his voice barely more than a whisper.

"Yes, I asked to leave but then he twisted it into making me an Enforcer, and he said I'll only get my doctorate if I do as he says."

"Still for your education project though?"

Bertram gripped Percy's arm and led him further into the shadows. Their tunics melted into the gloom so they appeared to be a single body.

"No. That's the worst thing. Not for that. But *in lieu*. For being a spy."

Percy put an arm around Bertie's shoulder.

"I'm sorry. They just don't see the value in what you do. Write it anyway. Others might still read it."

"That's not the same."

"No. But we must do the best with what we're given." Percy hesitated. He glanced behind them, into the open area of the pod, before continuing. "This is your best chance of finding your parents."

Bertram nodded. "I know. I think I was convincing. I don't think he guessed I knew about contacting the dead."

"There you go. You can get what you want. Just keep him happy too."

"But I can't report people, Percy. Remember? Even when we were small we said we hated Enforcers."

"I know. Be clever, Bertie. You have to be clever. They underestimate you, and that's to your advantage. Tell them nothing that sounds like something. Be inept. Use the time for our own purposes—find your mother, and write your project."

Bertram smiled. "I suppose you're right. What else can I do? So, how are you? I forgot to ask. I'll miss you."

Percy cleared his throat.

"I'll miss you too."

The clatter of bowls interrupted the silence. The two men walked back into the light and separated without looking back.

An hour later, a more disciplined group of children sat opposite Bertram, in rows, each at a desk, with a tablet open and ready. Bertram stood up and they copied him.

"Bless our day and the learning we do. We dedicate our efforts to God, the community, and the Prophets." The children looked at the pictures on the screen at the front of the class, bowed, and sat down.

"This morning it's algebra, again. So, let's see what you remembered." Bertram chuckled at the groans. "But before that, you should probably know that I'll be going away for a while. I've been sent on a mission."

"Oh no, Brother Bertram."

"Who's going to take over?"

"We'll miss you."

"Is it a secret mission?"

"Where are you going?"

Bertram disentangled the questions, deciding which to attend to. "I'll miss you all, too. Very much. I'm going to another community. So, it's not secret. But I will be back."

Chapter 3

BERTRAM RESTED HIS HEAD AGAINST the tinted window of the transport. He shifted on the bench, so the icy fingers of the air conditioning trickled down his back. The glistening dome slowly dissolved into the sandy haze. He sighed. The excitement at finally leaving had disintegrated into doubt. His worries had disguised themselves as lists of belongings he needed to pack. But now that all his things were safely stowed, they ambushed him. Could he avoid spying? How would the Historians welcome him? Might they turn him away?

"Going far?" the woman next to him said.

"Yes. Yes, I am. Very far. You?"

"No, only a few hours. My daughter's having a baby."

Bertram smiled. "I hope the delivery goes smoothly."

"I'm sure it will. It's not like the old days, is it?"

"No. I suppose not."

Bertram looked out of the window again. The dome had gone. He felt as if he'd left a part of himself behind, like a tunic, or a tablet, forgotten on a sleeping mat. The other passengers rustled as they unwrapped their snacks. Bertram smelt fresh bread. Might it taste different, away from home?

This must have been the road he'd arrived on. But at seven years old he hadn't been watching the scenery. And in those days ... he sighed again and wrapped his arms across his chest. *Do journeys make us different people? Can we return and slip back into our old selves? Climb back into our lives?*

He closed his eyes and felt the vibrations rolling through his body. It would take hours. Hours and hours.

The transport emptied slowly as the other passengers clambered out. The driver called their names and found their luggage. Some scrabbled with their muslins in the hurry to get out. His neighbour hesitated by the bench; he could see fear and hope fighting within her. *The next time she's in a transport she'll either be a grandmother or a mourner,* Bertram thought. He smiled at her.

"May the Lord be with you," he said.

The woman's face tensed momentarily. She nodded and got off without looking at him. The driver passed around containers of water. Bertram splashed some on his face, feeling the grit and sand scratching his hands. The transport juddered and clanked onwards, westwards. Small outposts became scarcer and Bertram looked at the emergency store, wondering whether it had been checked.

The brakes screeched, and Bertram jolted forward. His eyes felt sticky. Had he been asleep?

"Brother Bertram."

"Yes, yes. Here."

The driver held open the door, resting his body against the cool metal inside the transport.

"Luggage?"

"No. I have it here. Thank you."

The driver nodded.

Bertram wrapped his muslin tightly around his face and stepped out of the transport. His shoulders sank into the heat. He breathed heavily through the layers of fabric. His eyes stung from the swirling sand. He blinked and hid his face in the crook of his arm.

"Where is it?" he said.

The driver waved into the distance.

"Just over there. Fifty meters or so."

Bertram braced his body against the wind and walked sideways in the direction he'd been shown. He closed his left eye, to give it a rest. Then he switched to his right eye. He shuffled ahead until the sand built itself into a shape. A dome, a dome made of blocks of sandstone. Bertram found the door and kicked at it, his fear at what might greet him outweighing his discomfort. The sound vibrated, as if in a cave.

"Our visitor." The face peered around the door, shielding itself. "Yes. Blessings."

"Come in. What a horrible day to arrive. I promise it's sometimes quite pleasant here."

Bertram walked into the holding room and shook off the sand. He unwrapped his muslin, desperately resisting the urge to spit out the sand in his mouth. He looked up.

The woman facing him stood patiently, with her hands clasped in front of her. Her mouth seemed to hide a smile. She looked to be a similar age to him, with dark hair that partly covered her eyes. She picked up a bowl of water from the floor and held it out to him.

Bertram stood completely still, his hands by his sides and his mouth open. He shook his head to jolt him into action.

"Thank you."

He washed his face, rinsed out his mouth, and dried himself on his tunic.

"Welcome to our community. My name is Annabelle. Shall we go in?"

"I …" Bertram rubbed his face and blinked. "My name is Bertram."

"I know." Annabelle smiled. "We've been expecting you."

She held open the inner door and bowed as he passed her. She smelt of clean water.

The communal room was sparse and dimly lit. The air conditioners hummed. Bertram counted ten doors round the edges of the sandy dome. Annabelle led him to one. She held it open for him.

"This is your room while you're here. I hope you find it accommodating."

"My room?" Bertram peered in. A sleeping mat, a desk, a trunk, a water closet, and a small window looking out into the swirling sand.

"Yes. Your room." Annabelle looked at her feet.

"There are no dormitories?"

"There are dormitories, but we aren't many. We thought you'd like to rest alone."

"Yes. Thank you," Bertram said, willing Annabelle to look up at him.

"You've missed the communal meal, but I can bring you a portion, if you're hungry."

"Yes, I'd like that. It's strange how travelling makes a person hungry, even though they've really done nothing."

Annabelle nodded. "I'll leave it outside your door."

"Thank you. When …" Bertram fumbled with the belt of his tunic. "When is it convenient for me to meet …" He searched though his vocabulary, but all the titles he'd heard were insults. "When can I see …" He coughed, and found Annabelle's eyes watching his, enjoying his discomfort.

"You can just call him Edmond," she said. "He'll meet you tomorrow. As soon as you're rested."

"Thank you. I wasn't expecting to be welcomed."

Anabelle smiled. "I heard you've never left your community before. Is it strange, to be somewhere new?"

"It is strange … I feel out of place."

"We always appreciate the opportunity to show people our work. And we're pleased to welcome you."

Bertram frowned and fumbled with his gritty tunic.

"Rather than who they could have sent, you mean?"

Anabelle's eyes flickered around the room behind him, focusing anywhere other than his face.

"I'm happy I opened the door to you, and we'll do our best to make you welcome."

She turned quickly and closed the door behind her.

Bertram stared at where her shape had been in the doorway, trying to conjure her out of the grain in the wood. He ate sitting on his mat, conscious of all the sounds he made. He put his empty bowl outside the door and lay down on his mat. He tried to stay awake, to think and to plan, but his thoughts morphed into dreams in which he followed Annabelle's smile, and argued with a man made of sand.

The following morning, Bertram opened his door and found a bowl of oat porridge. Apart from the air conditioners, the communal room was still silent.

He ate his porridge on his mat. It stuck to his mouth and coated his teeth. His hand shook as he held the spoon. His ears ached for the morning shouts of the children. Was there a name, yet, for the new boy? Had he cried, and given up his story? Bertram's throat felt as if it could make no room for food. His eyes stung. He must focus on the coming day. He put down his bowl, closed his eyes, and counted his breaths slowly in and out. His heart responded and slowed.

Bertram got up, carried his bowl outside and stood in the centre of the communal room. He held his hands behind his back and waited. *I'm not skulking in my room,* he thought.

He heard a door open behind him, but didn't turn around. He heard light footsteps behind him, circling. Bertram resisted the urge to turn. He waited until the man appeared in front of him.

"Welcome, Brother Bertram. We're honoured by your visit." The man nodded and looked at the floor.

"Blessings. Thank you for your hospitality."

The man waved towards some cushions arranged around a low table. "Shall we sit?"

They sat down opposite each other. Bertram tried to gauge his age, but it seemed indeterminate, or shifting. The wrinkles on his forehead suggested age, but his skin glowed, and his dark eyes flickered around the room like those of a nervous child.

"You are Edmond, I assume," Bertram said.

"I'm Edmond. The message from your community said you are here to learn about us." Edmond spoke slowly, as if his mouth weighed each word before letting it out. And when words were released, he traced their effects on the face of his listener.

Bertram hoped he had his body under control. "Yes. I'm here to learn."

"But really you are here to report on our heresy."

Bertram coughed. "No, my interest is in education. I'd like to find out about how New Britain taught their children to be so … so … compliant. I think if we understand education, we understand the mind of a society."

Edmond laughed. "I don't remember the Brothers being so interested in understanding those different from themselves. I think they've sent you to spy."

"My intention was never to spy, on anyone. I want to learn from you. Your knowledge is important. And I also want to find out about my history."

"Your history?" Edmond frowned.

"Your records are still intact. I've read them—"

Edmond laughed. "Really? I thought they'd burned them?"

"No, they didn't. I think they would have done, but the archiving system is substandard. Half the things they want to burn they can never find. And the half they want to read they find they burned in error."

"Well, well, Bertram. Some things never change." Edmond relaxed into his cushions. "And what is it that you read?"

"That you can …"—Bertram paused, considering his words carefully—"find out about people who died."

"The study of history is the study of those who've died." Edmond's eyes narrowed.

"I read you go beyond that. That you can contact people."

Edmond sighed. "Perhaps it would be better if our records were burned. That's not exactly what we do."

"Tell me then—tell me what you do."

"If you're willing to listen." Edmond seemed to be trying to read his mind.

"Alright." Edmond waved at someone who must have been watching behind a door. A woman, not Annabelle, brought in water, and flavoured protein pod balls, and honey bread. Bertram pulled his tablet out of his pocket and opened it, ready to note down everything. Honey bread. And it wasn't even a Remembrance Day.

Edmond closed his eyes before he began to speak. He spoke with a fluency that suggested he'd told the tale many, many times before. He looked into the distance as he spoke, as if he were used to his listeners' disbelief.

It had begun with the study of history. With the study of the turning points in history. With the hope of preventing disaster.

"Most people study the big things, the governments, the wars, the big ideas. But after reconstructing the data, we found that small things, done by ordinary people, might also change the course of the world. We try to intervene."

Bertram put his tablet down. "What do you mean, *intervene?*"

Edmond frowned, as if he'd lost the flow of his thoughts. "Patience, Brother Bertram. We immerse ourselves in the history of people in the past. They put themselves in their data. They stored everything about themselves digitally. We merge our minds with theirs, we feel their lives flowing through us, and we try to speak to them."

"But how?" Bertram said.

"We get all their data, all the seemingly irrelevant things. People live in the details of their lives. Their books, their commentaries, the stories of their actions. Sometimes, with a few people, there is consciousness in their data."

Bertram's mouth hung open. "But they're dead? Yes?"

"Yes, they're physically dead. But our minds and bodies are different things. We can store our minds in machines."

"That's not possible, surely."

"How prejudiced you are. You haven't even asked to see what we do. We can put our minds into our machines, and our consciousness can travel back in time. We contact the people we've worked out were important."

"But how can you possibly travel back?" Bertram pulled at some loose threads on his tunic, watching the material begin to unravel.

"We began reconstructing the data that had been purged, and we found reports, instructions, information on machines. They'd been made just before the Great Flood. We couldn't make one our-selves, but we found one we could repair. The Brothers decided it was heretical to try to contact people who they say are dead. So, we left, and became the Historians."

"What kind of machines are these?" Bertram looked around the pod, as if expecting to see one.

"It makes particles that travel faster than light. It can transmit information, and consciousness is just information. We can't inter-act with the past in the way we interact with the world here, but sometimes we can talk with people. People whose minds are also in the data. It's those people we look for and try to affect."

"So, what have you changed?"

Edmond's face fell. "Nothing, yet. But we work on. The first Historians have died, and I carry on their work. We've made many ideas appear earlier in the past than they did before. So far, it's not enough to change events. We just need to change more ideas in more people. We have to try to do it."

"Try what?"

"To stop the New Britain. To stop the death and the pain and the evil. There are many possible paths we could have taken to get from the past to the present, and the one we took was not the best."

"But you can't change the past."

"No. But you aren't listening. Not being able to change it com-pletely doesn't mean we can't affect it. We can put ideas in people's minds. We can make them hear and see things that change their behaviour. We can appear to inhabit people they know, and some-times make them see people they don't know."

"But what evidence can you possibly have that any of this is possible?" Bertram said. He expected Edmond to crumple. But Edmond smiled.

"I made a mistake, once. I brought back evidence," he said.

"Can I see it?" Bertram's voice squeaked with the indignation in his head.

Edmond stood up and opened one of the doors. Bertram heard him speaking to someone before he sat down again.

"Honey bread? We've had a good year for the bees."

Bertram stared at Edmond. What evidence could he possibly have? Honey bread? Now? "No, thank you. Your morning meal was very substantial."

"Ahh, yes. Alfred is very generous with guests. Water?"

"No."

A woman walked into the room, stumbling slightly with the weight of a shining metal bowl. She held it inverted, with wires and attachments hanging off. Edmond held out his hand and helped her settle into the cushions next to him. He smiled at Bertram.

"I would like to introduce my evidence," he said.

Bertram couldn't find any words.

"Hello," the woman in a bird-like voice said, "you're going to meet Laura. She's a woman who has joined us from the past."

"I don't understand," Bertram said.

"I know this will sound strange." The woman leant towards him, reaching out with the bowl. "Put this on your head," she said.

"Get it away from me," Bertram said.

"Brother Bertram, you promised to listen to me. That's your task," Edmond said.

Bertram shook his head, and kept shaking it.

"Bertram. Please. If I'm lying, what can possibly happen to you?"

Bertram sat still for a moment. He placed his hands on the warm metal. He thought it hummed. The sound resonated through his body, making him sway.

The woman held his hand while Bertram put the bowl on his head. It felt less heavy than he'd expected. Edmond attached a tablet to one of the wires while the woman muffled his ears and moved a tinted screen over his eyes.

Edmond and the woman moved away from him. Bertram watched the brief glance they shared; it seemed that Edmond was nervous.

"Alright Bertram. You'll meet Laura. Be calm and speak to her like you might speak to any other person."

Edmond typed on the tablet.

The screen darkened. Bertram's ears rang.

"Hello, Bertram. I'm Laura."

The voice came from all around him, and inside him. It sounded odd, emphasising unusual parts of the words. Like a visitor from abroad.

Bertram raised his arms to remove the machine, but felt his hands gently restrained.

"You can speak to me like a normal person."

Bertram coughed.

"Go on. The first word's the hardest."

Bertram breathed slowly.

"Laura?" he said

"Yes. That's my name. Well done."

Bertram gripped the fingers that still held his hands.

"Who are you?"

"I'm a woman, from the past. I lived before the Great Flood."

"You can't be."

"I am. Edmond came to visit me. He spoke to me through my baby. I decided to come to the future with him."

"Where's your baby?"

Bertram heard a sigh.

"I never knew him. I just knew Edmond. But I regret that, even though I had no choice. Life is made up of our regrets and how we face them."

"That may be true. But … no. This is just a machine."

"Yes, but I'm in the machine. I'm still alive."

"You're dead."

The voice laughed.

"That's not very nice. I'm not dead. I'm here. I just don't have a body. That doesn't make me dead."

"It does. We can't raise the dead. You're a trick, an illusion."

The voice sighed. "It really upsets me when people say that."

Bertram flinched, sorrow saturated the words and leaked into him.

"You can't feel anything, you aren't real."

"I made a difficult choice, to come here, to live like this, away from everything I knew. The worst thing people can do is deny my humanity. Your confusion doesn't make me any less of a person."

Bertram blinked. "I apologise," he said. The words escaped involuntarily. Shame and confusion controlled him in equal measure.

"It's OK. It's hard to understand," she said.

"Yes."

Bertram paused while he gave a name to what he felt. Empathy.

"It is difficult to leave your home," he said.

"Yes," the voice said, sighing, "but I wasn't welcome there anymore. They didn't believe Edmond was from the future."

"Are you happy you're here?"

Silence. Bertram thought he heard breathing but couldn't tell whether it was his own or someone else's.

"Yes," the voice said, "it was the right thing to do. I had to follow my baby."

Bertram's mind reeled.

"Can you find another woman for me?" Bertram said.

"Which woman?"

"She died, twenty years ago. Probably."

"I don't know. You'll have to ask Edmond. But it depends if she left enough of herself in the data. Did she leave records?"

"I don't know. I barely knew her. But I need to find her."

"I can't help you. Sorry—you'll have to ask the others."

"I don't know what to say anymore. Can I go now?" Bertram said.

"Of course. I hope we'll speak again. It's nice to speak to someone new."

Bertram grappled with the machine on his head, and pulled at the wires. Edmond and the woman helped him. When they had finished, he slumped back against the cushions.

The woman left, and Edmond sat very still.

"I know it sounds strange. We contacted her, and I spoke to her through her child. It was hard work, but it's my most precious memory. No one gets to remember the love a mother has for her newborn baby, or to know the great cost it imposes. I couldn't leave her behind, knowing what was coming."

"I lost my mother, but some essence of her stays with me," Bertram said. "That's who I need to find, but I wasn't expecting machines, and people from the old days."

"Your mother?"

"My parents died, and I was found. Living in ruin, on my own. My parents were loyal to New Britain. But whenever I think of her my mind is filled with peace. And. And, something else that I don't have a word for. I want to find her. Can you do that?"

Edmond frowned. "I don't know. We find people through their data. There isn't much left from the end of New Britain. Laura has been invaluable in reconstructing the data from her time."

Bertram's mind was blank. He thought a better student would have known what to ask. But his mind babbled incoherently.

"Can you bring anyone to life like this? If I tell you a person's name, can you bring them into the machine?"

"No, it doesn't work like that."

Bertram blushed, and looked away.

"Our history is so much more than this though," Edmond said. "Historians are supposed to work out what made things as they are and, by implication, what would have needed to be different to change the course of events."

"I don't think I can believe you about that," Bertram said.

Edmond shrugged. "Perhaps if you stay with us for some time, you'll begin to see."

"But you haven't changed anything. The course of history is the same," Bertram said.

"There's the thing. We have affected things. Laura took actions we think are important. We haven't affected enough people yet. But we will."

Bertram blinked. "How many do you need?"

"We don't know, but we'll continue with our work. It's difficult because we can only affect those whose minds are already in the data, so we can only go back to the years shortly before the Great Flood. If we could go back further, we might affect more things. But we work with what we have."

"You really think you can change the past?"

"I have faith that one day we will."

Bertram turned away to examine the cushion next to him.

"We will talk more later. You're most welcome, so please make yourself at home," Edmond said.

Bertram watched him walking out through one of the doors. Once it closed, he felt as if he'd been asleep, or in a waking dream. The smell of the honey bread invaded his nose. How hadn't he smelt it before? He picked up the biggest bit.

The honey exploded in his mouth; the sugar raced through his body, awakening it, filling it with life. He chewed, and swallowed, and reached for another. He put this in his mouth with his eyes closed and felt honey running down his chin.

"Brother Bertram?"

Bertram hid his face in the sleeve of his tunic and wiped the honey off. He coughed, trying to swallow the sticky lump as quickly as possible. He looked up. Annabelle stood next to him, her face a mask.

"Annabelle. I didn't hear you. Apologies."

"The honey is delicious this year. Would you like to meet the bees?" she said.

Bertram stood up. "Please give me a few moments."

He turned away from her and walked back to his pod.

Bertram sat on his mat and tried to summon up the willpower to get up. He failed. The sun fell onto the floor of his pod in a thick column. The dust and sand in the air twirled through it like dancers. The sandstone walls of his pod seemed light and open, compared to the silver lining of the pods at home. He felt like he might be joined to the sky above.

A knock at the door made him jump.

"Bertram. Will you visit the bees with me now?" Annabelle said, tripping over the words. Bertram thought she pretended to be cheerful, and that he could see tension in her clasped hands.

"Yes. Please. That would be most interesting," Bertram said.

Annabelle led him towards the main door. Bertram took his muslin off the hook where he'd hung it the previous night. He ran his fingers over the material.

"It's been washed," he said.

"Of course. It was disgusting." Annabelle wrapped herself up and pointed towards the door. "Are you ready? It looks very different today."

Bertram followed her out. A blanket of soft blue sky nestled into the undulating red sand. He stopped and breathed in the air. It tasted acrid, like burned food.

"The bees are round the back," Annabelle said.

Bertram followed her around the edge of the pod. He could see, now, where the other doors led. The pod looked like a spider, burying itself in the ground. Annabelle led him to a large rectangular hole dug into the ground, with pre-Revolutionary materials holding up the sides—scavenged plastic, bits of ancient furniture. She led him down steps to the floor.

"The people who lived here before made their own micro-climate," she said. "Look," she knelt down, "we can grow things in the shadow of the walls. As the sun moves, the shadow moves, and everything gets enough shade."

"Ingenious," Bertram said, "but how long did it take to dig such a gigantic hole?"

"No one knows. We didn't dig it. We just spotted plants growing down here when nothing grows up there."

"And water?"

"We collect all the water we use from our pod and get it here with pipes. It leaks into the ground."

"But where does the water come from for your pod? I haven't seen storage tanks."

Annabelle frowned. "From the sea, of course."

"The sea?"

"Yes, over there." Annabelle waved her hand in a vaguely souther-ly direction.

"I didn't know the sea was here," Bertram said. He craned his neck as if he might be able to see over the huge wall.

"I'll show you, if you want?"

"Yes. I've often read about the sea."

"Well, see the bees first. That's what we came for."

Bertram introduced himself to the bees, although his impatience to see the sea had dampened his enthusiasm. They seemed content in their clay hives. Their intense murmuring enveloped him, speak-ing a language that felt within reach, if he only concentrated more.

Annabelle led him down the path to the sea. For most of the walk Bertram thought that perhaps she was lying. She led him up a steep sandy slope that shifted and swallowed him with every step. He sank onto all fours, gasping for breath through his muslin.

When he had gathered his breath, he looked up.

A living thing pulsed and swelled and oozed in front of him. Light skimmed off its surface, glinting at times and hurting his eyes. It roared gently as it moved towards him.

"That's the sea," Annabelle said.

"That's the sea," Bertram repeated. He sat unmoving, afraid it might escape.

"That's where we get water. There's a pipe from here. We take the salt out and flavour it."

"It's beautiful," Bertram said.

"It's beautiful today. It's terrible sometimes. It charges and crashes like it wants to kill us. I hear it at night, sometimes, and it keeps me awake."

"Have the fish returned here yet?"

"Sometimes, but it's dangerous here. There are rocks, and boats get pulled out. We get fish from further down the coast."

Bertram watched Annabelle's brown eyes, working out where her nose was from the bumps in the cloth over her face. Sand trick-led down from the hollows their bodies made in the sand. He willed her not to move, to stop the tick of time, to imprint his brain with the feeling of this moment.

"Do you want to touch it?" Annabelle said.

"The sea?"

"Come on."

He slid down the slope and landed on his knees again. Annabelle pulled her gloves off and planted her hand in the sea. Bertram copied her, flinching as the water ran over his fingers.

"It's as cold as refrigerated water," he said.

Annabelle sat down next to him.

"I understand what you experienced with Edmond must have been difficult," she said.

Bertram watched the light catching on the waves.

"We didn't think he was going to tell you everything he did. He took a risk. And now we're in your hands."

Bertram turned away from her.

He felt her hand on his shoulder.

"Your community told you things about us that are wrong. But I think you'll be able to understand. Give us time." Annabelle buried her hand in the sand and watched it swallowing her fingers. "I know something about growing up in places like you did."

Bertram turned back to look at her.

"What do you know?"

"I was an orphan child. I grew up like you, in a community. It becomes your life. But there's so much more. It's like being born, when you leave."

"When did you leave?"

"Five years ago. One of my teachers came to join the Historians and I came with her. She was the person I loved most in all the world. I couldn't let her leave me."

"Do you miss your community?"

"No. Life is so constrained there. Relationships so prescribed. There's freedom outside."

"Yes. I never felt quite understood. But now I'm no longer there, I feel cut adrift," Bertram said.

Annabelle put both her hands on his shoulders and looked into his eyes.

"Some people like to live life to some else's rhythm. Some of us don't. It feels strange when you first escape, but you get used to it. I hope Edmond was right to trust you."

Bertram felt her hands sinking into his shoulders, holding him steady. He didn't want to move.

Annabelle let go. She scooped up some water in her hands and threw it at him.

She ran through the sea, her limbs light and uncontrolled like those of a child.

Bertram felt calm. Watching her bound him to this place. He forgot his worries about his visit. The longing for familiar sights subsided.

He wanted to stay longer, but Annabelle began walking back the way they'd come.

"What do you do here?" he said on the way back.

"What do you mean?"

"Are you paid to work here? Or, or do you live here?"

"I work here. Everyone needs to contribute, just like at your home."

"Do you believe they contact people in the past?" Bertram said.

"Yes," Annabelle said.

"But how can it be true?"

"Because I've become other people, too. Edmond makes it sound easy, but it's not. Only some minds are open. But it's true; you'll see for yourself."

"You're a Historian?"

"Of course I'm a Historian. We all are. What did you think my work was? A servant, an assistant, a cleaner?"

Bertram walked purposefully on, his cheeks reddening. He looked away. "I assumed nothing."

"Brother Bertram. You assumed everything. Just because I showed you in and got you food. If you'd arrived tomorrow, Edmond would've done it."

"Surely not," Bertram said.

"Surely so. No one wants to cook, or fix the air conditioning, or clean up after the sheep. So, we all take turns."

"There's no hierarchy of tasks?"

"Hierarchy. No."

Bertram thought of his Master corralling the children, and laughed.

"It's not funny. Laura believes very strongly in sharing. She lived in a time when it didn't happen so well."

Bertram felt like someone had shaken his brain and left it aching.

"You speak of her as if she's a person."

"She is a person."

They walked in silence for a while.

"I think you should join us later. You might understand better," Annabelle said.

"My task is to join you in everything."

"I know. We all know why you're here."

Annabelle led him back past the herd of sheep sheltering behind a makeshift wall and a canopy of muslin. A man had an animal clamped between his knees. He held its back leg gently in his hand. Annabelle waved.

"Not got another stone in her foot, has she?"

The man looked up for a moment. "Unbelievable. Don't know what she does," the man said.

Annabelle frowned.

"Come on," she said to Bertram, "you'll meet everyone later."

As they skirted around the walls of the sunken garden, he spotted the bent backs of more people, raking at the ground and picking fruit off plants.

Bertram dragged his feet in the sand. It took Annabelle some time to realise that he'd dropped behind.

"Keep up," she said.

Bertram stopped, and leant against the wall of the pod. The smooth sandstone warmed his arm. He felt the heat sinking through him.

"Why do you believe?" he said.

Annabelle turned and moved into the shade. She looked out into the distance.

"I understand it must be difficult for you," she said.

"I don't know whether it's difficult, or whether there actually is anything to understand."

Annabelle sighed and loosened her muslin.

"It's hard to explain."

Bertram scratched his head.

"Do you really believe Laura is … that Laura was …" Bertram tried to look into Annabelle's eyes, but they were hidden in her muslin and gazing away from him.

"It can't really be true that Edmond was a baby. There's no one less like a baby."

Annabelle laughed. She covered her mouth with her hand and stumbled towards Bertram. She put a hand on his shoulder and shook him gently.

"Of course, I believe it. But it sounds mad the way you say it."

Annabelle's arm crept around his elbow and she led him along the edge of the building, her steps slow and purposeful.

"It's like this. People used to write everything down. They stored it. They saved it so their whole self was in their data. And when we have that data, we can reconstruct the data person."

Bertram sighed, and looked at her like he looked at his class. "But that's not the real person. It's just the record of them."

"Yes, mostly, but sometimes it is. Sometimes it is their real mind. Left behind. We convert our minds into data, too. And when we manage to talk to that mind, we can travel to the past."

"How?"

Exasperation flickered in her eyes. She began to let go of his arm, but Bertram gently clamped her hand in place. He found himself wishing they were inside so that he might see her skin.

"Edmond must have told you about that? With the machine? It makes particles that travel faster than light. When you travel that fast you unwind time. So, we send our minds back. But it needs that connection to work. A pull from another mind. It only happens with people whose minds became detached somehow. Often they were sick."

"And Laura?"

"She's the one who made us realise that. Her mind was broken. That's why it worked with her."

"Yes, but he said he was her baby, and that she came back with him."

"There are very few of us who can do that. Most of us just manage to contact people. Edmond managed it, but we've never done it again. We're not sure it's right to bring people with us."

"And she just appeared?"

"Yes. We stored her in a machine. Like the ones we use to transfer our minds in," Annabelle said.

"And where is this machine? This machine that lets you travel."

Annabelle pointed at the ground. "It's under there. We built it a chamber. It needs not to be disturbed, by light, or sound, or too much heat."

Annabelle leant in close to Bertram and spoke quietly into his ear.

"I don't think he liked being a baby. Can you imagine? Feeling and remembering all the things a mother does for you?"

"No. It would be strange." Bertram coughed, thinking that it might be the nicest thing in the world.

"But Laura was important. Many strands of history met at her. We had to try."

"Strands of history?" Bertram said.

"She was married to someone who came to control a big energy company. He had power over the government. Her life was close to many people who had the power to change things."

"So, Edmond tried to contact her?"

"Not just Edmond. Another Historian became her friend."

"How?"

"She went back, and made Laura see her as a person. She was the only one to manage that. Although Laura says she seemed very odd. Not quite real."

"And what did she want to change?"

"If they hadn't eaten mammals. It wasn't like farming now. If they'd used less energy, and got used to monitoring it in a healthy way. If they'd planned for rain, and floods, and heat. They knew their climate was becoming more extreme, but they didn't spot the pattern—they thought too much about warming. They did too little, too late. Imagine … imagine if they'd protected people earlier. If they'd had the tools New Britain used to tyrannise them, *before* New Britain came to power, used them on their own terms. If they had prepared for the flood. They might not have been so abused. It wouldn't have gone so badly wrong."

"And you really think you can do this?"

"Yes. And I'll spend my life trying. If I can't do it, maybe the ones who come after us will do it."

Bertram sighed. "It's a noble cause, the way you describe it. But you do realise that to talk of contacting people after they're dead is forbidden. It's heresy."

"Yes, but it is a noble cause. Brother, you take care of people today, we try to take care of those in the past so those today might live better. It shouldn't be forbidden."

They had arrived at the entrance. Annabelle scanned her wrist and the door opened. Bertram watched her taking her gloves off and unwinding her muslin. She hung it on a peg. Her lips hesitated as if she were deciding whether to smile. Bertram hung his muslin on the peg next to hers and tried to catch her eye.

"I will try to understand," he said.

"I know."

Her smile burst out like a flower in spring.

"I look forward to showing you," she said.

She held his hand for a moment.

"I understand why it's hard to take in."

Bertram closed his fingers around hers.

Once back in the main pod, Annabelle left him alone. Bertram sat in his room, the silence of it heavy in his ears. His breath seemed to bounce off the walls and return to him, whispering words he couldn't catch. The last time he'd been really alone had been … he looked at his hands in his lap. They had been so much smaller then, with dirty nails and smudges on the palms. He followed the trails of his veins through his wrist and sighed. It whistled around the room like wind. Bertram hummed quietly, but the sound clashed in his brain. This was a place for solitude, not singing.

He closed his eyes and replayed excited shouts, and smelt the sweet, dirty smell of children back from work. For the first time the failure of his project no longer weighed him down. But as soon as he thought of it, the words he'd written spun around his mind. No one would read them now. He would never finish his writing, and no one would ever care about the history and development of education. He shook his head and picked up his tablet. His Master hadn't communicated yet. He began to write to him.

> *I have been inclined towards melancholy since my arrival. My home is written in every particle of my body, and without it, I am empty. I hope to return soon. I have spoken to Edmond. They have sent a female to distract me, but I remain focused on my task. They can't explain what they do, and I think they delude themselves about contacting people who have died. They appear to be motivated by good intentions. I will discover if there is actual heresy here.*

Bertram read the message. Would it do? He closed his eyes and saw Annabelle's smile. His arm still felt the pressure of her hand. He winced at the shameful way he'd described her. But she would never know. But this was the message he knew he should send, and so he sent it.

The knock on his door almost seemed to rattle the walls. He leapt up.

"Come and eat." It wasn't Annabelle's voice, this time.

Bertram adjusted his tunic and walked into the communal room. He paused on the threshold, hiding his hands behind his back. He clenched his fists and rocked back and forth a few times. He took a breath in before he walked towards the group. The communal room seemed almost cheerful; eight people lounged on the central cushions, their limbs dangling lazily towards each other. Bertram lowered his eyes as he approached.

"Thank you for welcoming me into your community," he said.

"Welcome Bertram," one of the men said. "We don't have many visitors. Sit down."

Bertram sat down, leaving a space on his left. Another man walked in with a tray of bowls. Bertram took one and waited for the others. After the usual prayer, which showed that they had not moved so far away from the Brothers, they began to eat.

One of the doors flung open and Annabelle scampered towards them. She gathered her tunic in her hand and looked for a space to sit. Bertram moved closer to the man next to him without looking up. Annabelle saw the gap and sank into it.

"I apologise. I had an urgent message," she said.

Edmond stopped eating and looked at her.

"The data I requested. From the French Central Collection. They sent it," she said.

Edmond's face relaxed. "And can we use it?"

Annabelle shrugged. She picked up a bowl and hastily murmured the shortened prayer. She put a spoonful of stew in her mouth and swallowed.

"Yes. I think we can. It will need some cleaning. But yes."

Annabelle reached over to Edmond and placed her hand on his back.

"Don't worry. We'll solve this problem like all the others. Leave it with me," she said.

Edmond smiled.

"Thank you. I know."

Bertram no longer felt hungry. He wanted to pull Annabelle away from Edmond, get in between their smiles. As she moved into her place her hair fell across her face and swirled on her arm. Bertram watched the shadows it made on her skin.

A while later they all sat in one of the other rooms. Again, in a circle, but each with a large tablet on their laps, and wearing the metal upturned bowls on their heads. Unlike the one he'd worn earlier, these had more attachments. Thick wires ran from each of them through the floor. Bertram fumbled with the equipment. A metal plate had folded his ear over, squashing it against his head.

Someone helped him. The screen fitted over his eyes, blocking out the real world, and the side panels covered his ears. They connected a tablet to a communicator.

"So, sit back and relax. The tablet has all the data on a life we think is important. Watch, and listen, and let the data flow around you. Let it become you. Let it speak to you."

Bertram fumbled with the hem of his tunic, pulling it over his feet. What would his Master say? A child's game. A waste of time for a serious seeker of knowledge.

The screen glowed.

Bertram gasped.

A man's laughing face winked at him.

Brown hair, medium build, looking for someone who likes cycling and beaches.

I'm not sure this marketing plan is going to work …

Here's me on the final section of the marathon. Knackered but happy.

Anyone up for drinks on Friday?

Have you seen this video? Crazy.

Kate, seriously, you're not worried by this rain?

"Relax. You can't read all of it. Merge with it. Let it become you."

Bertram gripped the edge of his cushion. Words rushed past him. Lights blinked and swirled. Voices burst through his ears like shouting in a storm.

"Get it off," he said.

Someone put a hand on his shoulder.

"It's OK. Relax."

The screen blazed with colour. So much colour that it drowned and disoriented. So many words and thoughts and views. It smothered him. He struggled to keep breathing through it. His eyes burned with the light. His mind leapt, untethered, from one thing to the next. Cycling? Knackered? Before he could pause to decipher it, something else appeared. He clutched at one thing, then the next, like falling through a collapsing building.

"He's in there. He's in his data. Be him; be his world."

Bertram raised his hands to his head but couldn't touch it through all the equipment. His fingers scrabbled at the wires and metal plates until someone pulled his hands away and placed them at his sides. Someone held his shoulders and forced him back against the pillows. As his back touched them, he felt as if he were falling.

His stomach convulsed and he gasped.

"Breathe. Breathe slowly. In and out, that's it."

Bertram didn't know whether the voice came from the machine or from outside. He buried his fingers in the mat on the floor. Three of his nails ripped. He shook his head from side to side, but the machine amplified his movement and he swayed uncontrollably through swirling, blurred shapes.

The man's face swooped past him. Then a woman. Their clothes were tight and colourful. Their faces open and uncovered, even outside. The voices started again, coming from inside his head. He closed his eyes, but the faces still circled him.

Are you picking up the kids?

I don't see why I can't get paid more than that.

Date this Friday?

Bertram felt his mind ripping apart. One half attached itself to the words he knew he didn't know but could somehow feel the meaning of; the other half tried to stay his, and remain apart. He tried to pause, to think, to make order from the chaos, but whenever he did, the dizziness returned. So, he rushed along with it.

His fingers tingled. He could no longer sense the floor, or the cushions, or the air around him. He fell through the tunnel of noise and pictures.

The man seemed to lead him on, from above, as if Bertram were a child. He felt his hand being held.

If you stop whinging, I'll get you an ice cream. OK?

And then Bertram was at eye level with him.

I thought we'd agreed you wouldn't talk to him?

The man's face peered into his. Bertram flinched. An unfamiliar smell, sharp yet smooth, enveloped him.

What the hell were you thinking, hey?

Bertram clenched his fists. His broken nails cut into his palms.

Well?

"Leave me alone," Bertram said.

The man's eyes focused anew, as if he'd noticed him for the first time. They bounced around his face. Bertram felt the wind of his breath.

"What?"

"I don't know anything," Bertram said.

"I know you spoke to him this morning," the man said.

Bertram felt himself falling. Thoughts turned to pain behind his eyes. The part of his brain that he'd left behind screamed at him. The sound lost itself in the tangled mess of images, but it reached him as a whisper.

Bertram pulled at the headset, tangled his fingers in wires.

"Get it off. Get it off now."

The man's face blurred into the distance, a perplexed frown on his face.

Someone helped Bertram take off the headset.

Bertram slumped on the mat. He closed his eyes and tried to breathe normally. He covered his ears with his hands and shook his head.

"I think he made contact!"

"On his first attempt?"

"Brother Bertram. You're a natural."

"Have some water. You might feel nauseous for a while."

Bertram didn't want to move. He listened to the voices around him, focusing on each one, assuring himself that they were real. He felt the warm air, listened to the hum of the air conditioning, and smelt the salt and the sand. He touched his hair, and the mat, and his skin. Someone cleaned his fingers and wrapped tape around them. Then they left him alone.

Bertram lay on the mat for some time, moving one part of his body at a time, waiting for the nausea and the pain behind his eyes to stop. He rolled over and drank the water. They must have been listening, because as soon as he sat up, Edmond walked in.

Edmond watched him. Bertram looked away. He began sentences in his head and left them dangling. *These moments never arrive when we're ready for them,* he thought. His future taunted him. 'What did he say?' they would ask, and his words would follow him, either holding him aloft, or burying him.

Edmond waited.

"What happened to me?" Bertram said.

"I don't know. Everyone's experience is theirs alone."

"But you must know something."

"It seemed as if you made contact. We heard you speak. Was that it?"

"Who was that man?"

"One of the ones we think was important. We didn't expect you to get through on your first attempt. It seems you have talent, Brother Bertram."

"But how?" Bertram raised his hands and let them fall to his sides. "What?" Blood rushed to his cheeks. He looked away.

"I thought he spoke to me," Bertram said.

"I apologise. That must have been disorientating. As I said, we didn't expect you to do that. Normally, we have a script."

"A script?"

"Based on our analysis of the possible paths time could have taken, we have things to say to people who can change how things were."

Bertram nodded, not because he agreed, but because he had no idea what else to do.

"Who do you talk to?"

Edmond frowned. He examined Bertram's face, as if reading it. "I'm working in a more recent world," he said.

"Yes?"

Bertram scarcely cared what he might say. His eyes felt heavy, his body strung out like after a day picking protein pods.

"I'm trying to retrace the steps of the Revolution. We are struggling to change the far past, so perhaps we can make the near past have happened sooner."

Bertram frowned, struggling to make the words stick together coherently.

"The near past?" Bertram said.

"Yes. If the Revolution had happened sooner, the present would be better."

"Oh."

"Have I lost you, Brother Bertram?" Edmond said. Edmond smiled the smile of a patient teacher with an obstinate child. "I have also begun searching for your mother."

Bertram froze, afraid of looking at Edmond.

"I thought … You said … I didn't think you could."

"I don't know that we can. But we will try."

"Thank you," Bertram said, but his thanks was insincere. This was what he'd come for, after all. But his need had made him naked in front of this man; a child again.

Edmond coughed and smiled.

"Unfortunately, I keep stumbling against a bigger problem."

"What problem?" Bertram said.

"Something doesn't hang together with the one we call Evie," Edmond said.

Bertram blinked. His body tensed. Energy rushed through him.

"Edmond. What are you saying? You should be careful with what you're saying."

The corner of Edmond's mouth twitched.

"I am being careful. I could say more. I am failing to connect the past to the present, where it joins at Evie."

"Perhaps there's a problem with your data." Bertram stared into Edmond's eyes.

"We do have problems with the data, but this is a different thing."

"What sort of thing?"

"I can find no history leading to her martyrdom."

Edmond sat in silence, watching the phrases weaving their way through Bertram's brain. Bertram stared at the floor, fumbling again for the necessary words. *No history of her martyrdom? No history?*

"But she was a martyr. Why do you think there's no history?" Bertram said.

"She was a martyr. I don't deny that. She made the ultimate sacrifice. But why is there nothing from her before? No sign of rebellion, no hint of what was to come. She just appeared in the desert, as if from nowhere. No history. And no one asked."

"Their minds were on bigger things," Bertram said.

"Brother Bertram. You and the Brothers have never paid enough attention to people. Real people. If you found a woman in the desert, would you not ask her where she came from? They must have known," Edmond said.

Bertram frowned. "I have always been interested in people. That is the great difference between the Brothers and me. Perhaps they didn't record it. What we think important might not have seemed important then. It was a different time."

"Why is there no record of the letter? Did she show it to no one? Why didn't she begin the Revolution earlier? Rather than as she was dying?"

"It took a supreme act of courage. Perhaps she didn't dare. And she needed the Religious communities to start it."

"You Brothers have an unparalleled sense of your own importance. If it had been known earlier, the Revolution would have happened sooner, with or without the Religious communities."

Edmond stared at Bertram, waiting for him to react.

"What are you saying?" Bertram said. "My interest is in education, and in finding my mother. But you must know my vows oblige me to report heresy. Please be careful what you say, because I don't want to have to do … those things." Bertram opened and closed his mouth. He lifted his hands and let them fall.

"I know that. But I think you're more than your vows, Bertram."

"You're right to criticise, but the Brothers do much good. We take care of children and we devote our lives to learning, so we can all live better."

Edmond shrugged.

"You spoke to me about evidence. I follow evidence. I am telling you about my evidence."

"What you see in those machines isn't evidence. You're deluding yourselves."

"What is evidence then?"

"Visiting the sacred places. Reading about her work … and what people said about her."

"But she's a mystery to us. She appeared as if from nowhere. And I can't trace her in the data. She should be in the data."

Bertram shrugged. His lips quivered.

"I will disprove you," he said.

Edmond smiled.

"You can try."

Bertram stood up and wobbled. He tried to disguise the weakness in his legs by holding onto a cushion.

He sat in his room and read the message from his Master.

> *Brother Bertram, this is a task that seems to suit you. Once there is enough evidence we will move quickly. You must beware of the woman—they are trying to distract and confuse you. But you have done well. Even your suspicion is enough. I will send in the Enforcers. Please wait there until they arrive.*

Bertram's fingers shook. He put his tablet face down on his mat. He had voiced no suspicion. He read his previous message. Where was his suspicion? His Master had needed nothing from him but his presence here. Just that was enough. But then what of his plans?

The image of Annabelle, the distraction, smiled at him. He closed his eyes and listened to his breathing. His mind refused to focus; it leaped around, not attaching to any thought. He tried to control it, but it seemed afraid to form the thoughts Bertram wanted it to think. They had deceived him with that machine, made him dream, or see visions.

The room seemed calm—but if he wrote, the world would burst through the walls, smash this place into the desert. All traces of these people and their work would be gone.

Bertram picked up his tablet. He must delay.

Wait, he wrote, *there is something worse. We must tread carefully. It is not my place to decide what to do, but there is perhaps a greater heresy here. They question that Evie is a Prophet. I fear for the Amalgamation if this isn't disproved. We must disprove it, or it will spread and grow, and will threaten our faith. We can't just eradicate them without proving that they are wrong. They should be publicly refuted, to make sure it doesn't spread. That is my advice but tell me what you want me to do.*

He typed and retyped the message before sending it. He knew he could find Evie. He would find the origin of the Revolution, and he would expose Edmond as the fantasist he really was. That would be a project to be proud of. Perhaps, with evidence, Annabelle might be saved. But not Edmond. Bertram paused. Edmond. He had no distinct idea of his character, or his thoughts. He was a cypher, an image with no depth. Indistinct, and yet able to burrow into his mind and read his thoughts. Bertram's hand formed a fist.

His Master's reply came quickly. Bertram should go, and find evidence, he said. So, Bertram ordered a transport.

The following morning Annabelle took his empty bowl from him.

"I'm sorry to see you go. I liked having you as our guest," she said.

"I have something I need to do. But I will come back and see you."

He held out his hand to her and she pressed her palm into his.

Anabelle met Edmond in his room and sat on his mat. Edmond stared out of the window with his hands behind his back.

"You took a great risk," she said.

Edmond didn't move. His eyes focussed on the clouds outside.

"We've been talking. We all think you took too much risk."

Edmond turned around slowly and looked at Anabelle.

"We all decided that we had no option," Edmond said.

"No, Edmond. We all decided that we had to show him what we do. That doesn't mean you had to tell him everything. We could all—" Anabelle's body shook and she hugged her knees.

Edmond sighed. "I know what could happen to us. That's what I'm trying to prevent."

"Then why?"

"Belle." Edmond smiled and held his hand out to her. "When I saw him, he wasn't what I was expecting. When I spoke to him, he gave me an idea."

"All he has to tell them is that we contact people who are dead."

"But he wants us to contact the dead. He longs for his mother. He won't want us destroyed while that is possible."

Anabelle frowned. "You really think he'll put that ahead of his duty?"

"It's the best strategy we have. To align his interests with ours."

"And the idiotic search for Evie?"

Edmond laughed. "Idiotic?"

Anabelle put her head in her hands. "What good can possibly come of that? It's best left alone. You should have kept him here if you wanted to manipulate him."

"No, Belle. You're too cautious. When you fear attack, your best option is to prepare to attack first. When they do come for us, we will bring them down too. No one would ever believe the truth if we say it. But if it comes from one of their own …"

Anabelle stood up. "You're going to have to justify it tonight. For all of us. We don't like being at the mercy of your grand plans after we'd all decided on a strategy together."

Edmond nodded. He reached for Anabelle's hand as she turned and left his room, but she moved too quickly.

Chapter 4

BERTRAM ASKED THE DRIVER TO halt. He wiped the surface of his tablet with his arm and propped it up against the window. He and the driver peered at it.

"I'm not sure this is the way, Brother," the driver said.

Bertram blinked into the distance.

"A few miles more. It says there's a village here."

The driver shrugged.

"I'd rather not spend another night in the back, if that's alright with you. If we go much further, we can't get back before dark."

Bertram sighed. "I'd rather not, too. But it must be here. And it might be more comfortable than an outpost."

The driver whirred the engine back into action and guided the transport over the lumpy, sandy track. Bertram watched every bump ahead of them, willing it to be the village. Sand swirled in the distance, obscuring the horizon. He blinked, lurched and nudged the driver's arm.

"Look. Look. I saw something."

The driver shrugged.

"Really. Look. Something glinted."

The driver shrugged, and kept his eyes on the track ahead. The engine throbbed. They had been sitting there so long that their bodies had become attuned to it; it had become their pulse. Bertram's eyes remained fixed on the small patch in the distance where he'd seen something. The cabin smelt of oil and grease, and Bertram swallowed to control the nausea. The driver peered through narrowed eyes and the transport struggled through a patch of loose sand. The engine whirred and spluttered in protest.

"You're right," the driver said. "There is something there."

He forced the transport on, increasing its speed and bumping it along.

After another hour, they arrived. Bertram wrapped his muslin around his face and jumped down. His legs almost gave way. He hung onto the door and pulled himself upright. He approached the door of the pod eagerly. Someone opened the viewing hatch. A wrinkled eye peered out.

The door opened.

A very old man beckoned them in.

"We haven't seen a Brother for many years," he said.

"Blessings. Thank you for your welcome. May we claim the hospitality of strangers?" Bertram said.

"We have food to contribute," the driver said.

The man nodded.

"You may stay, for one night. We are unused to strangers, but your food will be welcome."

He led them into a communal pod that served as dormitory and eating area all in one. An old woman stirred a pot on a cooker opposite them. Bertram heard his driver sigh and knew that he'd been hoping for better.

The pod was poorly lit—a light hung from the centre of the roof, lighting the seating area. The air weighed on his shoulders and smelt thick with something Bertram didn't recognise. The edges of the pod were dark. Bertram peered into the darkness. He thought more figures moved on the mats. The driver gave the woman the food, which she smelt, and inspected questioningly. Bertram watched her hesitate, frowning at the driver. Then her face exploded in a smile.

"Is this honey?" she said.

The driver nodded.

"Real honey?"

The driver shrugged.

"I'll bake bread balls. We have honey!" Bertram watched the sleeping mats come to life. Three people sat up.

"Yes. Really. Make these people welcome. They've brought honey."

The old man rolled out sleeping mats and moved them in close to the air conditioner. He smiled at Bertram.

"You really are welcome."

The three others moved into the centre of the pod.

Bertram gasped, and then controlled himself. The driver busied himself with his sleeping mat, taking out his tablet and arranging his spare clothes at one end. He held his hands out in the stream of cold air, and avoided looking up.

Bertram stepped forward, unsure of whether to help. They didn't seem to want help. They leant on each other, and moved as one. A shifting, straggling shape with immobile limbs and scorched faces. They sat on the central mats.

Bertram lowered his eyes.

"Thank you for your hospitality," he said.

The old man sat down next to him.

"May I know your history?" Bertram said.

"We are grateful for your food, and will give you the hospitality of strangers, but we don't need converting."

Bertram coughed. Perhaps they should have turned back. But they couldn't leave now.

"I'm not here to convert anyone," he said.

The old man grunted. Bertram avoided looking at the others. He thought one might be female, but he wasn't sure.

"What are you here for then?" one of the others asked. His voice rasped, as if his throat were charred.

Bertram looked at him, and tried to focus on his eyes, rather than the melted face.

"I'm undertaking my final project. I'm trying to find out about the beginning of the Revolution." It wasn't entirely a lie, but Bertram's voice wavered with the dishonesty.

"Here?" the old man said. "Don't you stay in your pods, and eat yourselves fat, and steal children to work for you, and do your thinking there?"

Bertram cleared his throat. "No. That's not quite right."

The warm air weighed him down.

"The Revolution started in a Religious community near here. I'm trying to find where Evie appeared," Bertram said. He waited for his words to settle. His eyes traced the edge of his tunic.

"Do you know what we are?" one of the people said.

Bertram looked up again. "I can guess what you are. Senior officials in New Britain; only they have the resources to last this long. I'm grateful for your hospitality. We bear you no ill will, and …" Bertram wished he hadn't brought the driver. "I think that any harm done to a human being is a harm that should not be done. I have never agreed with …" He paused again. "I don't think they should have done that to you. Or to anyone else."

He listened to the driver still rearranging his belongings. The old man seemed to relax.

"Thank you. Then we can eat in peace," one of the others said.

"I'll eat in peace with anyone who brings honey," the old woman said.

Sometime later, they ate. Bertram calculated that the food they'd have eaten without their contribution would have been very little indeed.

"How do you live, out here?"

"We manage," the woman said.

"How long have you lived here?"

"Since the revolt," the old man said.

"It was Revolution, not revolt," the driver said. "Still waiting for the glorious return of New Britain?"

Bertram glared at him. "These people have given us hospitality. This is no time for quarrels."

"We may be old, and we may be broken, but we never shrink from quarrels. Especially with the Religious."

"It's right you were left out to burn. You destroyed our world and they should have left you out to die," the driver said.

"Enough." Bertram put his hand on the driver's arm. "Enough. This is an age-old quarrel and we aren't going to resolve it now."

"It's your duty to make a stand, Brother Bertram." The driver's voice dripped with malice. Bertram held out his fingers where he hoped only the driver could see. He tried to show him how out-numbered they were. Even disabled people might use weapons.

Bertram stared at him, and then at the others. "My religion is about love. These are human beings. I know it was directed, but it was wrong to cause them this much harm. We will never change minds with brutality like this." Bertram waved at the three people.

One of them could barely open their mouth and sucked at the food from their bowl. The old woman had cut it up as if for a baby.

They ate the rest of the meal in silence.

Afterwards, Bertram sat with the old couple and tried to find out about the Revolution. He asked if they knew where Evie had appeared. He asked if they knew her history.

"It was near here that she appeared. But we arrived after your Revolution. We sought out somewhere we could live in peace," the old woman said.

Bertram nodded. "It must have been a difficult time for you."

The woman laughed without joy.

"It was a difficult time."

Bertram hesitated. He should sleep, stay silent. But here was an unread book.

"What happened to you?"

The old man shuffled away, muttering to himself. The woman watched him go before replying.

"He still finds it too difficult to talk. We lived in a megadome back then. We did nothing more than obey the rules. We didn't know the Revolution had begun, until you surrounded our dome.

You stopped supplies coming in. You stopped us getting to our food. We starved. We tried to fight, but there were too many of you. And when you broke in you were monsters. The Designated Carers hid with our children. But you found them, and you dragged the children out, and you killed them. And then you killed the Carers, and then you killed all the adults who couldn't run away. Some of them you tied naked to the sand at night, and watched them burn as the sun came up. It took days for them to die. Some of them you tied to the back of transports and dragged around, others you sliced apart with wind turbine blades. Some of them you—"

"Enough," Bertram said. "That wasn't me."

"But you're one of them."

"I … I don't think that was right. It shouldn't have been done."

"It wasn't right? It was more than that, Brother. It was evil."

"It was. But New Britain killed people in the same ways, it was just hidden. No one was free. You can see why people were angry."

"I was angry. Many of us were angry. But you were murderers. New Britain only killed to keep the peace, to build a better future."

"It wasn't—"

"You. It wasn't you. And yet here you are, defending them."

"Our religion is about love. We have to build our society better this time."

"And what about all the people who died for your love?"

"I can't defend it. And I won't. I apologise for what was done to you. But …"

Bertram looked around the pod for inspiration, but found none.

The following morning, Bertram and the driver ate a hurried breakfast before getting back into the transport. The old woman followed them out.

"Will you report where we are?" she looked at Bertram.

Before the driver could speak, Bertram answered, "No. No harm will come to you because of us."

The driver's anger translated into erratic driving. He swerved and bumped the transport, turning the wheel viciously, and grinding the wheels in the sand.

"You didn't follow protocol."

"Protocol is wrong, in this case."

"We should report them."

"We should report them. But don't you think that by showing kindness they might come to realise that ours is a better way?"

The driver shrugged.

"Every community in every part of this country sends a representative to decide what happens. Every representative, every single one, voted that any supporters of New Britain must be reported. It's protocol now. You don't have a choice."

Bertram slammed his hand on the window next to him.

"Really! We still find their starving, traumatised children. Uncared for when their parents die, or are killed. Was that what the Revolution was for? Is that how we build our new society?"

The driver said nothing.

"And don't you see? They think as they do because that was what they were taught. And we think as we do because of our education. Controlling the mind of a child sets the adult on a course that cannot be changed. It's not they who are to blame."

The driver still said nothing.

Bertram watched the sand.

"There's another village in about fifty miles. We go there next. And if not there, then the next village, and the next. Someone must know something."

"And does this one have a name? Or is it another outpost of oppression?"

Bertram peered at his tablet. "It says it's called Eden."

"That sounds promising," the driver said.

Bertram let his body shake and sway with the transport. He remembered hearing the words the child, his student, had spoken. Hearing without comprehending. *We burned them.* Waves of panic fluttered in Bertram's chest. How had he never thought? The words had been empty, until now. Burning had been cooking. Burning had been stoking a furnace. He never knew that burning could be melting, and twisting, and contorting. Burning people. He stroked his cheek and felt the hairs prickling him. Burned skin would feel smooth.

We burned them.

The words had been so casual in his mouth. The thoughts attached to them just matters of fact. There had never been feelings before. Bertram began to wonder, again, about his parents. Had they been burned? He couldn't remember anything.

Three weeks after leaving Edmond, Bertram arrived in Eden.

Chapter 5

BERTRAM SAT CROSS-LEGGED IN THE doorway of his pod, staring out at the sea. His body swayed gently in time with the crashing waves. Small boats with red sails straggled into the harbour at the bottom of the cliff. He listened to the shouts of the fishermen, filled with words that were new to him. 'Come around, come around.' Bertram watched the sail jerk from left to right, the boat roll over before it righted itself. The breeze flapped the door of his pod, straining at the ties. Bertram pulled his muslin higher up his face as the heat from the settling sun soaked into his cheeks.

He nodded at the sailors as they walked past him carrying fish. Bertram smiled. In the distance he heard lessons coming to an end. The children clapped, and shouted, and ran back and forth. He knew he should offer to help, but didn't want to disturb the rhythm of the place. His limbs had relaxed into their position. For the first time since leaving home, he felt content. He had watched the children learning, and written down the stories they were told. Stories that shaped their minds, and showed them their place in their world.

One of the villagers approached him. Bertram pretended not to notice.

"Brother Bertram? The communal meal is nearly ready. Would you like to come?"

Her voice enveloped him like newly spun cloth, soft and vibrant.

"Yes. Thank you. I didn't realise how late it is."

"That's alright. You must be tired."

"Yes. But what a lovely place to rest."

He sensed hesitation.

"I've never been anywhere else. Is it?" she said.

"Yes, it is. You don't need to go anywhere else."

"My father is taking me to France. We have relatives there."

"Really? I've never been to France," Bertram said.

"It's only recently that the crossing's really been safe. We'll go after the next full moon."

Bertram followed her into the communal pod.

The group meal was extravagant compared to the food he'd shared on the way. Bertram stirred the fish, thinking of the almost empty bowls passed around elsewhere.

"Your driver wasn't staying?" the man next to him said.

Bertram scraped his spoon around the edge of his bowl.

"He had things to do. I can order another transport," Bertram said.

"You'll be lucky. It takes days."

"I can wait days."

"So, what is it exactly you're trying to do here?" A woman opposite had spoken.

Bertram's spoon screeched against the side of the bowl. He didn't look up. He chewed slowly before putting his bowl down in front of him, the edge of it lined up with the pattern on the floor mat.

"I'm trying to find out about the Revolution," he said.

"Here?" the woman said.

"Everywhere and anywhere."

"I don't think we can tell you anything," one of the villagers said.

"No one has been able to tell me anything. But I will continue to look."

"Shouldn't you be looking in the old megadomes? That's where it started."

Bertram folded his hands and placed them in his lap. He looked around the circle of villagers. They gazed back at him with the curiosity of people who have few visitors.

"I'm trying to discover the history of Evie," he said.

The villagers continued eating. A woman wiped a boy's face. One of the older girls picked up a tablet and began to read.

"Not during the communal meal," the woman next to her said.

"Mother, I was supposed to get a message this afternoon," the girl said.

"A message from Alex. A message from Alex," the boy said.

"Does he love you?" one of the other children said.

"Have you kissed him?"

"Leave me alone." The girl stood up and threw her muslin around her face. She left the communal pod, ripping the door aside as she left.

Her mother sighed.

"I apologise, Brother Bertram. Girls are very difficult at this age."

"Don't apologise. I know all about it."

"You were explaining what you want to do." The question came from someone on Bertram's left.

"Yes, I was. I'm trying to discover the history of Evie."

"What sort of history?"

"Where she came from. What good deeds she performed before her martyrdom."

"Why do you think we can help?"

Bertram smiled at the villagers, lingering over each of their faces as he looked at them in turn.

"I don't know that you can. But she was found somewhere near here, and none of the other villages I've visited know anything. I thought I might use Eden as a place to stay while I continue my investigations."

An old man coughed and scratched at his chest.

"You're welcome to stay with us, as long as you contribute fairly to our community. But you do know that we don't share your beliefs."

"I've never tried to convert non-conformists, or anyone else. I'm just trying to find information."

"'Non-conformists.' We've been called that before, but what it means to conform is always changing. We just live life in our own way and always have."

Bertram nodded.

"I understand."

* * *

Bertram held the knife firmly in his hand as he steadied himself against the wooden table. Despite his gnarled and aged fingers, Sam neatly cut between the skin and muscle, peeling the woolly hide off the carcass. Sam put the pelt to one side and passed the body over to Bertram.

Bertram sliced open the belly. The intestines spilled out. He cut them out and put them in a woven basket.

"Over there," Sam said, pointing to another table with his knife.

Bertram carried the basket across the pod, then returned to the table where he began butchering the meat.

"Your sheep are very healthy," he said.

Sam grunted, pulling free another pelt.

"I heard you ate meat, even before the Revolution," Bertram said.

"We live our own way. Always have."

"You have a pleasant life."

"We've had to protect it."

"From strangers?"

"From everyone," Sam said.

Bertram watched the stains on his own tunic spreading up his sleeves. He had a red line across his stomach where he'd been leaning against the table.

"You can go now," Sam said. "It's nearly done."

"I think I might go completely in another day or so."

"Really?"

"I've found nothing. Anywhere."

"Isn't that part of your faith? People appear from nowhere. Put here by God to do what he tells them?"

Bertram frowned and wiped his hands on his sleeves.

"Not exactly. I was hoping to find some grounding for our faith. Something to add to our story. It wasn't so long ago, after all, and we know a lot about the lives of Mohammed and Jesus."

"Perhaps what you know isn't true?" Sam said.

Bertram sighed.

"We believe it is true, even if the meaning is sometimes hard to discover. She was a real person—the letter came from her great-grandmother, so she must have a story."

Sam grunted again.

"I'm going to clean myself. I'll see you at the communal meal."

Sam nodded and focused on his work.

Bertram hesitated by the door.

"I sense fear here. But faith is supposed to comfort, to help. It doesn't try to change who you are."

Sam turned around, with a piece of bloody skin wrapped around his hand.

"It changes who you are," he said.

Bertram looked at the ground.

"It helps us to be the best we can be. That's all."

"We're already the best we can be," Sam said.

Bertram walked out of the pod and felt the heat pressing him down. The breeze smelt of salt.

* * *

Bertram welcomed the silence in his pod. The walls dampened the calls and shouts of the villagers. He closed the door, but left a small opening so he could still see people occasionally walking by. He watched his tunic swaying gently in the breeze. He reached over for his tablet. His Master asked, again, how things were going.

Much poverty remains, outside the larger communities, Bertram typed. *I have been shocked by the conditions in which people live. I had believed people live better now. There isn't enough food, nor medicine, nor education, nor happiness. We could do much good if we travelled and spread our knowledge more widely.*

I have come to a place called Eden—it is small, but well-provisioned. The people here are non-conformists, and mistrustful. But they have welcomed me, in return for labour. I do not know why I have stayed, except that the place is well-named after the villages I have passed before. I will not stay long. So far, I have discovered nothing about Evie. It does seem that she appeared from nowhere, to save us all. I will leave this place in a few days and return to the Historians. It is a tragedy that we can't disprove them. But we can't allow them to spread lies about a Prophet.

However, there is much we can learn from Eden. I have noted some ingenious solutions for desalinating water. Likewise, their water recirculation system is advanced. We could make some changes on my return that would considerably decrease our wastage. They are also skilled in cooking fish, but the women who cook guard their recipes closely. I am determined to learn their secret before I leave. The fish are spreading, year by year. Perhaps we could track this and plan a move to the coast. We might have a better life there, eventually. I sense the talk of sickness was never true—for a place ravaged by it the villagers are remarkably incapable of giving specifics.

Bertram frowned. The words about fish and farming jumped from his fingers, while those about eradication dragged. The face of Edmond dissolved into the burned faces he'd seen on the way. He tried not to think of Annabelle.

He shrugged and sent the message. His Master was so far away it scarcely seemed a real person he communicated with anymore. It was hard to think he had the power to make anything happen out here. The faces of the other Brothers blurred in his mind. He thought of them impassively. He thought more about farming, and fishing, and water reclamation these days. Perhaps he might have a future outside the community. He had never considered it before. He thought of his unsuccessful project on education without loss, as if it might have been a rehearsal, an introduction to real life.

* * *

Bertram sat in the centre of the communal pod, with his tablet on his lap. Two rows of children looked up at him expectantly. He looked at them in turn. He'd delayed the transport, again.

"And then ... she heard a noise. Behind her." He clapped his hands together and the sound bounced around the walls.

One of the little girls shrieked and buried her face in her neighbour's arm.

"Who do you think it was?" Bertram said.

"The Gramblebug. The Gramblebug."

"She turned around. Ever so slowly. Inch by inch. Peeping through her eyelashes."

The older children sat, wide-eyed; a couple of the smaller ones quivered in their places.

"And she saw her father. He'd followed her the whole time."

One of the children clapped. Another sighed with relief.

"I thought she was going to be eaten, or burned."

"Can you tell another one?"

"Go on. We have ages."

Bertram rubbed his hands on his tunic and laid his tablet down beside him.

"What do you want to hear about now?" he said.

"Where are you from and what do you do?" one of the girls said.

"What's your name?" Bertram asked the girl.

"Katie." She smiled. Her yellow hair fell around her face like the picture of an olden-day angel.

"Well, Katie, I'm a Brother. Which means I've spent my life in a faith community, learning."

"You had to learn the whole time?" Her eyes widened in horror.

Bertram laughed.

"No. Some of the time. The rest of the time we farm, and cook, and work, and look after children. Just like everyone else."

"Are they your children?"

"No. They're children we find. Who haven't any parents."

"What did they do with their parents?"

"Their parents were taken from them."

"Who takes parents? Didn't the children stop them?"

Incredulous faces stared up at him, indignant.

"Children, it's more complicated—difficult to explain. It wasn't …"

Bertram watched one of the children losing patience, and willed him to speak.

"Why are you a Brother?" the girl said.

"Because I've promised to continue the work of the Prophets," Bertram smiled again, happy to find himself back in a familiar groove.

"Who are they?"

Bertram frowned. "You don't know? Evie, for example. You've heard of her, haven't you?"

"We aren't Religious," Katie said.

"I know. But I thought you'd perhaps have heard about them, and what they taught. Even if you have no faith, their lives are examples we can all learn from."

"I've heard about Evie," one of the boys said.

Bertram looked at him calmly, and smiled.

"What do you know about her?"

The boy shrugged. "She used to live here."

Katie wrapped her arm around him and buried his face in her lap.

"Thomas always imagines things. He thinks stories are true."

"What stories have you heard about her?" Bertram said.

Hesitation flickered across Katie's face.

"She started the Revolutions, after the Religious had found her. She was a mater, or marter?" she formed the words as if they were foreign to her. But it seemed to Bertram that she acted.

Bertram watched her, keeping his face still.

"Thomas?" he asked the boy.

"She did live here," he said, voice muffled. "She did. My grand-mother told me. Evil Evie, Evil Evie, she said."

Katie wrapped her fingers around his hair and pushed his head further into her clothes. Her lips retained their smile.

"Owww. She's hurting me!"

"Please let Thomas go. He's only repeating a story. There's no harm in that, surely?" Bertram said.

Katie's hair shook, although her head barely moved. Her lips lost their colour.

"Of course. I apologise. My sibling always tells stories. I thought it would anger you."

"No. It doesn't." Bertram smiled at Thomas as his blotchy face emerged, gasping, from his sister's lap.

Bertram answered their other questions without paying attention to what they asked, or to what he said. He calculated. He saw the strings of time stretching into the future. There were many ways to get from here to there, and that which he picked made all the difference. Once the children had left, he picked up his tablet and postponed the transport. The villagers would believe it had been delayed. He sent a message to his Master that said something, while seeming to say nothing. 'Perhaps I have found something. Perhaps I have not. I will stay a while. We must refute the heresy.' he wrote, and buried it in geographical information, and advice for breeding sheep.

* * *

Bertram waited for the right time. That time was when he saw the boy, Thomas, struggling with his muslin in the morning wind. He walked over to help him, wrapping it around his neck and tying it in a knot at the back. His fingers lingered over their work.

"What was the story about Evie?" he said. "It sounded like a good story."

Thomas' eyes looked up at him from the folds of cloth.

"I made it up."

"All good stories are made up. What did you make up?"

Thomas shrugged. Bertram thought he saw fear.

"No harm will come to you from a story. I'm not going to get eaten by the Gramblebug, just because I told a story about him."

Thomas laughed.

"My grandmother did tell the story that Evie lived here. And Evie was bad. Evie was very bad. And then the villagers chased her away. And then the Revolution came."

"Oh. That's not that much of a story, is it?"

"No. I should have thought of a better one."

Someone called Thomas away, and Bertram watched him hopping around the circular stones in the middle of the village as he made his way towards a woman. Bertram lifted his arm and waved at her, making an effort to remember the shape she made as she turned away, seemingly without noticing him.

Bertram sat in the entrance to his pod, feeling the breeze cooling him. The sea crashing rhythmically soothed his mind so much that he almost fell asleep. But his mind remained alert, and worked on. 'Bad.' What might 'bad' have meant, at that time? If she'd opposed New Britain she would have been 'bad,' but not in a way that mattered. He formed a picture of her rebelling. But Eden had always non-conformed. What, then, would they have meant by 'bad'? Disagreeing with them? It seemed they never agreed with anyone about anything. Was that why she had sought out the Religious?

He reached into his pod for his tablet. He moved further inside to stop the light reflecting from its screen. He searched for records of Eden. The poor connection dragged out his search.

The record said Eden had not supported New Britain. Perhaps she had argued with them. Bertram struggled to see into the past, to form a plausible picture of what might have happened. In the absence of evidence, he stayed at sea, floating in his own images, knowing that none of them were anchored to firm ground.

Later that day Bertram waited outside Elizabeth's pod. She had smiled at him during each of the communal meals, and was, Bertram thought, related to Thomas and Katie in some sort of complicated way.

"Come in now," she said.

Bertram pulled the door aside and hesitated for a moment. She sat, cross-legged, on a blue mat and had laid out two bowls of water in front of her.

"Thank you," Bertram said. He unwound his muslin and sat down opposite her. Her hair fluttered in the breeze as the door closed again.

Elizabeth smiled again. Bertram tried to read her face. Her smile seemed detached from the worry lines that creased her skin. As if she had borrowed it.

"What do you want to speak of, then?"

Her eyes turned to him. Bertram stared at his hands, counting his fingers, and then recounting them. He picked up a bowl and sipped the water. He had thought of two beginnings, but neither felt right. He repeated them in his mind, but his lips resisted.

"I'm here to find out about Evie," he said. The words took him by surprise.

Elizabeth's mouth twitched. Her eyes glimmered momentarily.

"We don't know anything about her. Except for what we've heard."

Bertram watched the side of the pod rippling in the wind.

"I heard that she visited here," he said.

Elizabeth laughed, but the sound didn't travel. Then she paused, as if searching for words.

"Evie, the Prophet, didn't stay here. Of course, it's a common enough name."

Bertram looked up. Of course. What an assumption. But something … Elizabeth's face was a blank.

"Can you tell me about the Evie that did visit you here?"

Elizabeth frowned.

"Why do you want to know about her? I thought you wanted the other one?"

"Well,"—Bertram's heart raced—"well, sometimes history is about mistakes. It sometimes helps to know who isn't the person you're trying to find. It …" He scanned the roof of the pod. "It eliminates confusion. Otherwise, people might make the same mistake." He felt himself walking on sinking sand.

"Oh," Elizabeth said. She lifted her bowl to her mouth, with her eyes fixed on Bertram's face. She put it back down on the mat and scratched the back of her hand.

"A young woman came to stay with us. She left. I don't remember when. The Revolution started, and we forgot all but the most important things."

"Eden never supported New Britain. Is that right?"

"No. We never supported them."

"Why did the girl come?"

"I don't know," Elizabeth said. "I had my children to care for back then. I didn't pay much attention."

"Did you have many visitors?"

Elizabeth closed her eyes. "It was a different time. I try to forget. People did come from time to time."

"I thought the roads barely reached here before the Revolution. You can't have had many visitors?"

"No, we didn't have many visitors. Now I must sleep, Brother Bertram. It's been a pleasure entertaining you, but now you must go."

"I will leave you. You have a good life here. I can see why you want to defend it."

Bertram thanked her and said goodbye. He left her pod and stood at the top of the bank overlooking the sea. The children were swimming with some adult life preservers.

"You don't want to join them?"

Bertram jumped and turned around.

"Sam?" he said, peering at the eyes looking out from the muslin, and the sharp slope of the shoulders.

The man nodded.

"No. I didn't float very well last time."

"It takes practice."

"I won't be here long enough to learn," Bertram said. He thought he read a smile in Sam's eyes.

"When are you leaving us, Brother?"

"When I receive permission from my Master, and when I can persuade a transport to fetch me."

"You shouldn't have sent your driver away."

"I found him annoying," Bertram said.

Sam nodded again.

"I'm going for a swim. It helps my old bones."

"Yes." Bertram watched him turning away. "Sam?" he said.

Sam stopped without turning back.

Bertram felt braver not seeing his eyes.

"The woman called Evie who stayed here. I need to know about her."

Sam's body didn't move. Bertram looked out to sea. The children floated like crosses on the water. One of them flipped over and splashed water on the others.

"I wouldn't ask questions, Brother Bertram. None of it matters now."

Bertram clasped his hands behind his back.

"But she was just a visitor. No one of any importance. We just need to ensure no one gets confused about her, in the future."

Sam spun around, his eyes wrinkled with fury.

"Of course. No one of any importance. But no one remembers people of no importance. I can't help you."

"How did she get here? How did she leave?"

"I must go for my swim."

"We Religious aren't so bad, Sam. You should find out. And you should certainly let your children find out about us."

"We know that. We always traded with them when it wasn't permitted. You people wouldn't have survived without us. But then you had your Revolution, and you became the tyrants. I told you— we live our own way."

Bertram returned to his pod. He turned on his tablet, and flinched. Edmond had written. Unlike his speech, Edmond's words clung to each other and struggled to flow. They bundled up emotion and spat it out in clumps.

> *I know I shouldn't ask, but I would like to know, if you can tell me, if you have found anything. We have never done anyone any harm and I don't know what they are planning for us. Do you know? You think you can't tell me, but I would like to know. I'm responsible for our community. If I need to make preparations, I would like to do so. I think you know what I mean.*
>
> *I took a risk with you; one I was advised against. But we knew you were coming, and I found out what I could. It seemed our best strategy was to invite your sympathy. I would not have been so candid had they sent a Master. Have I misjudged you? I should not have talked of Evie. She is of no consequence to us. We don't care who you worship as a Prophet. Don't let my words condemn my community. By my doing we are at your mercy, Bertram. I hope you are not lacking in mercy.*

Bertram read the message again, and again. It transmitted fear, and doubt. But also a longing to protect. Bertram sat on his mat and tried to turn the paths between which he could choose into distinct roads, and to see where they would lead. In among the paths weaved the images of Annabelle, and the burned faces. Bertram tried to bring clarity to his thoughts. He breathed slowly, until he saw the way ahead.

First, he wrote to Edmond, telling him that he hadn't yet found the answer.

> *Someone called Evie did stay here, just before the Revolution started. They called her 'bad,' but I don't know what they meant by it. It seems she left, or was sent away. There is a chance she isn't our Prophet, but I will find out. There is some truth to what you said about missing data. I will find what evidence there is.*

But that isn't the real purpose of your message. I cannot let you spread lies about Evie. You must say that you will renounce that heresy and follow the correct teaching about the Prophets. Your belief that you can contact people from other times is surely a delusion and can be forgotten, but you cannot put faith in the Prophets at risk—that is what holds the Amalgamation together. I will tell my Master that you want to make amends. If you do so, all will be well. They show mercy to the penitent. I want no harm to come to you.

Bertram frowned. It wasn't exactly what he wanted to say, but someone else might read his communications. It would be better if the Historians conformed. Under cover of conformity and repentance they could do whatever they wanted with the data, and their strange machine. The strange machine that might yet give him a family.

The image splintered apart inside his head. Edmond would never conform. Just as Eden would never conform. The eradication would begin. They would be taken away and put on the path to redemption through work and prayer. Bertram felt cold inside his bones. His hand shook. He had no distinct idea about the work they did. He struggled to separate it from burning and killing. But no one burned now, did they? He hadn't heard of it. He would have heard of it, surely? But he hadn't known how hungry people were outside the domes. There were many things he didn't know.

Bertram wrote to his Master asking for more time.

And then Bertram sat with his eyes closed, weighing the two messages. A fine balance needed to be kept between them, just until he had evidence. Just like the boats below him, he felt he might tip either way. If only he could write to Percy and lay out everything before him. His advice would be sound. But someone would be sure to read his message. And a message approved by a Censor was no message at all.

* * *

For the next two days Bertram worked with the villagers and told stories to the children. He found their geometry lacking and taught them well. He avoided Sam, and Elizabeth, and tried to seem casual. He spoke often about the difficulties in arranging a transport. The credit from his community didn't extend this far, apparently, but it was sure to resolve itself soon. He asked innocent questions about the history of Eden. About how they had kept themselves so isolated. About how they'd survived. About visitors. They answered him politely, but their vagueness was a resistance he could not break.

After one of the lessons he sat on the floor of the communal pod. Two children, a girl and a boy, lingered on the mats, seemingly putting their tablets in their pockets but fumbling and drawing out their actions. The girl looked at him quickly, and turned away. The boy nudged her elbow.

"Is there something else?" Bertram said.

The two children stopped their fumbling and sat still. They watched Bertram warily, gathering their courage. Bertram sat completely motionless so as not to startle them. Any word might be the wrong word. The silence became uncomfortable, and the boy spoke.

"I know the others don't like lessons so much. But we like it."

"We like it a lot," the girl said.

"That makes me very happy," Bertram said.

"We wanted to ask. If we could learn more." The words tumbled out of the girl's mouth, and she sighed with relief once they were out.

"Of course. We can do more tomorrow, if you want. While I'm here I can teach you as much as I can."

The girl's face crumpled in exasperation. The boy frowned.

"That's not what we meant," he said.

Bertram stared at them.

"Is it possible for someone from here to go to your community?" the boy asked. "To learn like you said you do? To do it all the time?"

Bertram felt knocked back by their request. He sensed danger ahead. He weighed the answer he wanted to give against the answer he was expected to give. He spoke tentatively, feeling his way through the uncertainty.

"Life is good, here. Why do you want to leave?"

"Because we don't want this to be our life," the girl said. "It is the same every day and all the time. We can come back later."

"People travel now," the boy said. "We want to learn. I don't want to look after sheep, and fix irrigation systems for my whole life."

Bertram smiled at them briefly before burying his smile in a frown.

"I don't think your parents would like you to leave. You are needed here. We must serve our communities."

"But we can serve our community," the girl said. "Our community is the whole of Britain. Why must we just serve Eden?"

The boy nodded eagerly and reached out to hold the girl's hand.

"Have you spoken to your families?" Bertram said.

"No, but we will," the girl said. "We wanted to ask if it's possible."

"It is possible. There is space for children who want to learn. But they have to work hard. They have to earn their way too, by helping in the community. It is a hard life."

"But we can learn all of geometry, and all of algebra, and all of history?" the boy said.

Bertram laughed.

"I don't know that anyone has ever learned all of algebra, or all of history. But you can learn as much as you want. You can also, eventually, make your own contribution to knowledge."

The girl clapped her hands.

"I want people to read my name after I'm dead," she said. "I want to leave a thought behind. A useful thought."

Bertram looked away. To leave an idea behind. An idea that shapes the knowledge to come. A thought that shifts the path of learning a little, and helps determine the future. The children looked at him eagerly. How strange, he thought, that such dreams spring up in villages, among children who have barely learnt anything. He imagined himself gathering them all up, from all the villages, and watching their dreams flicker to life.

"It is nothing to do with me. You should speak with your family first," he said, surprised by the harshness in his voice.

* * *

The following evening, as he walked back to his pod after the communal meal, he noticed someone sitting on one of the circle of stones. Bertram sat down next to them. It was Sam.

"It's very relaxing, watching the sea," Bertram said.

"I don't think I could live anywhere else," Sam said.

"It's worth defending, a place like this."

Sam looked at Bertram, and nodded vaguely, as if he hadn't properly heard the words.

"Have you had to?"

"Had to what?"

"Defend this life." Bertram waved at the sea, which tonight was calm, shimmering with the light of the setting sun.

Sam said nothing, and his body remained still.

Clouds of sand and earth rose from the ground, and danced for a while, before collapsing.

"The villagers are angry," Sam said. "You must stop preaching at the children."

"I haven't preached. I taught them geometry." Bertram sat up straight, bracing himself against Sam's anger.

"They have no need for geometry. It's part of your life, a Religious life, not of ours."

"Can my life not be good, just as yours is?"

"You have no business preaching to them. Least of all encouraging them to leave. I forbid it."

"But the children came to me. They are clever children," Bertram said.

Sam clutched his knees with his hands.

"You must not try to take our children."

Words rushed around Bertram's head. He struggled to join them into sentences. He feared someone else would deal with this better. He felt his Master's presence, watching, and judging. His heart pounded and he breathed carefully.

"I have treated you with respect. I have done all the tasks assigned to me. I understand that we have different views, but why do you talk to me like that?"

Bertram sighed; his voice had remained calm. He imagined approval.

"Because you're wrong about Evie. You're wrong about everything. Evie was evil," Sam said.

Sam's voice floated between them and hung in the air while Bertram groped for a response.

"Why do you think that?"

"She tried to change us. She was loyal to New Britain. She would have killed us. And then she stole from us."

Bertram laughed.

"Elizabeth was right, then. It was a different Evie."

"No. It was the Evie you worship."

"It can't have been. She started the Revolution."

Sam stood up.

"Walk with me," Sam said.

Sam led Bertram between the living-pods and up the hill towards the energy farm. Bertram struggled up the hill, his feet sinking into the loose earth and sand. The wind was stronger at the top; it whistled through the wires of the solar panels. Bertram smelt the salt from the seaweed farm. Sam pointed at two wind turbines. Bertram could tell that they were old models, but they still turned slowly, like a clock counting ages, not minutes.

"She fixed those," Sam said.

"Yes?" Bertram said, unsure of the meaning or importance of what he'd heard.

"She had a way with machinery. They shouldn't have worked, but she fixed them."

"I see. That's impressive," Bertram said, looking down the slope, wondering how long it would take to get back down.

"She reported us, you know. She would have had us killed,

because we ate meat. And because we didn't live communally, in the New Britain way."

Bertram scratched his legs through his tunic. His boots had filled with sand. He wriggled his toes to try to dislodge it.

"But then she can't have been the same Evie. It's against everything she gave her life for."

Sam shrugged. "Perhaps not, then. But after she left, the Revolution started."

"Why did she leave?"

Sam sat down on a tuft of grass and adjusted his muslin. In the setting sun, his shadow stretched in front of him like a giant finger, pointing back down the slope.

"She could no longer stay here."

"What does that mean?"

"She stole from us. She deserved punishment. She walked into the desert. We assumed she would die."

Bertram's hand flew to his throat and he seemed to have difficulty breathing. He coughed. The wind buffeted him more strongly than before and he sank to the ground next to Sam.

"You killed her?" he said.

"No, she chose. But we didn't care. And then the Religious found a woman wandering in the desert, not far from here. You can see why we know it's your Evie."

"Yes ... but ..." Bertram let his mind race ahead of himself and gave up trying to catch his thoughts with words. A criminal. Loyal to New Britain. And they had found a woman, half-dead. He shook his head. The ways of God were unfathomable. Who knew what might have happened after she'd left?

"I'll give you something," Sam said. "She sent messages. It'll show I'm right. And then you must leave."

Bertram nodded.

"And we never want you back. Brother."

Bertram's mouth fumbled with his thoughts.

"If you come back, or send anyone to disturb us, we'll deal with you just like we deal with all outsiders."

Bertram's body shook.

Sam leant towards Bertram.

"Do you understand?"

It seemed to Bertram that Sam spat poison in his ear.

"I will leave and never return. But how do I know it's true?"

Sam looked down on the village and squinted into the distance. Bertram tried to read his eyes, but they were blank.

"I'll give you something so there's no doubt."

Sam stood up and led the way down the hill again.

"I think you misjudge me," Bertram said as he scrambled after him.

Sam hesitated.

"Who do you think I am?" Bertram said.

Sam didn't speak.

"My parents fought and died for New Britain long after their cause was lost. The Brothers took me in, and we still take such children in. I chose to stay in this life because it's better. It's the way forward."

Sam began walking again.

"I don't care who you are. After you've seen what I'm going to give you, you'll see why we hate you, and everyone like you. Especially when you plan to take our children."

"Hate is a sin, Sam. We should approach the world with kindness," Bertram said.

Sam laughed a slow, loud laugh.

"We do. It's the world that isn't kind to us. Without people like us your Religious communities could never have survived. We traded with you, we helped fix your machinery. We passed messages on. But you were only kind to us when you needed us."

"You can't hold the actions of others against me."

"But you're one of the Religious. You just told me you've chosen to live like them."

Bertram paused.

"I choose to live how they live now. It doesn't mean I agree with everything that happened in the past … What did they do to you?"

"New Britain fanatics swapped for Religious fanatics. It's all the same. They wanted to take our resources, and they wanted us to worship Evie."

"Did you tell them about her?"

"No. We killed them, and threw them into the sea."

"Sam ..."

Sam stood still, staring into the distance. "I would have been a different person, if I'd grown up at a different time."

"What do you mean?"

Sam's shoulders slumped. Bertram felt sadness enveloping them both. He looked at the village below, trying to imagine fighting, screams, chaos.

"It must change you. Living through that."

Sam nodded.

"You're all so certain, you outsiders. All so sure of yourselves. All of you come here to teach us how to live. But we live as we've always lived. And rid ourselves of threats."

Bertram shivered.

"I understand."

* * *

Bertram lay on his sleeping mat, but couldn't sleep. His chest was heavy within him and his breaths came jerkily. The heat pressed down on him, forced him into his mat so that he hurt wherever his bones touched the ground. He rolled onto his back.

Tomorrow he would be gone.

He covered his eyes with his arm. Is it better not to know, or to seek the truth? He scrunched his eyes together until they hurt.

When the truth is a burden, what do you do?

Bertram dug his nails into his skin.

The words filled his mind, leaving no room for anything else. They had thought him a poor student, but what would they say now? If they knew what Sam had given him.

Bertram tried to fill his lungs with air, but filled them only with heat. He coughed. He looked at his tablet, no longer a communication device, but a bomb.

What would they do if they knew? If they knew what Evie had said? If they knew what Evie had thought? And yet ... Bertram struggled to disentangle his thoughts. And yet ... she had been afraid. She had so clearly been afraid. A young woman, away from home, and afraid.

He tried to recreate her mind. How might he react to strangers? What might he have done? After what she had been taught? After New Britain had given her stories that shaped what she saw.

Bertram rolled over again. His narrative clashed with her final message. She had tried to have them killed. She had called for them to destroy Eden, and the Religious. But they had deceived her, they had caught her. They had saved themselves.

Should they remove her name from the list of Prophets? Would they no longer celebrate her name day with roasted sheep and honey bread? Bertram tried to unpick the lessons he'd taught, and the lessons he'd been taught. Would this be the final thing to break the Amalgamation?

She had started the Revolution. But she had been bad before. How much did that matter? Perhaps her mind was changed, in the desert. Perhaps enlightenment had come. Perhaps the Religious had changed her. Perhaps ... perhaps a story should be made.

But she had written in her private confessions that the Religious were evil. That they threatened the future. That they would bring the end of the world.

Bertram rolled over again and noticed daylight creeping through the pod. He rubbed his face, put on his tunic and muslin and walked outside. He sat on one of the stones watching the sea.

Edmond had been right, then. Bertram rubbed his eyes. Could it all be destroyed, and a new fiction put in its place? Bertram squirmed and his head swam. That could never be right.

After breakfast the transport arrived. The villagers said fare-well, but looked relieved that he was going. Sam held his hand momentarily.

"May your God be with you, Brother Bertram," he said.

Bertram could see the metallic glimmer in his eyes.

"Which way is it?" Bertram said.

Sam pointed into the desert.

"I hope you find what you need."

Sam laughed.

Bertram climbed up next to the driver.

"Blessings, Brother. Where're you going?"

"Into the desert. That way." Bertram pointed in the direction Sam had shown.

The driver frowned at the desert, and then at Bertram.

"You're lucky we're fully provisioned. Your loan of this transport expires in three days. You're aware of that?"

"Yes, yes."

The driver started the engine and moved onto a small track that ran along the far side of the hill with the wind turbines on.

"What are we looking for?" the driver said.

"Just drive."

Bertram settled back in his seat and let the vibrations roll through his body. He watched Eden disappearing into the dust and wished it had never existed, or that he had never found it. The breeze from the sea fell away and the crushing heat returned. He heard the engine labour as dust swirled, rising in waves around the front wheels. Out in the desert he couldn't communicate. He felt his tablet in his pocket, dreading to touch it. Perhaps he should stay in the desert and keep his knowledge to himself.

The sun climbed into the sky. The transport moved slowly, often losing the track, then sticking in sand. The driver disliked turning around and following his tracks back to firmer ground. Bertram hardly spoke, except to encourage him on.

Late in the day Bertram spotted a circle of pods. Rips in their sides had been patched roughly. The wind picked at the ragged edges of the repairs. A rusty wind turbine lurched in the centre, squeaking and struggling. The driver stopped by the turbine, but no one came to greet them.

Bertram got out of the transport and walked up to the largest pod.

"Blessings. Is there anyone here?" he shouted outside the doorway. He thought he heard rustling.

Bertram shouted again.

An old woman pulled aside the door.

"Yes?"

"Blessings. My name is Brother Bertram, and this is my driver. May we come in?"

The woman looked around before beckoning them inside.

Bertram and the driver walked in and unwrapped their muslins. The air conditioner was old and the air crushingly hot.

"What do you want?" the woman said.

"We're trying to find out about a woman who came to your village, many years ago." Bertram found his words had gathered a tempo all their own.

The woman blinked quickly.

"The woman was Evie."

She frowned.

"Brother, I have no idea what you mean."

She turned away, and walked to the tap.

"Water?" she said.

"Yes. Water is welcome," the driver said, then made his way towards a mat and sat down.

Bertram paced impatiently.

"Please sit," the woman said.

"Can we stay for one night?" the driver said. "We can't get back to a transport hub today."

The woman nodded.

"We have provisions," the driver said.

The woman nodded more enthusiastically.

"I've come from Eden," Bertram said. "They told me what happened with Evie. So, I want the truth. I want to know."

The driver stared at him, open-mouthed. The woman put down her bowl of water.

"I need to know what happened. Without delay." Bertram watched her flinch as he spoke.

The wind picked up and began to whistle through small cracks in the lining of the pod.

The cloth of the woman's sleeves vibrated. She clasped her hands together to calm them.

"I don't know," she said. "I don't know what happened."

The driver stretched out on the mat and closed his eyes. Bertram paced up and down. The woman moved away from him and stood by the driver. Bertram followed and leant over her. He smelt her hair, and the dust on her clothes. Her tunic was covered in light brown stains. The wind squealed as it charged through the pod. The wires on the turbine outside whined, sounding like they might break. Bertram raised his hand as if to stop the noise, and the woman flinched again. He kept his arm raised and looked down on her.

"You hardly know the importance of this. But you must tell me. Now," he said, stepping away from her. As he spoke, the dust and sand got into his mouth.

The woman stared at the floor.

"They did it for the best," she said, sighing.

"I know. Tell me."

Bertram sat down, and the woman followed him.

She looked into the distance as she spoke.

"I was only young. We thought she could save us. The one who'd save us. You have no idea how it was, in those days."

"I know how it was. Please continue."

"We feared for our lives. We thought we might die, every day. And then she brought this knowledge, she brought the truth. All we were missing was hope, an idea. Something for people to unite behind. Our Father spoke with her, but he said she hadn't brought the letter to us, she only had it because she was ashamed."

"Ashamed?"

"About what it said about her. That she was descended from traitors."

Bertram nodded.

"She was very badly injured. She was in pain, they said. Her body and her mind were in terrible pain. So, they gave her sleep."

"Eternal sleep," Bertram said.

"Yes. But if she'd lived, there wouldn't have been a Revolution. We wouldn't have saved ourselves. We would have been destroyed."

Bertram looked at his boots and picked at a worn piece of cloth.

"Leave her alone," the driver said. "These are good people."

Bertram hesitated. *Good people.* Perhaps that was right. They had started the Revolution. The sacrifice of one for the many was a noble thing. But they had killed a woman, heartlessly killed a woman because … He struggled to see through his feeling. They had done it because they thought it was for the best. Bertram picked at his boots for a few more moments, stopping only when he realised he could see his foot through the hole he'd made.

"Did you try to speak to her, to understand her?" he said.

"Yes. We told her New Britain was evil. But she didn't see."

"How long?" Bertram said.

"How long what?"

"How long did you talk with her, try to convince her?"

The woman shrugged. "A few weeks."

Bertram's hands entwined themselves in his sleeves as if he were washing a particularly stubborn stain. His shoulders sank.

"A few weeks?" His voice was a whisper, but the force of it made her flinch. "You sacrificed her to your idea of the future. You shouldn't have done that. There must have been another way." Bertram's words hung in the air like smoke. They soaked through the walls, through the woman.

"It wasn't like that, Brother. She was evil. She would have destroyed us. And look what good came from it. We overthrew them."

Bertram's face twisted. He struggled once again to find the words he needed. He searched the walls, and then let his eyes fall again on the woman.

"We always see evil in things we don't understand," he said. "You knew what they did? She was a child, once. A child they denied a family, who they denied a loving home, who they denied fun, and laughter. And you thought she was evil. You failed, utterly, in imagination. You failed in compassion; you failed in every way."

The woman didn't reply, but shook her head.

"What's your name?" Bertram said.

"Rachel," she said.

"We leave tonight. We're not staying here."

The driver jumped up. "It's unsafe, Brother. We simply can't."

"We simply can, and we will. I refuse to remain here. Before I go, we will take your testimony."

"I refuse," the woman said.

Bertram took out his tablet and began to type.

"You can either tell me, and I will write it down. Or I can send Enforcers to get it out of you. I promise you, my way is better."

The woman shrank from him.

As she did so, her arm appeared from the folds of her tunic, thin, and blotchy. Bertram could see her skull through the matted strands of hair that she'd tied at the back of her head. He shook his head. Why had no one told him about this hunger and sickness?

"Why don't you get the food out?" Bertram said to the driver. The driver sighed and moved towards the door.

"How many of you live here?" Bertram said.

"Five of us. I'm the youngest." The woman smiled. Some teeth were missing. Her eyes followed the driver as he fetched his bag. Her fingers twitched at the sound of the unwrapping of food.

Bertram watched her eat in silence.

"I promise I'll be fair to you," he said. "But I must have this evidence."

"It's heresy. What will they do to me?"

Bertram ran his fingers over the gritty surface of his tablet and wiped it clean.

"Why did you tell me?" he said.

"Because you already knew." The woman paused, looking towards the door. "I always wanted to tell someone. It seems right to tell someone. But I don't want them coming for me."

"I don't think they will," Bertram said. "I will be fair to you."

As Bertram typed, and the woman spoke, the wind died down, and the turbine began to turn normally.

When they had finished, Bertram stood up and walked towards the door.

"We're leaving," he said.

The driver followed, with his hands reaching out to stop him. Bertram turned to face him before telling him to leave most of their food behind.

* * *

People didn't travel at night. Apart from during the full moon the tracks and roads blended with the countryside, and merged into olden-day paths that no longer led anywhere. The driver gripped the steering wheel, peering into the gloom. The transport rocked and jolted and stuttered its way. Bertram sat impassively, watching the driver's struggles, but doing nothing to alleviate them.

The driver brought the transport to a halt.

"I can't go on," he said. "If I do, we'll be lost."

Bertram shrugged and wrapped his muslin around his head, covering his eyes. He listened to the driver making himself comfortable in the hard, upright seat. He thought he heard the murmur of complaint.

"Turn off the motor," Bertram said.

"But we need the air conditioner."

"We might run out of power. Turn it off."

"I'm sure we can—"

"I said turn it off!"

The motor faded out, leaving them in silence. The lights died and the hot air hung, undisturbed, in the cabin. Bertram sat completely still, pretending to sleep. He tried to order his thoughts. He began as far back as he could, with his project, which suddenly seemed vital for understanding this world.

New Britainers had lived communally, with children held in common. At seven they put them to work. They ranked them, according to their heritage. Physical contact was forbidden. And they filled them with fear of imminent death if they didn't sacrifice themselves to build a perfect future.

Bertram tried to inject the facts into Evie. The Evie he constructed in his mind. She went to Eden, where they ate mammals.

She must have been afraid, and uncertain. Her education made her unable to see a different way. Any relaxation of the rules meant death, to her. They said she stole something. And then she left. The gaps between the facts opened up chasms of possibility. She had carried the letter with her all the time, not to bring about Revolution, but to hide her history. Why hadn't she destroyed it? Was that the work of God? The Religious had killed her so they could write a story that inspired the frightened and the cautious to rebel, or stand by while others rebelled. Perhaps that was for the best.

Could it be for the best? The Religious had caused so much misery themselves, in this Revolution. Do all lives lost count the same?

He would have to tell his Master what he'd found. And risk the Amalgamation. If they found out Evie was a lie, the religions might splinter, separate to become the old religions again. Britain would no longer be a model of unity, and peace, and equality. Bertram opened his eyes. Was it a model of equality, and unity? Rachel's thin arm, and Eden's poorly educated children stretched the meaning of equality beyond recognition. And Edmond should be told. Bertram felt calm.

Bertram heard the motor start again, and realised that he must have slept. They arrived at a transport hub as the first signs of dawn lightened the air. The driver almost fell out of the transport, his legs unable to support him. Bertram walked up to the transport coordinator and demanded another transport, and another driver.

And so it was that an astonished Annabelle opened the door and found Bertram, dirty, tired, and hungry just a day later. She let him in. Someone prepared a bath, and found him bread.

Bertram sank into the water and closed his eyes. He hadn't had time to work out the structure of his thoughts, to weave his ideas together into a pattern that he might display, or defend. He found himself unable to do it, and went to sleep.

The following day, he met Edmond.

They sat, as before, in the middle of the dome, half-sitting, half-lying, staring at each other across bread, and honey, and water. This time, Edmond fidgeted with the cushions.

"I found evidence," Bertram said.

Edmond looked away. "Is it the evidence that will sweep us away?" Edmond covered his mouth momentarily with his hand.

Bertram looked at the ground.

"Things kept hidden have found their way out," he said.

Edmond shifted on his cushions.

"You were right about Evie. That something didn't fit."

Edmond nodded. Bertram felt the power of his words and weighed them carefully, like balancing a sword before beginning combat.

"She wasn't a martyr, or a Prophet. She was just a woman."

Edmond sat up. He leant forward. His mouth opened, as if he were about to speak. But he remained silent.

"The letter. The call to Revolution. She'd hidden it because she was ashamed of her heritage. Perhaps she also kept it to inspire her to overcome her tainted background. She was loyal to New Britain. The Religious found her in the desert and saw the value of what she had. But they couldn't convert her. Although they didn't really try. So, they killed her. And used a story about her to start the Revolution."

"You know all this?"

"I have the messages she sent. And I found the place where she died."

Bertram laid his tablet between them. Edmond reached for it, and hesitated, looking at Bertram.

"Yes, please, read it," Bertram said.

Edmond looked at the tablet, but seemed not to read.

"I was hoping for something like this. But I feared you would hide it."

"I've sworn to look for truth."

"Many people swear many things. What they do is often different."

"I keep to what I swear."

"I can see. Thank you."

"Why are you grateful?" Bertram said.

Edmond hesitated. He seemed to try out different words and reject them. He sighed.

"Because you've saved me from an unpleasant task."

Bertram frowned.

"You've been open with me, so I shall be open with you. The only way I could see to stave off the Enforcers was to find a bigger problem than us. I had my suspicions, and I hoped you'd discover it. I'm grateful that you've told me. If you had not …" Edmond straightened a cushion next to him and rearranged is tunic. "… I already know what you found."

"How?" Bertram said, fist clenched.

"We put a reader in your tablet while you slept. We already have your data."

"That's intolerable. How dare you?" Bertram stood up.

"I apologise. But I have to save my community. We are under attack and I must be able to defend us. I see now that I didn't need to do it. Please forgive me."

Bertram stood up and strode to the door to his room.

"Please stay," Edmond said.

Bertram turned around.

"You have little idea how much I risked for you. I could have called down the Enforcers as soon as I arrived. I put myself at risk. And now you say you spied on me."

"I thought you wouldn't call them immediately. You seem more open minded than many of them. So, I trusted you. But I needed something more than trust. Surely you must see that? What would you have done?"

Bertram turned away and walked into his room, slamming the door behind him.

He walked around his pod, thrusting his possessions into his bag. When he was packed, he sat on the mat and took out his tablet. He began to send a message to his Master, but got no further than the greeting.

Bertram practiced his breathing exercises, trying to slow his thoughts, letting them run in and out of him in time with his breaths.

Evie was not a Prophet.

Edmond must have known this, or nearly known this. He'd manipulated him.

But only to save his community.

Bertram noticed the dread he felt at the thought of returning home. A dread like an ache.

A brisk knock at the door interrupted his thoughts.

The door opened. Edmond stood there, looking down at him.

"What will you do?" Edmond asked.

"I was just thinking. But you interrupted."

"I felt I had to, given what's at stake. Once again, Bertram, we depend on you. So, what will you do with your knowledge?"

Edmond slumped against the doorframe with tiredness.

Bertram moved to one side of his mat, and asked him to sit. He intended to speak with outrage, but his voice seemed unwilling to match his mood.

"I'm angry that you spied on me ... but ..."

Edmond looked him fully in the face.

"I understand your motive."

"Yes," Edmond said.

"That doesn't mean I trust you."

"It's so difficult to trust anyone."

The two of them sat for a while, the discomfort between them increasing.

"How do you feel? About all of this? It must all be a shock," Edmond said.

Bertram flinched. Edmond's concern felt like a wound. He looked at the dirt still under his fingernails.

"My parents defended New Britain, until they died. I lived alone after that, as a child, until the Brothers took me in. I learned their lessons well. I followed their rules. I lived like them; it's my way of life. But I've always felt apart."

His eyes searched the roof. He hesitated before beginning again.

"Evie wasn't a Prophet, but she wasn't evil. I imagine it took courage to travel to Eden. It took courage to speak up for her way of life. And they equipped her so badly. They infected her with fear, and suspicion, and the end of the world. I might have done the same as her."

"I didn't expect that from you," Edmond said.

Bertram shrugged.

"I think you're right," Edmond said. "When we experience other lives, we learn what it's like to be other people. It's hard to express, but you're right, Bertram."

"I planned to write a project about education—about how what we teach our children makes them see the world in certain ways. They never saw the point, but I see it more clearly than ever now. Evie was formed by her upbringing. It made her closed to differences. I must return to my community. To tell them. Her life is still a lesson for us. But a different lesson."

"And what about us?"

"I think this news will be a distraction. It may even end the Amalgamation. But you must stop this nonsense about talking to people who've died. You should formally ask forgiveness, and rely on their mercy. I wish it were true—I came here wanting to find my mother, but it all seems so implausible."

Edmond smiled. "We might find her in the records still. In a more conventional way."

Bertram looked away and coughed.

Edmond's face flushed and he ran is fingers through his hair, pulling at his temples. "I will always be grateful they sent you, and not someone else."

Tiredness swept through Bertram and he leant back against the wall. The strain of continually being on his guard drained away and his eyelids sank. Tears gathered in his eyes.

Edmond looked away, as if mesmerised by the roof.

"Do you think the Brothers will welcome you back?"

"No," Bertram said, "I don't think they will."

"I think your project has merit. I can offer you somewhere to work, if you have nowhere else. And I will try to find your family. We owe you that."

"Thank you. After I've reported back, may I stay here for a while? I don't think I can stay with the Brothers, after what I'm going to tell them."

Edmond laughed. The first time Bertram had ever seen him do so. It made him seem old.

"You'll always be welcome here."

Bertram sighed.

"Thank you."

"I'll arrange a transport as soon as possible."

Bertram and Edmond stood up. Edmond held the palm of his hand out to him, and they held their hands together. Bertram thought Edmond's skin felt like olden-day paper, smooth, neither hot nor cold, retaining only the memory of life.

* * *

Bertram waited in the pod for the transport to arrive. A door opened and Annabelle walked in.

"Bertram. Were you going to leave without saying goodbye?"

Bertram's mind had had no space for Annabelle, and his complicated thoughts about her. But she stood in front of him, small, injured.

"No. I'm sorry. This has been hard for me," he said, and winced. "I should have been more aware of your feelings. I'm sorry."

"It's alright. I had thought you might have had … It doesn't matter."

Annabelle shook her head and pulled out her tablet from her tunic.

"Look, I found Evie, in London North. We have some of their records."

"You knew this, even before I left?"

Annabelle winced. "We suspected. But the story you found is like a thread, stitching together the scraps of data. Without you the story is nothing. Without you telling it, it can never be true."

"What does it say?"

Bertram moved closer to her so he could read her tablet.

"She had a tainted heritage, from her father, as well as her great-grandmother. They didn't fully trust her, even though she reported a lot of people. They sent her away because she took something that should have been held in common."

Annabelle's finger traced the line of text.

"Here, see, two children reported her for taking a 'red hairband'."

"So, they sent her to Eden?"

"Yes. It was on her record and it marked her. They thought about sending her to learn about wind turbines. She had a skill with mechanical things, it says. But instead, they sent her to the end of their world."

"Because two children said she took something," Bertram said.

"And she had a bad background. They saw things differently then." Annabelle let the screen and her hand sink to her waist.

"They would ruin a life for a children's squabble."

"They killed adults for less, Bertram. This isn't the worst of it."

"I know. And then we burned them for it."

Annabelle flinched.

"I didn't. We didn't."

"We didn't. But our words skim over it, not touching the horror of it. That's if we ever talk of it at all," Bertram said.

"We talk of it here."

"And do what, exactly, to help?"

"Nothing. Some things still aren't safe. We hide, and we record, and we try to make it not have happened. Don't you see?"

"I do see. But it's not enough. We need to show people, to talk of these things. More than that ..." Bertram could see Annabelle's scalp where her hair was parted. It looked very pale.

"More than that, we need to understand how to teach our children better."

He sensed her body flinch.

He waited for her to speak but she said nothing. He watched her tunic moving as she breathed.

They both heard a noise.

"That's my transport," Bertram said.

They walked to the entrance together and Annabelle helped him with his muslin.

"I need to return to my community. But I'll be back, Annabelle. I'd like to talk with you again."

Annabelle's eyes flashed like a light had turned on.

"I'd like that. Perhaps we could check on the bees again."

"And go to the sea again."

"Yes. I'd like that."

"But first I must deal with this."

"Of course."

Bertram pressed his palm into hers and felt his arm tingling. He closed his eyes to let the feeling imprint itself on his body.

* * *

Bertram watched his home growing on the horizon. He wished it would stay suspended there, close enough for comfort, but far enough away from conflict. The transport moved too quickly.

He tripped as he climbed out. In the dormitory he laid out his belongings in their familiar pattern. They connected him to the past, but his feelings no longer matched.

Everyone was teaching, or doing tasks, and he walked into the communal pod to wait for them. He thought about going to his class, but decided not to. He was no longer their teacher.

The tables had marks and scratches on them that he'd never noticed before. One of the air conditioners clicked and wheezed unfamiliarly. The air hung uncomfortably.

* * *

Bertram stood outside the Master's room. He heard the assistant's footsteps and turned around to face him.

"The Master is very busy this morning, Brother. He's preparing for an envoy from Barcelona. Could you return after the communal meal? He is eager to speak with you."

The assistant stood aside to allow Bertram to make his way back down the tunnel.

Bertram remained where he was.

"I will see the Master now," Bertram said. "It's important."

The assistant gasped and placed himself between Bertram and the door.

"Move aside. I will see him now."

Bertram walked towards the door as if the assistant were air. He knocked on the door with his fist, and pushed it open.

The Master looked up from his tablet, and his eyes contracted in fury.

"Brother Bertram, what are …"

"I've come to tell you a number of things that you need to know. And you need to know them now."

The Master fell back in his seat.

Bertram walked towards his desk and looked down on him. He didn't pause to find the words, or search his mind before he began. He told him plainly, and clearly, what he'd discovered. There was no doubt in his mind that the Master would listen.

* * *

A couple of hours later Bertram sat at the head of an oval of Masters, his seat slightly out of alignment with theirs. They talked as if he no longer mattered.

"I vote for eradication. We must remove all evidence," one of them said.

"If we move quickly, it might be possible. But we must be thorough. Eden, the old Religious settlement, the Historians, and anyone they may have contacted."

"Bertram, now that we're decided, will you help to implement it? You will be our avenging angel." Their eyes found him and glimmered.

Bertram met their gazes and wallowed in their expectation. He opened his mouth to speak, knowing that his next words would fall like a knife.

"Unfortunately, it's too late for eradication," Bertram said.

His Master's eyes turned cold.

"The information, Evie's messages, Rachel's confession, everything I found has been broadcast to all the Religious communities, and all the domes, and all the villages that care to turn on their communicators. And the party from Barcelona."

His Master rose to his feet, quivering. Indistinct sounds of outrage fluttered past Bertram. He smiled.

"You've always taught me to seek the truth. So that is what I have done. I can't allow you to sacrifice people to hide the truth."

"You have no idea what you're saying. Truth? The truth is whatever leads to the greatest good." His Master's face reddened, his cheeks vibrating as he fumbled with his words.

The next thought pierced Bertram's brain so that it almost hurt. "This is what the letter meant," he said, looking out above their heads, his lips moving as if by instinct. "Never be certain. Evie was certain so she wanted to destroy Eden, the Religious community's certainty justified killing her, and your certainty is going to destroy more people. Never be totally certain. We never knew what those words meant. But this is what they mean: don't sacrifice people to an idea, or a dream of perfection. The truth is never whatever you want to believe. The truth is never known by a single person. We circle it, grasp at it, see it indistinctly, and must change ourselves to match it. Not lie about it to preserve ourselves."

Bertram sat back, suddenly tired, and waited for the silence to break.

One of the Masters broke it. He raised his voice and shouted.

Bertram didn't hear him. He sat enveloped by calm. He watched the Masters as if they were a dream, or a play.

He stood up, walked to his sleeping mat, gathered his belongings, and went to order a transport. While he waited, he found Percy.

"Come with me," Bertram said.

"Bertie, I can't. My life is here."

"But the world is so large, and full of things we've never known. Come with me, and see the sea."

Percy smiled. "I would like to see the sea."

"Then pack, quickly. Leave with me."

"I may join you later."

"Don't let them tie you here, or let fear of the outside stop you leaving. Please join me."

Percy squeezed his arm.

"You aren't safe yet. You do realise that, don't you? They may still come for you, and Eden, and all the others. Don't you want a spy?" Percy smiled.

Bertram frowned. "I know. I spoke with the delegation from Barcelona. I hope they will—" He paused. "That their presence will prevent any 'excess'."

"Ahh, the words we use for dangerous things … Perhaps they were right to teach us to understand our words before we understand our deeds. I will watch them for you."

"Thank you. Can you warn Eden too? They are perhaps in more danger than anyone."

"There's a delivery of beans due today. I'll send a message with the merchants. Commerce travels faster than religion," Percy said, laughing coldly.

"Of course. Thank you. And I hope we'll see each other soon."

Many hours later Bertram was back outside the dome made of sand. A familiar face opened the door and Bertram smiled. For the first time he felt he was walking into a place he had chosen to be his home.

Acknowledgements

IT IS TEMPTING TO THINK THAT this book sprung, fully formed, from my own imagination. In reality, it is the result of people who have influenced me over many decades, most of whom have no idea of the impression they made. This is therefore the appropriate place for me to thank them.

Mr. Derrick, my history teacher at Ivybridge Community College, for teaching us the fine line between scepticism and conspiracy.

I owe my life-long interest in authoritarian regimes to another history teacher—Rick Wells at Farnborough Sixth Form College, whose A-level history syllabus covering Nazi Germany, Soviet Russia, and Franco's Spain never left any of us quite the same again.

John Rumsey at Institutional Investor for teaching me how to write. His exasperated pleas to turn a 500-word story into a 250-word one taught me more than years at school ever did.

Prof. Jason McKenzie Alexander at the LSE, without whose quest to make my PhD thesis clear and simple to read, my writing would not be what it is.

Everyone at the Sevenoaks Writers' Group for their excellent advice and encouragement.

My friends—Pirkko, Caroline, Jenni and Katharine—for their support, patience, and walks.

My family for putting up with me.

Finally, the editors without whom this book would not have been possible. Amanda Rutter at Cornerstones. Justine Hart and Michael Mirolla at Guernica—thank you for taking this on.

About the Author

SINCE AN EARLY AGE CATHERINE GREENE has been fascinated by totalitarian regimes and the ways in which they use utopian dreams to subvert people's sense of morality. This book is an exploration of this theme. It has been a longstanding ambition of Catherine's to become an author, but it wasn't until she returned to university later in life that she felt able to write coherently. She has had a varied career including working as a journalist, an academic, and latterly as an ethics consultant. She lives in Kent with her husband and son and enjoys walking in the countryside, camping, and TV she'd be embarrassed to be caught watching.

www.catherinegreene.co.uk

MIX
Paper
FSC® C100212
www.fsc.org

Printed by Imprimerie Gauvin
Gatineau, Québec

a love story

"The Open": Epigraph from Heidegger, who was, according to Giorgio Agamben, from whose *The Open: Man and Animal* I've drawn this quotation and title, inspired by Rilke's eighth *Duino Elegy*.

"The Snake": Lines quoted and (in one case) paraphrased are drawn not quite randomly from *The Swerve*, by Stephen Greenblatt.

"The Understanding": Hannah Green is the author of *Little Saint*, from which the quotation identified in section three is drawn. My thanks to Jenny Irish for the gift of this exquisite book.

Biographical Note

Described in the *New York Times* as having "a knack for intensity," Cynthia Hogue has published twenty books of poetry, translations, and criticism, including such volumes from Red Hen Press as *Revenance* and *In June the Labyrinth*. She is coauthor of *When the Water Came: Evacuees of Hurricane Katrina* (interview-poems with photographs by Rebecca Ross), named a Notable Book by *Poetry International*. *Revenance* was listed as one of the 2014 "Standout" books by the Academy of American Poets. Hogue's honors include two NEA Fellowships and the H.D. Fellowship at Yale. She lives in Tucson.